W9-BXW-092

PRAISE FOR CHRISTINE MCGUIRE'S LEGAL THRILLERS STARRING KATHRYN MACKAY

Until the Final Verdict
"[McGuire creates] human characters who . . . leap right off the pages."

—*The Pilot* (Southern Pines, NC)

Until We Meet Again
"A great legal thriller . . . fascinating and complex."

—Barnesandnoble.com

Until the Bough Breaks
"Full of the sort of twists and insider looks at criminal investigation that fans of legal thrillers adore."

—*Booklist*

Until Death Do Us Part
"Starts with a bang—literally—and never lets up."

—*Publishers Weekly*

Until Justice Is Done
"What sets McGuire's novels apart from the pack is the level of realism she brings to the legal aspects of the story."

—*The Sentinel* (Santa Cruz, CA)

Until Proven Guilty
"A tense, nerve-jangling thriller that should satisfy fans of *The Silence of the Lambs*."

—Peter Blauner, bestselling author of *Man of the Hour*

Books by Christine McGuire

Christine McGuire

UNTIL JUDGMENT DAY

POCKET BOOKS

New York   London   Toronto   Sydney   Singapore

An *Original* Publication of POCKET BOOKS

 POCKET BOOKS, a division of Simon & Schuster, Inc.
1230 Avenue of the Americas, New York, NY 10020

Copyright © 2003 by Christine McGuire

ISBN: 0-7434-2230-9

First Pocket Books printing April 2003

10 9 8 7 6 5 4 3 2 1

POCKET and colophon are registered trademarks of Simon & Schuster, Inc.

For information regarding special discounts for bulk purchases, please contact Simon & Schuster Special Sales at 1-800-456-6798 or business@simonandschuster.com

Cover design and illustration by Matt Galemmo

Printed in the U.S.A.

Until Judgment Day
is dedicated to
Survivors
of Sexual Abuse

Our heartfelt gratitude is, as always,
extended to
our agents, Richard Pine and Sarah Piel,
Nicole who inspires Emma and
our editor, Amanda Ayers

and the fond memory of Arthur Pine,
without whose encouragement and support
no Kathryn Mackay novels would be in print

✝ CHAPTER 1

"EVERYBODY ON THE FLOOR! Close your eyes and cover your heads with your hands."

Silhouetted by a bright neon light in the parking lot that read BAY LIQUOR EMPORIUM, a gunman dashed into the store and slammed the door behind him. "Get down, now!"

He quickly checked out the situation. Stuffed with unopened cases of beer, wine, liquor, and food, along with Thanksgiving decorations, the store had barely enough room to walk through the aisles, much less hide someone from view.

Except for a lone customer—a pudgy bald man in a business suit who looked like an accountant—and one clerk, it looked empty.

The clerk behind the cash register looked up, startled. "What the hell—"

"I said drop to the floor!"

The clerk's hand inched toward the edge of the checkout counter but before it reached the silent alarm button, the bandit squeezed off three quick rounds from his old nickel-plated .45-caliber military automatic. They reverberated through the room like a howitzer.

The first slug shattered the beer cooler's glass door, launching a foamy yellow wave of pressurized Corona Extra that spewed over the beancounter who was studying the champagne selection.

The second bullet hit the snack display like a freight train, pulverizing a chest-high stack of canned nuts and a couple dozen bags of pretzels and chips. The remnants rained down on the head of the terrified man who dived to the floor, rolled behind the wine rack, curled up in a fetal position, and clasped his arms over his head.

The third slammed into the clerk's sternum, driving him backward into the whiskey display, killing him before his body slumped to the floor.

The bandit sprinted around the counter and spat on the clerk. "Tol' you to get down, you dumb asshole."

He punched the No Sale button, yanked the cash drawer open, scooped up a handful of bills, and started to flee. Then he turned around and licked his lips.

"What the fuck." He grabbed a pint bottle of Wild Turkey, twisted off the top and took a deep swig, then vaulted the counter and bolted for the door.

Before he got there, another clerk ran in from a storage room in the rear carrying a 12-gauge shotgun. "Stop, you son of a bitch."

Before the clerk could raise the scattergun's muzzle the robber fired again. The bullet tore through the clerk's left shoulder, spun him around, and knocked him to the floor. The shotgun discharged and obliterated a set of shelves full of cognac and brandy.

The bleeding clerk moaned. When he heard the engine roar, he climbed to his knees and crawled to the door just in time to see the getaway vehicle fishtail into the early evening traffic.

✝ CHAPTER 2

SANTA RITA COUNTY SHERIFF David Granz flipped the wipers to high speed and squinted through the wet windshield to watch the narrow, steep, pitch-black road. Above the trees, he could make out the faint glow of Felton Village five miles ahead.

A tinny female voice crackled through the police radio that was tucked under the dashboard of his unmarked motor pool Ford Taurus and, startled, he swerved slightly into the oncoming lane. "Shit!" He corrected, grateful that old Highway Nine was deserted on Thanksgiving eve.

"All units, all units." The County Communications Center dispatcher's voice was tense but controlled. "Stand by for an all-points bulletin."

Granz reached under the dash and twisted the

radio's volume-control knob to drown out the rhythmic slapping of the windshield wipers.

"All units, Comm Center—Santa Rita P.D. reports an armed robbery at Bay Liquor. Shots fired. One store clerk dead. Second injured. Suspect is a lone white male, late twenties, fled in a late-model white Ford minivan, California license 4-S-L-R-7-2-9 reported stolen this afternoon in San Jose."

Although the CHP patrolled major highways into and out of Santa Rita, the old road over the mountains into San Jose no longer carried much traffic. And, Granz lamented, cuts to the Sheriff's Department budget had necessitated severe reductions in the Valley's police coverage. He was alone.

He grabbed the radio mike and keyed the Transmit button. "Comm Center, One-A-One."

The tinny voice came back immediately: "Go, Sheriff."

"I'm northbound on Highway Nine south of Felton—how long ago did that two-eleven at Bay Liquor go down?"

"The clerk called 911 seven minutes ago—at five forty-two P.M.—immediately after the suspect took off."

"I left the County Building at five-thirty. If the shooter's headed this way, he's not very far behind me. I'll— What the hell!"

A white minivan slid around a sharp curve on the wet pavement, recovered, then roared up close to the rear of the Taurus, bumped it hard, blasted its horn, and blinded Granz with its high beams.

The minivan swerved into the southbound lane, sideswiped the Taurus, accelerated, and pulled back into the northbound lane a few car lengths in front of the unmarked police car.

Granz cranked down the driver's window, grabbed a magnetic portable red light off the floor, dropped it onto the roof of the car, and plugged the cord into the lighter socket. The flashing red light lit up the rear of the van as it tried unsuccessfully to open up some distance between itself and the police car.

"Comm Center, One-A-One." Granz steered with one hand and keyed the radio mike with the other. "A white Ford van just passed me going like a bat outta hell."

He speeded up to within a few feet of the van and read the license plate: "License 4-S-L-R-7-2-9. I'm in pursuit of the two-eleven suspect three or four miles south of Felton Village."

"Copy, One-A-One."

"My Valley substation closed at five o'clock. Ten-twenty-one the resident deputy, and advise."

"Ten-four, stand by."

The van sped up to seventy, lost control on a sharp turn, skidded, knocked down a 25 MPH speed-limit sign, then recovered.

"One-A-One, Comm Center."

"Go," Granz answered.

"I contacted Deputy Smith by landline. He's ten-seventeen from home to Felton."

"That's—"

Suddenly, an arm extended from the van's driver

window and a flash erupted. Granz ducked instinctively, momentarily blinded. The bullet shattered the Taurus' windshield, showering him with glass shards, and plowed into the seat back. A second bullet knocked out the police car's left headlight, but a third missed.

"Comm Center, ten-thirty-three, ten-thirty-three," Granz shouted into the mike. "The son of a—the suspect's firing at me."

The tinny voice dropped into a matter-of-fact, professional monotone: "One-A-One, copy that shots are being fired. Stand by while I dispatch backup. All units, ten-three—switch to channel C. Communications Center will direct radio traffic on this channel."

A brief pause was followed by another calm radio call: "One-A-One, all available units are ten-seventeen to your location. Ten-twenty-six, five minutes."

"Copy ETA of closest unit five minutes, Comm Center, but that's gonna be too late. If I don't stop this guy before he gets to Felton, a lot of people are gonna get hurt."

Granz tailgated the van around another curve. When it opened into a short straightaway, he kicked the Taurus into passing gear. The big V-8 surged the car forward. He pulled into the left lane and eased alongside the van, aligning the Taurus' right front fender a few inches from the van's left rear.

When the van started into another left-hand turn, Granz jerked the steering wheel sharply to the right. The Taurus' right front fender smashed into the van just beneath the left rear side window.

As if in slow motion, the Ford van spun counter-clockwise and flopped onto its right side. Sparks flew from under the sliding van. Then it rolled again, teetered on the soggy shoulder, and toppled over a steep embankment. It crashed into the bottom of a deep ravine and exploded into a fireball, but the rain-swollen San Lorenzo River doused the fire almost instantly.

Meanwhile, realizing his own car was out of control, Granz pulled the steering wheel to the left, but it was too late to countersteer into the high-speed spin. Before the Taurus could regain traction, it slammed into the southbound guardrail, caving in both left-side doors.

Granz' momentum drove his skull into the door post at sixty-plus miles per hour, opening a huge gash over his eye.

The car careened back across the road, and when it hit the opposite guardrail Granz' head smashed into the driver's window. The car slid backward along the guardrail for about thirty feet, finally slamming into a huge oak tree. The front end lifted slightly into the air, then settled back into the mud, engine racing and red light flashing.

Granz kicked open the front passenger door and staggered from the car, shaking his head. His vision was blurry. He pulled his off-duty weapon, jacked the slide back to cock it, and glanced around quickly, unsure where the suspect was. Seeing nothing, he grabbed a four-cell Maglite from inside the car but he couldn't see anything in the flashlight's beam except thick, slanted sheets of driving rain.

Before he could make his way back to where the van had flown off the road, he heard a siren coming from the direction of Felton Village. The police car rounded a turn, its high beams lighting up the scene, then skidded to a sideways stop beside Granz' Taurus.

Deputy Sheriff Douglas Smith threw open the car door and sprinted toward Granz, gun drawn.

"Where's the suspect?"

Granz pointed toward the river.

Smith aimed his flashlight at Granz: "Man, your head looks like it went through a meat grinder, Sheriff. You all right?"

"Yeah, sure."

Granz touched his forehead and pulled away bloody fingers. "Damn, I think I'm—"

He collapsed onto the wet pavement and rolled onto his side, a bloody pool spreading from his head and running into a culvert.

✝ CHAPTER 3

DISTRICT ATTORNEY Kathryn Mackay hovered at the foot of the hospital bed watching her husband, absently gnawing a thumb nail. Petite and intense with dark brown eyes and curly black hair, Mackay still wore the heather-green wool Gianni suit she'd worked in that day.

A huge bloody gauze bandage was wrapped around Granz' head, and blood matted his dark sandy-blond hair. His breathing was labored and he moaned softly.

A young carbon copy of her mother, thirteen-year-old Emma Mackay had on Gap jeans with her blue and white sweatshirt and sat on the bed holding Dave Granz' hand.

"Will Dave be okay?" Emma's voice quivered.

Several years earlier, Emma's father, also a prosecutor, had been murdered in a courtroom shooting. She knew her mother's and stepfather's jobs were dangerous, and, despite their continual reassurances, she worried they might also be taken from her.

Doctor Morgan Nelson shook his head. "I need to do a test to find out."

"What kind of test?"

"It's called an MRI—a magnetic resonance imaging scan—it'll let me look inside Dave's head to see if everything's okay."

"What if everything isn't okay?" Emma asked.

"Then the test will tell me how badly he's hurt and what I need to do to fix it."

When County Communications called to tell Kathryn that Granz was injured and paramedics were transporting him to the hospital, she phoned their best friend, forensic pathologist/coroner Morgan Nelson, and asked him to be Dave's admitting physician. She knew that, although Nelson had been Coroner for twenty years, he retained his privileges at County General Hospital. She also knew her husband would be an uncooperative patient.

She had little trouble convincing him. Dave and Kathryn were his closest friends since his wife had died from cancer a few months earlier, and he was waiting at the ER when the ambulance brought Granz in.

Granz' eyes fluttered open and he tried to sit up. "I—oh, shit, my head hurts. Where am I?"

"County General." Nelson pushed him back down. "Be still, you'll rip the IV out of your arm."

Nelson was tall and lanky and wore thick tortoise-shell bifocals that magnified his bloodshot eyes so he looked like an owl that was in bad need of a good night's sleep.

"IV!"

"The accident damn near tore off your scalp. Paramedics stopped the bleeding and I stitched you up, but you lost enough blood to supply the Red Cross."

"What time is it?"

"Ten o'clock," Mackay told him.

"I've been here four hours?"

"Yes. Smith said you passed out right after he got to the scene. Luckily, he had dispatched paramedics while he was code three."

"I didn't pass out, I was resting." He tried to smile.

She gave him a stern stare. "Dammit, Emma and I have been worried sick. This is nothing to joke about."

"Sure it is." He winced as a sharp pain shot through his head. "What happened to our liquor-store perp?"

"DOA at the scene," Mackay told him. "Parolee just out of San Quentin three days ago."

"He's my next patient," Nelson told him.

Nelson checked the IV, scanned the monitors that recorded Granz' blood pressure, pulse, and respiration. He nodded and jotted a note on the clipboard he had removed from the door to the room. "I'll autopsy him tomorrow morning."

"On Thanksgiving?" Mackay asked.

Nelson shrugged. "Not ready to celebrate the holidays yet."

He stood and told Mackay, "Now I've got to leave instructions. The tech might be able to run the MRI tomorrow—I'll try to talk him into coming in on a holiday. Meanwhile, the night nurse'll monitor the vitals overnight. I'll be on call—he's in good hands."

"I ain't staying overnight," Granz protested. He started to sit, but moaned and fell back immediately.

"Why not?"

"Don't need to—I feel fine."

"You can't even sit up by yourself."

"Just a little dizzy's all."

"You're damn lucky you've got a head left."

"You're a master of overstatement."

"Oh really? A minor knock on the head might make you lose consciousness for a few minutes, but not almost four hours. I can't dismiss those head blows as insignificant."

"I've got a hard head."

"You sure as hell do."

Mackay sat on the bed. "Don't be stupid, Dave. Let them monitor you here in the hospital until Morgan can evaluate your MRI—make sure you're okay."

Nelson nodded in agreement. "You think you're invincible, Dave, but you're not. There's no way to know you haven't suffered a deep brain bruise or other serious head injury without an MRI, and it might take a day or two to schedule. Meanwhile, you need to stay right where you are."

"Nope. Tomorrow's Thanksgiving. I'm going home."

"If those head blows caused intracranial swelling or bleeding, you might not make it to the hospital again in time."

"Ain't gonna happen." Granz pointed at the IV and nodded at Nelson. "Take the IV out, Doc."

Nelson shrugged in exasperation and started to disconnect the monitors and tubes.

"Morgan!" Mackay implored.

"Can't keep him against his will, Katie, you know that. If I don't disconnect him, he'll do it himself."

"Tomorrow morning," Granz said, "I'm gonna drive back up Highway Nine and pick up that free-range bird I ordered special from Felton Market, then we're gonna feast on turkey, stuffing, gravy, and pumpkin pie with whipped cream. I ordered a surprise for Sam, too—a big bone with lots of meat on it."

Sam was the yellow Lab Dave had bought Emma as a companion after her father's death. "Can't let it go to waste."

He winked at Emma. "That work for you?"

"No."

"What do you mean, 'no'?"

"Doctor Nelson said you might be hurt really bad. I think you should do what he and Mom tell you. "

Mackay started to join in, but he held his hands up, palms out, in a "stop" gesture. "I'm not staying in the hospital tonight—I'm okay."

Mackay knew that when her husband made up his mind, there was no changing it and the more she tried, the more he dug in. But she could sometimes cut a deal with him. "Just to make sure, will you at least let Morgan schedule an MRI for Friday?"

"Nope."

"Why not?"

"Friday's a holiday, too."

"Jesus Christ! How about Saturday?"

"Nope."

"Why not?"

"Going Christmas shopping."

"Dammit, you're being macho and stubborn."

"No, I'm being practical. Doc's just being overly cautious—prob'ly afraid I'll sue him for malpractice if he doesn't do an MRI."

He glanced at Nelson. "Just kiddin'."

Then he looked back at Mackay. "And you're being overly protective."

"I'm being your wife."

"I know, but I'm fine."

"Sure you are."

"Look, make you a deal. If I don't feel a hundred percent better by the time the holiday season's over, I'll think about it."

CHAPTER 4

IN ORNATE RED AND GREEN letters bordered by multicolored bows, green holly boughs, and red berry clusters, the white canvas banner hanging above the double oak doors of the community room read:

WELCOME TO SACRED HEART CATHOLIC CHURCH
ANNUAL CHRISTMAS BENEFIT RAFFLE
FOLLOWING THE 10:15 A.M. MASS

A flyer posted beside the doors listed the prizes: autographed books by local authors; Annieglass; matching men's and women's Trek mountain bikes; six box-seat tickets to a Sharks hockey game; a week in Maui; a round of golf for four at Pebble Beach;

champagne brunch on the seventy-foot *Chardonnay II*; watches, jewelry, and dozens of less valuable items.

The announcement in the Religion Section of the *City Post*, a weekly tabloid, said that at noon, Reverend John Thompson would personally draw the final ticket and present the grand-prize winner with a check for $10,000.

He stood for a few seconds at the back of the hall and watched the Monterey Diocese Finance Officer spin the wire-mesh basket, pluck out a ticket, and ceremoniously announce another winner's name.

He checked his watch: 11:45 A.M.

"Just in time," he muttered to himself.

Then he swung the oak door open and slipped quietly outside, walked around the corner of the community hall, pulled an Advil bottle from his pants pocket, popped a couple of tablets in his mouth, and swallowed them without water. His rapid, shallow breaths came out in a thick fog that rose lazily into the cold, clear air and slowly dissipated.

He strode quickly toward the rectory, stepping over small cracks in the old concrete path that connected the community hall to the front door of the detached stucco structure that had served as the parish priests' home, office, and sanctuary for more than seventy-five years.

Through the window, he saw Reverend Thompson sitting at a huge oak rolltop desk.

The priest was tall and wide with a thick shock of salt-and-pepper hair and was smoking an ornately carved briar pipe. A steaming coffee mug sat beside the ashtray on one corner of the desk. On the other corner, a thirteen-inch color TV was tuned to a San Jose State–Notre Dame football game.

Thompson drew on the briar, inspected the bowl, tamped the tobacco, relit it, then leaned back in the leather high-backed chair and blew a perfect smoke ring at the ceiling.

He rapped on the rectory's heavy wooden door.

"Who's there?" Thompson's voice was deep and powerful, the result of many years' sermons designed to reach the rear pews, where the people who most needed to hear them usually sat.

"Reverend, there's a problem with the raffle. May I come in?"

He heard Thompson tap the briar pipe in the ashtray, then a desk drawer opened and closed.

"Enter, please."

He twisted the knob. It wasn't locked. Stepping inside, he closed the door behind him and engaged the dead bolt.

Thompson snapped the top onto an air-freshener can and rotated his chair to face the entry. "Nasty habit, smoking—wasn't expecting company." He stared at his visitor quizzically. "You look familiar. Are you a member of my parish?"

The room was expensively but sparsely furnished, with thick beige cut-pile carpeting. Besides the matching desk and chair, there were glass-fronted oak bookcases, a set of straight-backed visitor chairs, and a huge ancient leather sofa that looked like it had heard more than its share of church secrets.

"We were acquainted years ago."

"What's your name?"

"That's not important."

"I don't understand."

Thompson took a noisy sip of his coffee and cupped the mug in his big hands. "So, what's the problem?"

"You." He crossed the room in two quick steps.

"Excuse me?"

He reached under his coat and pulled out a pistol, then felt the front of his pants tighten. He looked down, horrified to discover a throbbing erection.

He jammed the muzzle against Reverend John Thompson's forehead, and squeezed the trigger.

✝ CHAPTER 5

THE FIRST THING DA Kathryn Mackay spotted when she rounded the corner onto Paseo Delgado at 1:15 P.M. was a green coroner wagon parked in front of the small lawn between the Sacred Heart Church community hall and the main church building. At the back of the lawn, recessed slightly from the street, sat the rectory building, its front door slightly ajar.

Yellow crime-scene tape was stretched from the corner of the community hall across the lawn and sidewalk, to the railing of the stairs that led to the church's main entrance.

A sheriff's patrol car was parallel parked in front of the coroner; two unmarked detective units and the CSI van angled in toward the curb nose-first, rear ends sticking into the blocked-off street.

Mackay parked her Audi and greeted the uniformed deputy who stood sentry outside the crime scene. She was wearing a simple black dress and a gray cashmere jacket. Her makeup was still fresh, her hair still perfectly in place.

The deputy recognized her and lifted the tape so she could pass. She ducked under and, walking up the concrete path, nodded at the two deputy coroners who stood by with a gurney, talking quietly, waiting for the go-ahead to remove the body from the crime scene. She pushed the rectory door open. A lone investigator was hunched over a tripod-mounted Pentax camera whose macro lens was aimed at the dead priest.

"Oh, God, Charlie." Mackay crossed herself. "That's Reverend Thompson."

Sergeant Charles Yamamoto, head of the Sheriff's Crime Scene Investigation unit, glanced up. "Ms. Mackay."

Yamamoto was a solemn man and a meticulous investigator whose expertise Mackay greatly respected and appreciated. "You knew him?" he asked her.

"I've attended mass at Sacred Heart a few times but I didn't know him personally. I do know he was beloved by his parishioners. Where's the rest of your CSI team?"

"Small room, gotta work here alone."

Mackay nodded. "Where's Sheriff Granz?"

"Not here yet. County Comm not get hold of him till five minutes ago."

"What detective got called out?" Mackay asked.

"Big boss. Miller. In community hall interviewing witnesses."

"Is it okay for me to come in?"

Yamamoto shook his head. "Haven't vacuumed yet."

"Okay, I'll stay out."

Mackay examined the body from a distance. Thompson's lifeless hands held a coffee mug, but it had tipped over and dumped its contents onto his lap. His head was slumped onto his left shoulder, and except for open, vacant eyes and a hole in the center of his forehead, he looked like he'd fallen asleep in his chair.

"What can you tell me?" she asked.

"Single shot. Close range. That door in wall by desk go into church, behind altar. Locked. Front door unlocked when RO get here." Yamamoto was referring to the responding officer, the patrol deputy who was dispatched initially by County Comm. "No forced entry," he added.

"So, how'd the perp get in?"

He pointed at the window beside the entry door. "Dirt wet under window, no prints. Look like walk right through front door."

"Hmm." Mackay was thinking out loud. "Someone the reverend knew, or was expecting."

"I'd say so."

"Find any empty cartridge casings?"

"No."

"Meaning the shooter used a revolver." She was thinking aloud again.

"Could be automatic, perp pick up ejected brass before he take off."

"True."

Yamamoto shot a few more frames and disassembled the camera, then removed a battery-powered vacuum from a case and switched it on. He vacuumed the floors, furniture, window ledges and other flat surfaces, emptied the contents into a bag, sealed and initialed it, and set it aside.

The bag would be turned over to the Department of Justice laboratory where a DOJ criminalist would log it in to maintain the evidential chain of custody, then examine the contents under a microscope in hopes of identifying bits of fiber, hair, or other particles that could be traced to a specific origin.

Yamamoto motioned to the two coroner's deputies. They rolled the gurney in, wrestled the heavy corpse into a thick black plastic bag, and zipped it tight. Yamamoto helped them hoist it onto the gurney. When they had rolled it out to the waiting wagon, Yamamoto ran the vacuum over the floor where the body had been, dumped the contents into another bag, and stored the vacuum.

"How about the Woods Lamp?" Mackay referred to a special handheld infrared light that illuminated microscopic fibers snagged off a perpetrator's clothing, usually on doorjambs, furniture edges, or rough fabrics.

"Room not dark enough. Seal crime scene, come back tonight when Woods Lamp be effective."

Yamamoto fidgeted, a sign he wanted to get back

to work gathering evidence, but he was too respectful to tell her.

"Thanks, Charlie," Mackay said. "I'll go to the community hall, check in with Lieutenant Miller."

Miller was sitting at a folding table interviewing an elderly man, jotting down notes on a yellow legal pad. When he finished, he thanked the witness, stood, and walked over to where Mackay was waiting.

The antithesis of Yamamoto, Miller was personable and talkative, with a perpetual smile. Tall, with a florid complexion and bushy red beard, he wore blue jeans and a 49ers T-shirt. His nickname, Jazzbo, resulted from his avocation as trombonist-saxophonist in a jazz band.

"Afternoon, Kathryn."

"Any witnesses that can tell us what happened?" Mackay asked.

"Everyone was inside at the raffle."

"Anyone hear a shot?"

He shook his head. "Apparently it was a pretty boisterous crowd. They were raffling off some expensive prizes."

"So, we don't know what time the reverend was murdered?"

"He delivered the ten-fifteen mass. Sometime between when it ended at eleven-twenty and noon, a parishioner went to the rectory to get Thompson for the grand-prize drawing and found his body. We've got more people to interview, but I doubt they'll be able to add much."

When Mackay walked out, the bright sun

blinded her, and she didn't see Sheriff Granz climbing out of his unmarked car. He called to her and waved.

When her eyes adjusted, she smiled and waved back.

He kissed her. "How long've you been here?"

"About ten minutes. I got paged out of noon mass and dropped Emma off at Ruth's on the way here." Ruth was a friend who'd been her daughter's sitter for years. Mackay hesitated, then said, "Emma and I missed you at mass."

"Kate—"

"You're Catholic, Dave. I don't understand why the three of us can't go to church together as a family, and neither does Emma."

"I stopped going to church when I was a teenager, and don't want to ever go again. I don't expect you to understand," he told her.

"If you'd explain your reasons to me, I'd try to understand."

"I don't want to talk about it."

"As usual." She knew a crime scene was neither the time nor place to pursue the touchy personal issue further, and let it drop. "You said you were going to catch up on some work this morning. I tried to call your office before we left for church, but you weren't there."

"I think I had to go out for a while."

"You think?"

"You know what I mean. What's up here? County Comm said there's been a murder."

She quickly filled him in on the skimpy details

she'd gleaned from her conversations with Yamamoto and Miller.

"Someone just walked past a couple hundred people into the priest's office, shot him in the head, and walked out without anyone noticing?" Granz asked.

"Apparently. Miller's team is still interviewing. Maybe they'll get lucky and find someone who heard it, tell us exactly what time Reverend Thompson was killed."

She glanced up and noticed him staring absently at the sky. "Dave?"

"Huh? What?"

"Did you hear me?"

"No, sorry. What did you say?"

"I said your detectives haven't finished interviewing witnesses yet."

"Why don't I check in with Miller, wrap things up here, then meet you at the morgue."

"Sure. Are you okay?"

Without answering, Granz turned and walked away.

✝ CHAPTER 6

MACKAY RODE THE ELEVATOR to the basement of County General Hospital and unconsciously wrinkled her nose as the doors swished open into the hallway of the morgue, anticipating the unmistakable stench of formaldehyde and death.

At the far end of a spotless tile-floored hall, double doors opened to a loading dock where coroner wagons backed up to discharge their lifeless cargo. An adjacent door accessed the cold storage vault where an assistant called a diener cleaned, weighed, measured, photographed, X-rayed, and stored bodies before autopsy. The door on the opposite side of the hall opened into an atmospherically self-contained isolation unit called the VIP Suite. There, bodies harboring contagious diseases or those in advanced stages of decomposition were examined while powerful extraction fans sucked up noxious or offensive gasses, forced them into a high-temperature incinerator, and neutralized them.

Mackay sucked in a deep breath, then hurried down the corridor past several doors that opened into various autopsy suites. Each suite was, she knew, equipped with an autopsy station that comprised slanted stainless steel tables, scales, sinks, and sluices enclosed in booths so the pathologist could dictate notes.

One of the doors stood open. Inside, lying on its back on the table, she saw a sheet-draped body that she assumed had once been Reverend John Thompson. She diverted her eyes and knocked on Nelson's office door.

"C'mon in, Kate."

Not much bigger than a walk-in closet, the room contained a desk, a bookcase full of dog-eared medical references, and wall shelves stuffed with diplomas, awards, newspaper clippings, and forensic journals. One shelf held specimen jars filled with human brains and tissue samples preserved in formaldehyde.

Nelson sat at his desk wearing freshly laundered surgical scrubs.

"You X-ray the body yet?" Mackay asked.

"Yep, the diener just finished."

"And?"

"Bullet's lodged in the brain, probably a small caliber. The slug from a larger weapon would've exited and taken the back of the head with it unless it was loaded with wadcutters or dum-dums."

"Loaded with what?"

"Wadcutters are flat-nosed target ammo with low muzzle velocity. Dum-dums are soft bullets designed to flatten and fragment on impact, causing extreme internal damage. We'll know for sure after I open the head."

Nelson glanced at his watch, a stainless Oyster Perpetual Rolex that, along with a new BMW, were the only luxuries he indulged. "Where's Dave?"

"Checking in with his detectives. He'll be here soon."

"We'll wait."

She smiled. "I'm sure he'll appreciate that."

Several years before, Granz was almost killed by a serial killer the press had dubbed the Gingerbread Man. That experience triggered a fresh appreciation for the tenuousness of life that, for him, a trip to the morgue invariably threatened.

"How's he feeling?" Nelson asked.

"He swears he's fine."

"Maybe, but he's got to have an MRI, Kate. Is he having headaches?"

"He says he's not."

"Even so, onset of noticeable symptoms from a serious head injury often takes weeks or months. By then it could be too late. I don't mean to scare you unnecessarily, but you need to be damn sure he has that MRI."

"You know Dave when he makes up his mind."

"Try, Katie. Try hard. His life could depend on it."

• • •

When Granz arrived, Nelson slid on latex gloves, pushed a black plastic brick-shaped block under the corpse's head to hold it up for examination, switched on two intense white overhead lights and a camera, pulled down a microphone, and started dictating.

"The body is that of a well-developed, well-nourished Caucasian male, late fifties to early sixties, seventy-six inches in length, weighing about two hundred forty-five pounds. Rigor mortis is absent. Hair is medium-length gray. Nose and ears are unremarkable."

He lifted the upper and lower lips. "Teeth normal."

He rolled the body from side to side to examine the back of the torso, then lifted each arm and leg to check underlying tissues. He looked into the ears, nose, mouth and eyes, then visually inspected the other body openings.

"Chest is symmetrical, abdomen flat," he dictated in a soft monotone. "External genitalia normal, upper and lower extremities show no deformities. Hands and nails clean and evidence no injury. No visible scars or tattoos."

Then, Nelson directed his attention to the head. "A single contact gunshot wound displaying black soot outside the skin, lacerated skin that has been seared by the weapon's discharge gasses, and lack of powder stippling. Entry wound is in the center of the forehead, five centimeters below the hairline.

"Projectile perforated the medial anterior cortex

on a front-to-back"—he consulted the X ray hanging on the lighted film reader—"slightly downward track. The opening measures approximately six-point-five millimeters. There is no exit wound.

"Pull up your face masks," Nelson instructed. "There'll be some aerosolization—airborne particulate material is unavoidable with a cranial saw."

Granz and Mackay, both wearing surgical scrubs, placed their masks over their faces.

Nelson combed the corpse's gray hair forward, then covered his own nose and mouth and switched on the Stryker saw, a special vibrating instrument that cuts bone but not soft tissue.

It bogged down slightly as the blade bit into the occipital bone, and threw off a faint mist of powdered bone and smoke as the saw cut toward the front, around the periphery of the skull below the hairline.

"Now for the fun part." He set aside the saw. "Gotta be careful when I lift this off so the dura—the cover of the brain—stays with the calavarium."

He tugged gently. As the top lifted free the skull grated together, like two halves of a split coconut being twisted, and made a slight sucking sound. He set the skull aside, then severed the spinal cord attachment and tentorium, lifted the brain out, and set it on the table.

"I'll put it in a jar of formalin for a couple of weeks to firm up the tissue before dissection," he explained, "but first I'll remove the bullet."

With long-nosed, soft-plastic forceps Nelson carefully probed the wound, pulled out the bullet, and dropped it in a clear plastic evidence bag, which he handed to Granz, who sealed and initialed it.

"The slug's not badly deformed. DOJ shouldn't have any trouble IDing the weapon that fired it."

He rolled the body onto its right side and slid another body-block under the back, forcing the chest to protrude and the arms and neck to fall back. Then he pulled a black-handled Buck knife from a leather case, sharpened it on a sheet of extrafine sandpaper, and drew the razor-sharp blade down an eight-by-ten sheet of paper. The paper sliced cleanly into two pieces, which he tossed in a trash basket.

"Better than a scalpel."

He sliced V-shaped incisions from each shoulder to the abdomen, and a horizontal cut from hipbone to hipbone, then pulled the chest flap over the face, and peeled the skin off the rib cage. With a small battery-powered Stryker saw, he removed the rib cage to expose the inner organs.

He nudged the innards with his hand, but before lifting out the lungs and organ block, he glanced at Granz. "I see nothing unusual. Cause of death was the bullet to the brain. Why don't you two take off."

"Gladly." Granz removed his scrubs and helped Mackay with hers. "Wanta stop at Starbucks for coffee on the way home, Babe?"

"Sure," she told him. "I could use it."

"Me too." Granz turned to Nelson. "Give us an

hour, then if you find anything unexpected, call me at home."

"Will do." Nelson started to lift the organ block out of the body, but stopped.

"Kate?" Morgan called at their backs.

She turned. "Yeah?"

"Remember what I told you."

✚ CHAPTER 7

"What'd Doctor Death mean by 'Remember what I told you'?"

A newspaper had once run an article that hung the nickname on Morgan Nelson, and it had stuck, at least with the cops.

Granz bit a corner off his lemon tart, set it back on the saucer, and washed it down with a cautious sip of steaming espresso.

"Please don't call him that," Mackay said.

"Sorry. What'd he mean?"

They sat at a window table in the mall Starbucks, watching last-minute shoppers hustling back to their cars loaded down with bags of food and Christmas presents.

"He reminded me to be sure you keep your promise," Mackay said.

"I always keep my promises." He took another sip of coffee. "What promise?"

"That you'd go in for an MRI."

"I said I'd think about it after the holidays if I didn't feel a hundred percent. I feel two hundred percent."

"Have you been having headaches lately?" she asked.

"No worse than usual."

"I didn't know you usually had them."

"Don't twist my words, Babe. Everyone has headaches."

Mackay rolled her eyes. "Not everyone got knocked unconscious and landed in the hospital less than a month ago."

"They're nothing," he assured her.

"How often are you having headaches?"

"Not too often."

"That's helpful. How bad are they?"

"Not too bad."

"Don't be evasive."

He grinned. "Sorry."

"So—how bad are they?"

"I'll bet at law school you got an A-plus in ruthless cross-examination, but I already have a mother."

"I'm not trying to be your mother." She set her coffee down and picked up one of his hands. "I'm your wife. I love you and I worry about you."

"I love you, too, but there's no need to worry."

"Promise?"

He held up his right hand. "Scout's honor."

"Don't be insincere. How bad are they?" she persisted.

"I told you, if I don't feel better after the holidays I'll think about an MRI."

"You'd better, because I'm going to bring it up again on January second."

"Figures," Granz conceded with a lopsided grin. "Can we talk about something else?"

"Like what?"

"Reverend Thompson's murder."

"Sure."

Granz finished his espresso. "What do you think?"

"I think Emma and I would be devastated if anything happened to you."

He kissed the back of her hand. "I meant what do you think about the murder."

"I know what you meant." She slipped her hand from his and thought for a moment. "His desk drawers weren't dumped, the room hadn't been ransacked, and the raffle proceeds were inside the community hall. His wallet was in his pants pocket with almost a hundred dollars in it when his body arrived at the morgue. It wasn't a robbery."

"That's my take on it. What else?"

"I suppose he could've gotten in an argument with someone, it heated up, ended in a shooting. But there were no offensive or defensive injuries on his body."

Granz contemplated. "That bothers me, too."

"An execution?"

"I don't think so."

"Why not?"

"Even as old as he was, Thompson was still a big man, an ex-jock."

"Ex-jocks can't get executed?"

"Sure, but if it were an execution pure and simple, why would the shooter get close enough to chance having to fight off a man that size?"

"You tell me."

"He wouldn't. He'd stand out of arm's reach, shoot Thompson, and walk away. No muss, no fuss, no risk."

"Maybe the murderer was bigger than Thompson, or a martial arts expert, someone confident in his ability to defend himself."

"Even then, why risk it?"

Granz shrugged. "Damned if I know."

"I think Thompson either expected his killer or knew him well enough to let him in while remaining seated," Mackay speculated. "Someone he didn't perceive as a threat until it was too late."

"And someone who wanted to see the fear in Thompson's eyes up close and personal when he pulled the trigger."

"Why do you say that?"

"Instinct. I think we'd better rummage around in his past—see what skeletons he's got in his closet."

CHAPTER 8

TUESDAY AFTERNOON, DECEMBER 24

BENEATH A GRAINY PHOTOGRAPH of a Catholic priest with a bald head and thick horn-rimmed glasses, the Teen Beat Section of the *Santa Rita Centennial*'s Christmas Eve edition carried an article that read:

LOCAL ATHLETES HEAD FOR MIDDLE EAST

High School principal/coach Reverend James Benedetti and four varsity basketball team players will spend January in war-torn Afghanistan, assisting Christians in rebuilding their churches. During its 20-year reign of terror, the Taliban regime destroyed nearly all non-Muslim places of worship.

To permit the volunteer athletes to embark on their "mission of mercy and compassion," Benedetti's players voted unanimously to forfeit its five January games. The paper losses will disqualify the team from the State Championships at Sacramento's Arco Arena in March. Many pundits thought the Mustangs had a solid chance of winning the state title this year.

The team's star center, 6'10" Tim Bethay, considered one of the best high-school athletes in the country, is being heavily recruited by many major colleges. Asked how this affects his chances of getting a scholarship from a top program, Bethay said, "I'm sure college recruiters realize that a few basketball games mean nothing compared to the suffering of our Afghan brothers and sisters. It's an honor to help them."

Benedetti said he and his players will celebrate Christmas at home, and leave for Afghanistan from San Francisco on December 26.

"These are sooo yummy."

"Don't talk with your mouth full, please."

Emma swallowed her cookie and washed it down with a sip of milk. "Can I have another cookie?"

"Where do you learn that grammar?" Kathryn Mackay asked her daughter.

"Huh?"

"*May* I have another cookie?" Kathryn corrected.

"Sure, go ahead," Emma told her, "but if you get to eat another one, so do I."

Kathryn smiled. "Deal, but only if you promise not to tell Dave how many I had."

Emma grabbed a frosted bell with red sprinkles, broke off a corner, popped it into her mouth, then handed her mother a green Christmas tree. "Cross my heart."

The kitchen was warm and cozy, filled with the comforting aroma of cinnamon, almond, and vanilla. As the late winter sun melted into the horizon, its rays refracted through the tiny prisms formed on the fogged-up window, and fractured into tiny rainbows that splattered the walls and ceiling with dots of primary colors.

A rack of brightly decorated Christmas sugar cookies cooled on the counter while a timer on the range ticked off the minutes until the dozen baking in the oven would be ready.

Kathryn Mackay wore Ann Taylor jeans and a black T-shirt, both spotted with flour and powdered sugar. She hummed softly.

"I like cooking together, Mom," Emma said.

"Me, too, honey, but with work and all I never seem to have time. I'm sorry."

"That's okay, I understand."

"Thanks."

Emma contemplated the likelihood that she might be able to compound her mother's goodwill into one final treat.

Kathryn spotted her daughter coveting the plate.

"I know what you're thinking, young lady. Forget it."

"Jeez, I thought we were having a Hallmark Moment. They're better with a cookie in your hand."

Kathryn laughed. "You crack me up. That's worth one more, but that's it. I don't want you to spoil your dinner."

"What're we havin'?"

"After Dave finishes his last-minute shopping, he's picking up French bread and a deli tray for us to nibble on while we decorate the Christmas tree."

Kathryn retrieved the last tray from the oven and slid the cookies onto a cooling rack.

As Emma savored her cookie and prolonged the pleasure, she glanced at the newspaper that lay on the table, left over from breakfast. It was turned to the Teen Beat Section, where she had left it. "I'm sure glad I don't go to high school till next year."

Kathryn shook multicolored sprinkles over the fresh, steaming, star-shaped wafers. "Why?"

"When me 'n' Ashley 'n' Lindsey go to high school, our basketball team's gonna win the state championship every year."

Kathryn arched her eyebrows but resisted the urge to correct her daughter's grammar. "Really?"

"Yup, but they won't win it this year."

"They won't?"

"Nope, listen to this."

Emma read the article about Benedetti and his players out loud. "Those guys're so dumb."

"Those boys are doing a fine thing. You should be proud of them."

Emma shrugged. "I s'pose, but I'd be a lot prouder if they won the state championship."

"Emma—"

The phone interrupted her. "That's probably Dave, wanting to know what we want for Christmas."

"Let me get it!"

Emma picked up the phone, listened, then a frightened look crossed her face. Wordlessly, she handed the phone to her mother.

Kathryn frowned, wiped her hands on a paper towel, and held the handset to her ear.

"Hello?"

"I have a message for Sheriff Granz."

The hair on Kathryn's neck bristled when she recognized the eerie monotone generated by an electronic voice changer. The artificial voice was high pitched, like a female, but that told her nothing about the real caller's identity.

"Who is this?" she demanded.

"I have an urgent message for Granz," the falsetto voice repeated.

"How did you get this number?"

The caller ignored her question. "I need to talk to Granz immediately."

"That's not possible."

"Why not?"

"He's not here," Kathryn said.

"Where can I reach him?"

"You can't. Give me your number, I'll ask him to call you as soon as possible."

"That'll be too late."

"Too late for what?" Kathryn asked, but the line was dead.

"Who was it, Mom?" Emma wanted to know.

"I don't know, honey."

"What did she want?"

"To talk to Dave."

" 'Bout what?"

"She didn't say."

"She had a weird voice. What was wrong with it?"

Kathryn absently sprinkled powdered sugar on the final batch of Santa Claus cookies. She picked one up and nibbled off Santa's head.

"I don't know."

✝ CHAPTER 9

SHINY POOLS OF STANDING WATER left over from a rain storm littered the empty parking lot in the early evening darkness. On the far side, a mercury-vapor light lit up the side entrance to Holy Cross High's gymnasium.

He crossed the abandoned school grounds, stopped beneath the light to glance briefly at Reverend James Benedetti's photograph on the cover page of the Centennial's Teen Beat Section, then wadded up the newspaper sheet and dropped it in a deep puddle of muddy water.

The door was locked—no problem for professional tools. With expert manipulation, three carefully selected picks inserted into the pick gun and stuck in the key slot released the tumblers with a gentle snick.

He replaced the tool in his pocket, cracked the door to listen, stepped inside, eased the door shut, and paused to let his eyes adjust to the dim light.

The baskets used for varsity games, at opposite ends of the main court, had been winched up into the open-beam ceiling by steel cables, and two sets of cross-court intramural baskets lowered.

Except for one ten-foot section that remained open, the built-in retractable wooden bleachers that paralleled both sidelines of the main court were nested into the walls. A gym bag, a heap of clothes, and a spare basketball sat on the lower bench of the open bleachers section.

He watched the lone man in gym shorts and sweat-soaked Holy Cross Mustangs T-shirt mop his shiny, hairless pate and brow on a towel with one hand, and bounce a basketball with the other. He was tall, skinny, and stooped, but looked to be in good shape and wasn't wearing glasses.

Clamping his palms over his ears to drown out the sound didn't work—the bouncing ball's deafening echo slammed around the huge room like marbles in an empty bucket, landed on his head, and amplified through his brain.

Benedetti tossed the towel to the floor.

"On this holiest of Holy nights—" the Reverend spoke aloud, putting the final touch on his Christmas Eve sermon in his most efficacious pulpit voice, "let us learn from the example set by our selfless basketball players, who have sacrificed an extremely important event in their young lives to help less fortunate people in Afghanistan."

Benedetti stopped preaching to concentrate on basketball. He bent at the knees, dribbled to the paint on the far end, finger-rolled in a left-handed lay-up, and raised his clenched fist over his head.

• • •

When the priest ran to the opposite end, he strode purposefully but silently across the court, pulled the priest's horn-rimmed glasses out of the gym bag, and crushed them on the floor with his shoe, then sat on a bleacher seat near the top.

Benedetti dribbled the basketball back toward the near basket, reciting the sermon under his breath, pulled up, and launched a jumper from beyond the three-point line. The ball whispered through with a swish and bounced back to him on the backspin.

"Father Benedetti?"

"Yes." The priest stopped. *"Who's there?"*

"May I talk to you?"

"I suppose so." Benedetti picked the towel up off the floor, wiped his face, and trotted toward the bleachers. *"Is it important?"*

"Very."

"How did you know I was here?"

"I called your secretary. She told me where to find you."

"How did you—" Benedetti paused, confused. *"I locked the doors."*

"I let myself in."

"I don't understand. Where are my glasses?" Benedetti fumbled in his gym bag, then dumped its contents on the seat and squinted toward the voice. *"Do I know you?"*

"It's possible."

"I'm not sure I like this."

Benedetti frowned and took a step backward, but pulled up abruptly when he stepped on the remains of his eyeglasses.

"What do you want to talk to me about?"

"Business."

"What kind of business?"

He reached under his jacket and pulled out a 6-inch .357-magnum Colt Python.

"The unfinished kind."

Benedetti involuntary gasped. "Wha-what are you doing?"

"Finishing business."

"Don't do that!"

He aimed the Python, tightened his sphincter muscle, and squeezed the trigger.

The high-velocity slug ripped through Benedetti's left hip, spun him around, tore his femur out of its socket, and shattered his pelvic bone, releasing great rhythmic spurts of blood.

The priest collapsed, groaning, falling onto his back, his left toes still pointed unnaturally down toward the floor. Blood coursed down his thigh and pooled under his buttocks.

The shooter clomped down the bleachers and stood over the priest, his right hand dangling at his side, still grasping the pistol.

Clutching his thigh, Benedetti tried to crawl away, but made it only a few feet before the shooter stuck the bottom of his shoe against the top of the priest's bald head.

"Help me, please," Benedetti looked up at his attacker and pleaded.

"Go to hell."

"My God, I'm bleeding."

"Yes, you are."

"Why do you want to hurt me?" Benedetti whimpered.

"I don't want to hurt you, I want to kill you," he spat, then blew away the top of Reverend James Benedetti's head.

The shooter stared at the twitching body for a moment, dropped the pistol, and strode across the shiny hardwood floor. He pulled out his tools, locked the door behind him, tugged off the latex gloves, and shoved them in his front pants pockets with the pick gun.

✝ CHAPTER 10

"Emma, come in here, please." Kathryn Mackay was at her computer in the spare bedroom that she and Dave shared as a home office, e-mailing last-minute Christmas greetings to her relatives in Detroit and Cleveland.

Emma stuck her head around the corner of the door and peeked in.

Their yellow Lab squatted on his haunches, staring at Kathryn adoringly. The dog's muzzle, beyond the reach of his long tongue, was dusty white and powdered sugar hung from his whiskers like fresh snow clinging to bare tree branches. He licked his lips, yawned, and burped.

"Jeez, Sam, you're so uncouth!"

"Yes, Mom?" Emma asked.

"Did you feed cookies to Sam?"

"A couple."

"Define 'a couple.' "

"Four."

"Why did you do that?"

" 'Cause it's seven-thirty, and Dave's not home with dinner yet, and me 'n' Sam were starved."

"*Sam and I* were starved."

"You too?" Emma lost the battle to keep a straight face. "Sorry."

"Don't give the dog any more sweets."

"It's Christmas Eve."

"You'll make him sick."

"What a Grinch."

"Emma—" The sound of a key in the front door interrupted Kathryn's lecture on canine nutrition.

"That's Dave." Kathryn clicked the Send key, zapping her e-mails into cyberspace, and logged off her computer.

"I hope he's got lots of Christmas presents."

"I'm sure he does. I'll clean Sam up. You go help Dave."

Emma arranged four sets of silverware and red Christmas plates with green napkins at each corner of the glass-topped coffee table, while Dave set out a spread of French bread, Brie, snack crackers, sliced avocado, and a bowl of fresh cracked crab on ice.

Kate carried in a tray with two stemmed glasses of white wine and one with Martinelli's sparkling apple juice, and sat on the sofa beside her husband.

Emma took her glass. "Mom said you were picking up a deli tray."

"Changed my mind when I drove by the wharf and saw a crab boat offloading a fresh catch."

"M-m-m, I love crab."

"You must be starved," Kathryn told Dave.

"What makes you think so?"

"You haven't taken a bite of food yet, but you were chewing like crazy."

"I was? I didn't realize it. Who's the fourth plate for?" he asked.

"Sam," Emma said.

Dave looked around. "Where is he?"

"Must be in my room."

"Usually you can't keep him away from food."

"He already ate," Kathryn answered.

"Well, after dinner I'll give him a couple of cookies for dessert," Dave said. "After all, it *is* Christmas."

"Yeah," Emma said, then told Dave, "I'm glad you're not a Scrooge."

"What?"

"Private joke between Mom and me."

"Oh."

Dave tinked his wineglass against Kathryn's and Emma's. "To our family."

Emma ate some crab, avocado, and a piece of bread, then reached for more bread.

"Try some Brie," Kathryn suggested.

"I like Jack cheese," Emma said; then, eyeing the new gifts, she asked, "Anything under the tree for me?"

"I doubt it," Dave teased, "but why don't you check before we decorate the tree?"

Emma plopped down by the tree, started four piles—including one for Sam—and announced the recipient of each gift. When all the gifts were separated, she methodically rattled each of her own and guessed what it contained. She saved the biggest one for last, held it to her ear, shook it, and turned it upside down and shook it again. "What is it?"

"Gotta wait till tomorrow morning," Dave answered.

"That's torture."

"I know," Dave conceded with a smile.

"It's child abuse."

"Tough."

"Gimme a hint."

"Nope."

"Silver Bells" was playing on the stereo. Kathryn stopped humming along, leaned over, and whispered in her husband's ear, "What *is* in that big package?"

"The CD Walkman and French language disks you asked me to buy. When I had it wrapped, I asked them to put it in a larger box so she couldn't guess it."

"Very devious—I like the way you think."

"You like the way I do anything else?" he whispered back.

She checked to be sure her daughter wasn't watching and ran her hand up his thigh. "Maybe—I'll let you know later."

"Didja tell Dave about that weird phone call, Mom?" Emma asked.

"I forgot, thanks for reminding me." Kathryn quickly described the voice-changed call. "Whoever it was hung up when I asked for a number so you could call back."

"What time?"

Kathryn thought for a moment. "Five, maybe five-fifteen."

"You sure the voice was mechanically changed?" he asked, arching his eyebrows.

Kathryn tilted her head. "Maybe I'm wrong—maybe there was just a bad connection."

"I'll bet that's it. I checked my office voice mail with my cell phone while I was driving home—there were no messages on it, so it couldn't have been very important."

"Well, there's nothing you can do about it now," she said. "Let's decorate the tree."

Dave strung the lights, but they wouldn't come on until he tightened the bulbs. When he found the errant bulb the multicolored strand sprang to life. When he finished, Kathryn hung ornaments, singing to herself.

Emma pretended to supervise. She was working on a cookie when the phone rang. She jumped up and dashed toward the kitchen. "I'll get it."

Emma listened, said, "Uh-huh," and handed Dave the phone. "It's County Comm," she told him, her voice reflecting her disappointment. She knew a call from County Comm meant either her mother or Dave—or both—were being called out.

He listened for a minute, said they'd be right there, and hung up. "There's been another one-eighty-seven," he told Kathryn with a shake of his head.

"One-eighty-seven means murder," Emma said. "I knew it—you have to go out."

"Afraid so, honey. Your mom, too. I'm sorry."

"That's okay, Dave, I'm used to it."

Kathryn stood up. "I'll call Ruth, ask her to come down and stay with Em."

"Mom! I'm old enough to baby-sit."

"That's different," Kathryn protested.

"No it isn't—why do you think I'm taking baby-sitting classes at the Red Cross? I'll finish decorating our tree."

"Get a pillow and blanket off your bed," Dave told Emma, "lie on the sofa and watch TV with Sam. Call us if you get scared. We'll only be a couple of hours."

"You're sure it'll be all right?" Kathryn asked when Emma left.

Dave picked up the phone. "I'll call Ruth, ask her to drop in and wish Emma Merry Christmas, eat some cookies, watch television for a couple of hours."

CHAPTER 11

SHERIFF'S CHIEF OF DETECTIVES Miller, Granz, Mackay, and forensic pathologist Nelson stood quietly in a tight circle around the body as if by not acknowledging what they saw, it might turn out to be a terrible mistake.

"Reverend James Benedetti," Miller finally commented grimly.

Mackay stuffed her hands in her coat's hand-warmer pockets. "Two priests shot dead in three days."

Miller nodded. "That's why I asked you to come out, Doc," he said to Nelson. "Figured it'd help if you saw it up close and personal."

"You were right," Nelson told him.

"Any idea how the perp got into the gym?" Granz asked.

Miller shrugged his shoulders. "Not yet. Yamamoto's team's checking all the doors and windows—there's a shitload of 'em—so far, no sign of forced entry."

Nelson bent over at the waist and studied the body, then straightened up and rubbed his lower spine. "My damn back isn't getting any younger. The crime scene been photographed yet?"

"You know Yamamoto—if he hadn't finished shooting his crime scene, we wouldn't be standing here," Miller told him. "They're scouring the rest of the gym for evidence now."

Nelson pinched his lower lip between his thumb and index finger. "The head wound was inflicted second, as an afterthought."

"What makes you think so?" Mackay asked.

"Those bloody smudges on the floor that start ten or fifteen feet from the body and end under the buttocks."

"Meaning?"

"I'll know more after the autopsy, but the hip shot damn near tore Benedetti's leg off, severing the femoral artery in the process. I figure he fell and tried to crawl away, but didn't get very far because he was as good as dead from blood loss. The head shot entry wound's in the forehead—he was lying on his back when the second round was fired."

"Looking at his killer," Mackay observed, "just like Thompson."

"Yep."

Nelson knelt, rolled the priest's head to the side, inspected the gaping exit wound in the back of the head, and pointed to a hole in the floor that had filled with blood. "Probe that, you'll find the slug."

"If Benedetti was obviously dying, why would the murderer take the time to stand over him and shoot him in the head?" Mackay wondered.

"My guess—to watch him die," Granz answered.

"Like Thompson," Mackay interjected. "Same MO—could it be the same shooter?"

Miller rubbed his palms together to warm them. "I don't think so. Thompson's shot once with a little .25-caliber automatic that the perp takes with him. Benedetti's killer blasts him twice with a cannon, drops it, and hauls ass."

Granz' eyes widened. "We've got the weapon?"

"Yamamoto recovered a Colt Python on the floor beside the body."

"I haven't seen a Python in twenty years," Nelson said, "but a .357-magnum would certainly do the kind of damage to the body that we see."

"That's another MO dissimilarity," Miller said. "With Thompson, there was just enough force used to get the job done, not to mention Thompson was offed in his rectory, while Benedetti was in a gym playing basketball."

"Thompson was a parish priest," Mackay pointed out. "Benedetti was a basketball coach. They were both killed where they worked."

"True," Miller conceded. "But Thompson's killer walks up and sticks the pistol barrel against his head and pulls the trigger once, execution style. To me that says 'I'm pissed.' Benedetti's killer stayed at a safe distance."

"Doc says the second shot was unnecessary, fired from an arm's length," Mackay told him.

Miller nodded. "You're right."

"That says 'I'm pissed' just as loudly."

"Possibly."

"They were both about the same age, they were both alone when they were shot to death," she argued.

"Most murders go down without witnesses," Miller noted.

"True, but there are too many similarities in these two for them to be coincidence."

"It might be the same perp," Miller conceded. "I was just yankin' your chain."

"Let's not rule out the possibility there are two killers out there," Granz said. "On the other hand, if there's not, we've got a shooter with a serious hard-on for Catholic priests."

Nelson nodded. "Maybe a hard-on literally."

Granz looked at the pathologist. "Meaning?"

Nelson licked his dry, chapped lips and pulled away a piece of dry skin with his teeth, which he spat on the floor. "With two dead priests, if it *is* the same perp, it might be a sexual-molest victim."

Granz glanced at the body and unconsciously brushed his hair back off his forehead, thinking. "Nothing about it suggests a sex-related or homosexual killing. Let's not jump to conclusions, Doc."

"Jump to conclusions?" Nelson challenged. "Hundreds of pedophile priests have been exposed in the past year or so, all across the country. Some guy in Baltimore tried to blow away the priest that molested him. Too bad he was such a lousy shot, or he would've succeeded. Who's to say Thompson and Benedetti weren't molesters?"

"Who's to say they were?" Granz retorted. "New church guidelines require a Diocese to report any allegation of sexual abuse of a minor to civil authorities. We've received no such reports."

"Not yet," Nelson told him. "Besides, they're only required to report *future* offenses to civil authorities. For past molestations, only an internal church investigation and removal of the priest from the ministry are required."

"True, but neither Thompson nor Benedetti had been defrocked so there must've been no prior allegations against them," Granz pointed out. "We ought to keep it in mind, but I say it's no more than a remote possibility."

"You're probably right." Nelson motioned for two of his deputy coroners, who waited by the door. When they started loading the corpse into a body bag, he said, "I'll autopsy him tomorrow."

Granz turned to Miller. "How about you attend the autopsy instead of me for a change?"

"I was hopin' you'd let me."

Miller, Granz, and Mackay walked away to let Nelson and his team do their jobs.

"Who found the body?" Granz asked.

"His secretary." Miller checked his spiral-bound notebook. "Name's Mary Shotwell."

"How's she handling it?"

"Surprisingly well."

"Is it possible she's the shooter?"

"I doubt it, she's in her late fifties or early sixties."

"So was Benedetti. Maybe he was involved with her."

Miller puffed his cheeks out with air. "She weighs at least two-twenty."

"You got something against overweight people?" Mackay challenged.

Miller patted his stomach. "Not me, I kinda like 'em, but Shotwell's also got white hair, thick bifocals, and false teeth."

"Different strokes," Granz commented. "You interview her?"

"Not yet."

"Where is she?"

"In the gymnasium office. I posted a uniform outside the door."

Granz turned. "Let's go talk to Secretary Shotwell, see if she can shed some light on the Reverend's murder."

✝ CHAPTER 12

"IT'S MY FAULT." Mary Shotwell lay on a sofa with a folded damp washcloth on her forehead, but sat up when Granz and Mackay entered the gym office. Her eyes were red and puffy, but she wasn't crying.

"What's your fault?" Granz asked.

"Reverend Benedetti's death. I think I killed him."

Mackay slid a chair close to the sofa. "Mrs. Shotwell, I'm District Attorney Kathryn Mackay, and this is Sheriff David Granz."

"I know who you both are, I read the newspapers."

"Before you say anything more, I need to advise you of your constitutional right to an attorney, and to have the attorney present with you while you answer questions."

"Why would I need an attorney?"

"You were about to confess that you shot Reverend Benedetti."

"I didn't shoot him."

"I'm confused." Mackay glanced at Granz, who turned his palms up. "What did you mean when you said you killed him?"

"I think the murderer called, and I told him where to find the Reverend."

Granz took a chair beside Mackay. "Please explain."

"Reverend Benedetti liked to play basketball while he prepared his sermons. This afternoon, he didn't want to be disturbed for any reason because he wanted tonight's Midnight Mass sermon to be perfect. But then the man called—I considered it urgent enough to disregard the Reverend's directions."

"Tell us about it."

"The caller said his university was in a hurry to grant Tim Bethay academic and athletic scholarships before he left for Afghanistan."

"Didn't you think that was unusual?"

"Not at all. Tim's being recruited by UCLA, Duke, Kansas, and several others to play basketball. They sometimes call at odd times."

"When did you get this call?"

"About five o'clock."

"Did the caller give you his name?"

"No, and I neglected to ask, but I gave him directions to the gym. I killed the Reverend as surely as if I'd shot him myself." Her lips trembled but she stopped herself. "I guess it hasn't sunk in yet that he's dead—I haven't cried."

"We'll understand if you need to cry, Mrs. Shotwell," Mackay assured her. "It's all right."

"No, it isn't. The Reverend continually advised me to be strong. Ten years ago, when my husband died, I realized how valuable that advice was. I need to be strong now, too."

"You're okay to answer a few more questions?"

"Yes, he would expect me to help."

"Thank you. Why did you come to the gym?"

"Once he gets the gist of his sermon in mind, he dictates it to me, and I type it up for him." She looked at her feet. "We're pretty old-fashioned."

"I still use shorthand I learned in high school," Mackay told her. "My secretary takes dictation, too."

"Anyway," Shotwell continued, "when the Reverend didn't return to the office by eight-thirty, I became irritated with him, and drove over so I could scold him and get the sermon typed." She squeezed her eyes shut. "That's when I found his body."

"How long have you worked for Reverend Benedetti?" Granz asked.

"More than twenty years. The Reverend hired me as his secretary right after he was transferred here. We've been together since."

"Do you know of anyone who might want to hurt him, anyone who was angry with him?"

"Reverend Benedetti was the finest man I ever knew. Everyone loved him—especially his boys."

"His boys?" Granz asked.

"In addition to being the high school principal, he coached boys' basketball and wrestling. He called all his athletes 'his boys.' It was a rare month that one of his players from years past didn't stop by to say thanks."

"You said the Reverend was transferred to Holy Cross. Do you recall from where?"

"Goodness no, it's been so long. Southern California, I believe. Is it important?"

"Probably not," Granz assured her. "If it turns out to be, we'll check Diocese personnel records."

Granz contemplated his next question. "The sooner we can eliminate dead ends, the faster we'll catch the Reverend's murderer. Where were you between five o'clock this afternoon and now?"

"I'm a suspect?"

"Everyone's a suspect until they're eliminated," Mackay told her. "Of course, you don't have to answer the question if you don't want to."

"I was working at the parish office, putting together travel documents, itineraries, and attending to everything else for their trip to Afghanistan."

"Can anyone verify that?"

"I was alone all day. Staff get Christmas Eve off to be with their families."

"I see," Granz said. "Will you submit to a GSR test?"

"A what?"

"A gunshot residue test to establish that you haven't fired a gun recently."

"Does it hurt?"

"No, and it only takes a few minutes."

"I don't see why you suspect me, but I'll take the test." She sniffed, as if clearing mucus from her nostrils would get rid of the indignity as well, then absently tugged at the tops of her support hose. "Is there anything else?"

"Just a couple more questions," Granz told her. "When you came into the gym, which door did you use?"

"The side door by the parking lot, as always. The Reverend and my cars are still in the parking lot."

"Yes, ma'am, we parked by them. Was the door locked when you arrived?"

"Absolutely; the Reverend invariably locked the doors when he was here alone."

"How did you get in?"

"I have a key."

"May I borrow it, please?"

"Mister Miller took it."

"What else does that key fit?"

"Nothing, just the side door. It was the Reverend's private entrance."

"How many other people have keys to that door?"

"Just the Reverend and me."

"How about the other doors?"

"Lots of people have keys."

"Do his players have keys?"

"No. Reverend Benedetti had tremendous patience with his boys, but he wasn't a saint. Sometimes he wanted to escape—teenagers can be very demanding."

Granz stood, and Mackay did likewise.

"Thank you very much," Granz said. "If you'll wait here for a few minutes, I'll ask Lieutenant Miller to administer the GSR test, then you may go home."

"Thank you."

Mackay stopped at the door. "I'm very sorry for your loss, Mrs. Shotwell."

"It's all our losses, Ms. Mackay."

"Yes, ma'am."

They found Miller inspecting the side door to the gym.

"Did you determine how the shooter got in?" Granz asked.

"Damn strange." Miller scratched his scalp. "No forced entry. Every door and window was locked, including this one, where Benedetti and Shotwell apparently came in."

He pointed to the floor. "There're some dried footprints that lead from this door to the bleachers, up and down the bleacher seats, around the body, then return. I'd say the shooter came and went through this door."

"The prints good enough to ID?"

"Yamamoto says 'no' but he's a fuckin' pessimist. Thinks the 49ers won the Super Bowl five times outta sheer luck and ain't ever gonna win it again. Never heard such bullshit."

"Jazzbo—"

"Yamamoto photographed the prints anyway. Maybe we'll get lucky."

Granz thought for a moment. "Tell Yamamoto to remove the lock in the side door, send it to DOJ. If the perp picked it, the tumblers'll show microscopic tool marks, no matter how good he is. Either the shooter was an accomplished B-and-E man or had a key, and Shotwell says she and Benedetti had the only keys."

"Will do, boss. Anything else?"

"Nada."

"Why don't you and Kate go home. I'll wrap it up here and buzz you if anything turns up."

As they walked toward the door, Mackay asked, "What made you think the door lock might have been picked?"

"Just a hunch."

✝ CHAPTER 13

Tucked in a third-floor corner of the ugly five-story concrete County Government Center, the Sheriff's conference room overlooked San Lorenzo Park, now submerged under a month's worth of stagnant rain water.

"Good morning, Sheriff."

Granz scowled. "Inspector."

"The District Attorney will be up shortly."

"That's good of her."

DA Inspector Donna Escalante took a chair facing a beat-up blackboard on which strategy had been plotted for longer than she'd been a cop.

In her midthirties, Escalante's conservative

pleated trousers, button-front shirt, and double-breasted jacket couldn't hide her taut athletic figure. Except for a little lipstick she wore no makeup. Short, jet-black hair accentuated chiseled Mayan features, and she moved with a lithe, aloof, exotic feline grace that compelled second looks from men and women alike.

Miller opened the door, checked out the room, aimed a forefinger at his boss, thumbed a make-believe hammer, blew the imaginary powder smoke off his fingertip, and dropped into a chair beside Escalante. "Merry Christmas, Chiquita."

"Hola." Her stoic expression didn't change. "Christmas was yesterday."

"No shit? You mean we spent all day watchin' an autopsy and gettin' shuck-n-jived by uncooperative Mackerel Snappers—and missed ol' Saint Nick?"

"Please don't use derogatory terms like *Mackerel Snappers*," Escalante reprimanded Miller. "We're 'Catholics,' and we're no longer required to eat fish on Fridays."

"Sorry."

"And there's no need to swear."

"Sorry again." Really sincere this time.

She couldn't suppress a small smile. "Apology accepted, Lieutenant."

Miller was the only person with whom anyone had ever seen her make jokes.

Granz checked his watch. "Inspector Escalante, do you have any idea how long before—"

Nelson and Mackay rushed in, followed by DA Chief Inspector James Fields.

Fields combed his thinning hair over his bald spot, disguised his teenage-acne skin pits with makeup, and tucked his suit coat's right sleeve into the empty space where his hand had been until a courtroom bomb blew it off a few years earlier. Shunning disability retirement, he'd converted to left-handed, then picked up where he left off as if nothing happened. Mackay's first official act as DA was to promote him to Chief.

"When I called everyone last night, I said the briefing would start at eight-fifteen," Granz said.

Nelson passed each person a manila folder. "My fault we're late. I wrapped up Benedetti's autopsy protocol this morning, and stopped by the DA's office."

"The District Attorney hears it first, and the Sheriff second?"

"Didn't know my autopsy protocols were top secret until you saw them. I walked up from the second floor with Kate and Jim. They asked about it, and I told them."

"Well, maybe you could fill the rest of us in."

Nelson shot Granz a quizzical look. "Yesterday's autopsy confirmed Benedetti died from a bullet that penetrated the brain's frontal lobe, transited the parietal, and exited the occipital."

Nelson pulled an eight-by-ten color photograph from his folder and motioned for the others to do the same. "It was the second shot fired. See the hemorrhaging at the point of entry?"

Escalante leaned forward in her beat-up,

chromed-plastic chair and studied the picture. "Yes. How does that mean it was the fatal shot?"

"The heart stops pumping at death and blood pressure falls to zero. Benedetti was alive when the perp fired the head shot, or there'd've been no bleeding. The hip shot shattered the pelvis and femur, severed the femoral artery, and caused massive blood loss that in itself would've been fatal except—"

"The killer shot him again," Fields finished.

"That's right—stood over the top of Benedetti and shot him at close range."

He pulled out a close-up of the priest's forehead, taken before the skull was removed, on which he'd circled numerous black dots near the entry wound.

"Fired from a distance of three feet or less, a gun expels gunpowder and other residue with enough force to tattoo the victim's skin—the closer it's fired, the more stippling and tighter the pattern. Beyond about three feet, there's no tattooing."

"Every rookie cops knows that," Granz told him.

Nelson ignored the jab and pointed with the tip of a roller-ball pen. "This spread tells us the gun was fired from two to three feet—the stippling pattern I'd expect if a six-footer held a Colt Python at arm's length and stood over his victim, who was lying on the floor."

"Did you examine the slug in the floor under Benedetti's head?" Fields asked.

"Yep." Nelson's medical knowledge was equaled only by his firearms and ballistics expertise. "And the one I recovered from the pelvis. Yamamoto removed the slug in the floor along with a square of wood about eighteen-by-eighteen inches, and—"

Miller whistled softly. "The Diocese is gonna be pissed when they find out how much it costs to repair that bird's-eye maple."

"Knock off the wisecracks." Granz glared at his Lieutenant. "Go on, Doc."

Miller glanced at Escalante. The slightest of shrugs lifted her shoulders.

"Looks like the same gun fired both bullets," Nelson continued. "Land and groove spacing and right-hand rifling twist are consistent with a Colt. The Python recovered at the scene was probably the murder weapon. Let's hope we get lucky when DOJ test-fires it and runs the serial number."

"This guy's too smart to leave a calling card," Granz commented. "The Colt's a dead end."

"What about the test for gunshot residue on Mary Shotwell's hands?" Mackay asked.

Miller turned serious. "Needed to nail her or eliminate her as a suspect ASAP, so to be sure it wasn't fu— botched, I swabbed her for two samples—one for atomic absorption and one for scanning electron microscope. I hand-carried them to DOJ for analysis. Negative for GSR. With both AA and SEM negative, it's conclusive that Shotwell didn't shoot Benedetti."

"No surprise," Granz said. "We figured that much at the scene."

"I don't believe in coincidences," Mackay said.

"Benedetti's murder's got to be related to Thompson's."

Granz wasn't sure he agreed. "Maybe and maybe not. But if they are, and if we're going to find out what they had in common that's worth getting whacked out over, we've got to dig deep into their backgrounds, see what surfaces."

Granz turned to Miller. "You and Escalante talked to church reps yesterday—what'd you learn?"

"Zilch. We got stonewalled. Nobody knew anything, kept referring us to someone else—a big circle jerk."

"Who did you talk to?"

"At Sacred Heart Parish, a guy named Ronald Leahy." Miller glanced at Escalante. "What's his title?"

"Pastoral Associate," Escalante answered, "and I agree he's following orders to keep his mouth shut. We asked to see Thompson's personnel file, but Leahy said it had been transferred to the Diocese in Monterey."

"That's what Shotwell told me about Benedetti's when I called her," Miller added.

"So Escalante and I drove to Monterey to see Monsignor Donald Winfield, the Vicar General."

"The what?" Fields wasn't Catholic.

"A Vicar's a mouthpiece for a Bishop—in this case, Bishop Jeffrey Davidson, who didn't make a personal appearance, and according to Winfield, doesn't know anything either. Winfield's also Diocese Operations and Personnel Director."

"Then he's got Thompson and Benedetti's personnel folders."

"That's what we figured." Escalante's face showed a rare emotion—frustration. "But he wouldn't confirm or deny that their files were transferred to Diocese headquarters or, for that matter, that they even have personnel records."

"Of course they have records." Granz sighed. "Did Winfield say anything at all?"

"Yes, he said if police want personnel files, we've gotta get 'em through legal channels."

"That's what he said?"

Miller pulled an unfiltered Camel out of his pack, started to light up, glanced around and thought better of it. "Can't smoke anyplace anymore. It's un-American."

He dropped the cigarette on the table. "Escalante sugarcoated it. Winfield said if cops want to see their records, they have to get a court order, and they better be ready for a, quote, 'hell of a legal battle.' "

"Great." Granz ran his fingers through his hair.

"It gets worse. Winfield says we can't contact any Diocese employee without clearing it through the Bishop first."

Mackay frowned. "They can't tell us who we can and can't talk to."

"No, but they can make it as difficult as possible if they want to," Miller told her.

"Did you ask whether or not the Diocese has received complaints of sexual misconduct against their priests?"

"Yeah, we did. Winfield said the Diocese handed over a dozen cases involving allegations of sexual abuse of minors by priests to the Monterey County DA. I checked with Monterey—they're looking into cases from nineteen fifty-three through ninety-four but haven't filed any charges yet."

"What about our county?" Mackay asked.

"According to Winfield, there've been no reportable cases in Santa Rita."

"Did you remind him of the four civil lawsuits filed against the Diocese in the past twenty years, alleging sexual misconduct on the part of priests at three of our local parishes?"

"Damn straight."

"And?"

"He said they involved consensual sex with adults and the cases were settled—there was nothing to report to authorities. He says they've cleaned house."

"You think he was being truthful?" Mackay asked.

Miller glanced at Escalante, who answered, "It's impossible to say for sure, but he emphatically denied that any priest now serving in the Monterey Diocese is a pedophile. My gut instinct says he was telling the truth."

"Let's hope so," Mackay said. "On the other hand, let's not overlook the possibility they're misleading us. When there's a coverup, it usually comes from the highest level."

"That's true," Miller continued, "and it looks like word got to Monterey that we wanted to talk to them before Escalante and I did. Winfield gave me this." Miller handed Mackay a sheet of paper. "Legal Department letterhead."

"Gerald Scalisi, of Counsel," Mackay read aloud.

Nelson arched his eyebrows. "In-house legal staff?"

"Why not?" Mackay turned toward Nelson. "The Diocese oversees four counties, fifty parishes, an eight-digit annual budget, and half-a-million Catholics. The church is no different from any other big business that has to deal with complex finances, contracts, litigation, employee relations, you name it."

"What now?" Fields asked.

Mackay looked at Miller, then at Escalante. "Would it do any good if the Sheriff or I contacted Winfield or Bishop Davidson personally?"

Escalante shook her head.

"Not a chance." Miller eyed the Camel. "They've already circled the wagons."

Mackay thought for a moment, then told Escalante, "Prepare a subpoena duces tecum for the records, and a subpoena compelling appearance before the Grand Jury."

"Will do. Who do I subpoena to appear?"

"I'm not sure yet."

"Jesus, Kate!" Granz slapped his palms on the table. "If we don't get those records before they're destroyed, we're screwed. How are we going to get someone in front of the Grand Jury if you don't tell her who to serve?"

Mackay gave her husband a stern look. "I'll let

her know after one o'clock. She can serve the subpoenas this afternoon."

"That could be too late."

"I'll convene an emergency session of the Grand Jury for first thing tomorrow morning."

✝ CHAPTER 14

THE COUNTY BUILDING'S cement stairwell rose from the basement to the roof and reeked of paint, disinfectant, and mildew, so Mackay stopped in the hallway outside the Sheriff's conference room to speak with Escalante.

"I'll have my secretary round up as many grand jurors as possible, and I'll call the foreperson personally, to explain the emergency session. Tell the Court Administrator we need a courtroom all day tomorrow."

"Anything else?" Escalante asked.

"Yeah, have the subpoenas ready for service when I get back to the office," Mackay told her.

They headed down quickly, heels clacking on the stainless steel stairs.

"Kate!" Granz' shout echoed back and forth between the bare cement walls. "Kathryn, wait."

Mackay and Escalante stopped on the landing while Granz charged down.

"Glad I caught you. Can we talk a minute?" he panted.

Escalante turned to leave.

"Stay please, Inspector."

Granz' face flushed. "I was rude to you both at the briefing. I don't know why I've been so irritable lately, but I was out of line."

"I didn't notice," Mackay lied.

"I'm sorry," he answered.

"No need to apologize to me, Sheriff," Escalante told him.

"Everyone but you calls me Dave."

"Yes, sir."

"See you later." Granz sprinted back up the stairs two at a time.

Mackay watched until he was gone, then turned to her Inspector, frowning.

"If I'm off base, Ms. Mackay, tell me," Escalante said. "Are you okay?"

"I'm fine."

"You don't look fine."

Mackay hesitated. "I'm seeing my gynecologist at eleven o'clock," she finally said.

"If you'd like to talk, I'm a good listener, and you can trust me to honor a confidence."

Mackay laid her hand on Escalante's forearm momentarily, in an unusual gesture of friendship.

"Thank you, Donna, I might need to take you up on that."

She turned away. "If I don't get moving, I'll be late for the appointment—and my gynecologist can be even grouchier than my husband."

Mackay crossed her right leg over her left knee, bounced her foot furiously, and stared across her doctor's desk. "Well?"

"You're pregnant, Kathryn."

"I know, I've missed two periods. I must have conceived in mid-October."

"Congratulations."

Doctor Diedre Burton leafed through Mackay's medical file and read a page. "Your blood is RH-negative. I'll arrange for your prenatal blood test, and a blood test for your husband, to see if he's positive."

"How long can we wait before his test becomes critical?"

"Even if he and the fetus are RH-positive, which they probably are, we've got until the twenty-eighth week before we start RhoGam injections—assuming you didn't form RH antibodies during a previous pregnancy."

"Is that the only way antibodies could form?"

"It's possible to form antibodies as the result of an abortion or miscarriage," Burton said, then asked, "You've either aborted or miscarried?"

Kathryn nodded. "I miscarried once, in college. What if antibodies are present?"

"I'll monitor you closely and if antibody levels get too high, take special measures."

"Like what?"

"Blood transfusions to the baby or early delivery."

"What happens otherwise?"

"Your antibodies can pass through the placenta and attack the baby's red blood cells, causing severe complications—anything from jaundice to stillbirth."

"Emma's my only child. Her father was RH-negative, and so is she. Couldn't this baby be negative too?"

"Depends."

"On what?"

"If your husband's RH-positive, so is the fetus."

"What are the chances my husband is negative?"

"Not good, but statistically better than Asians—or us blacks, who are ninety-five percent positive—eight out of ten Caucasians test positive."

"So, it's possible the fetus is RH-negative, and there's nothing to worry about."

"It's possible, but there's no way to know without testing your husband's blood. Send him in for a blood draw this afternoon."

"I can't."

Burton leaned forward, elbows on the desk, deep brown eyes boring in on her patient. "Why not?"

"I haven't told him yet that I think I'm pregnant."

"Are you saying you might want to discuss abortion?"

"Not unless my baby has *no* chance of being born healthy." Mackay dropped her eyes. "Even then, I'm not sure I could abort."

"Your baby has an excellent chance of being healthy, but only if we know what problems we face as early as possible. So, trust your husband—tell him about the miscarriage and the RH factor as soon as you get back to your office. Then send him in today for a blood draw."

✠ CHAPTER 15

SEVERAL YEARS BEFORE, the County Board of Supervisors had appointed Kathryn Mackay to fill the remaining term of DA Harold Benton, himself a murder victim, poisoned by County Health Officer Doctor Robert Simmons.

Mackay immediately tossed out the office's hand-me-down furniture and spent her own money to buy beige wool carpeting, a modern executive desk, a plush off-white leather sofa with matching end tables, love seat and interview chairs, then hung a few pieces of original artwork she had acquired over the years from a small art gallery in Zihuatanejo, Guerrero, Mexico.

County employees had gone home for the day when Escalante dropped into a chair and slid the unserved subpoenas across the desk to her boss.

"Their lawyer was waiting when I got to the Diocese. I didn't push when he refused service because he told me the Diocese filed a motion to quash."

"You did the right thing."

"Where does that leave the investigation?"

"Judge Woods set the hearing for nine o'clock tomorrow morning."

"Woods handles juvie," Escalante pointed out unnecessarily.

"Juvenile Court's dark on Fridays. He's the only judge whose calendar was clear."

"Maybe we got lucky, he's an ex-prosecutor."

"Luck shouldn't have anything to do with it. I rescheduled the Grand Jury session to one o'clock, in hopes he'll rule in our favor, so we can get on with it."

"You think he will?"

Mackay's shoulders lifted momentarily. "Let's hope so."

FRIDAY, DECEMBER 27, 9:00 A.M.
SANTA RITA SUPERIOR COURT

The calendar posted outside the door read:

SUPERIOR COURT OF THE STATE OF CALIFORNIA
COUNTY OF SANTA RITA
DEPARTMENT 12

In his sixties, His Honor Jesse Augustus Woods remained trim and fit with a full beard that matched a mop of wiry white hair. During testimony he often turned aside and gazed into space or closed his intense green eyes to concentrate, but missed nothing.

"In the Superior Court of the State of California, in and for the County of Santa Rita, case number 120211," Court Clerk Cathy Radina announced, "the Diocese of Monterey versus the State of California."

Woods surveyed the almost-empty room. "The record shall reflect that District Attorney Kathryn Mackay is present on behalf of the People, and representing the Monterey Diocese, Gerald Scalisi."

Wearing a rough-textured wool suit and a narrow 1950s tie, with a pouty-thick lower lip and black-plastic horn-rimmed glasses, Scalisi could have passed for an old, wrinkled reincarnation of Buddy Holly.

Woods acknowledged each attorney with a slight nod of his woolly head. "The Diocese has brought a 649 motion to dismiss subpoenas issued by the District Attorney seeking to produce certain Diocese personnel records and compel the testimony of a church official before the Santa Rita County Grand Jury."

He turned to the defense table. "It's your motion, Mr. Scalisi. What say you?"

When Scalisi stood, Mackay expected the Crickets to rush in with their guitars to join Scalisi in a few high-pitched bars of "Peggy Sue."

Instead, he addressed the Court in a deep, melodious tenor that Pavarotti would've envied.

"The Monterey Diocese thanks Your Honor for

hearing its motion on such short notice, and shall not consume an excessive amount of the Court's time.

"The motion before the Court poses only one question: Must this Court fervently enforce—or may it frivolously and forever invalidate—the venerable First Amendment to the United States Constitution, by which our Founding Fathers guaranteed our right to worship without government intrusion, government oversight, or government insertion between a Church—any Church—and that Faith's Believers?"

Scalisi cleared his throat. "The future of the fundamental American right to a distinct, total, and inviolate *Separation of Church and State* shall be determined for the next two hundred years by Your Honor's answer to that deceptively simple question."

Scalisi spoke extemporaneously, a gift Mackay admired but lacked, always presenting her courtroom arguments from meticulously prepared notes.

"The answer is obvious—the subpoenas must be quashed. Not only because the records and testimony the District Attorney seeks won't further her investigation, but because they pose a dangerous and unconstitutional invasion of Church affairs that are, and must remain, beyond the reach of government.

"I promised the Court I would not take up too much of its time and I shall not. However, I would like to assure the Court" he turned to Mackay— "and the honorable District Attorney"—he returned his attention to the Bench—"that the Church desires to neither obstruct justice nor thwart law enforcement's investigation into the deaths of two of its most revered clergy.

"The Diocese has engaged an independent investigator, whom I shall supervise, to conduct its own investigation into those deaths. As liaison between the Church, the Sheriff and District Attorney, I will make all relevant information immediately available.

"I offer this compromise in the hope the District Attorney will withdraw her subpoenas and preserve the sanctity and privacy of the Church and its parishioners, while still accomplishing her purpose."

Scalisi sat down at the defense table and folded his hands.

"Ms. Mackay, are the People willing to cancel the subpoenas on the basis Mr. Scalisi proposed?" Woods asked.

"No." Mackay stood. "The subpoenas seek not to violate the sanctity of the Church but, for limited investigative purposes, to identify what commonality exists between those two murdered priests. To that end, the subpoenas seek very specific documents, namely the personnel records of the two priests, and testimony from a single Church official to interpret the records on that narrowly defined issue."

"It is unprecedented, Ms. Mackay," Woods observed.

"Not entirely. In *Internal Revenue Service* vs *Church of Scientology of California*, the Court ruled

88 CHRISTINE MCGUIRE

that the IRS could subpoena and examine records of
the Church for the limited purpose of ascertaining
the Church's correct income tax liability. The Court
ordered Scientology to produce books and records
and provide testimony relevant to that purpose.
The People contend these subpoenas are similarly
specific and limited in purpose, and therefore ought
to be enforced."

Woods turned to the defense table. "What about
that, Mr. Scalisi?"

"I admire Ms. Mackay's resourcefulness, but that
obscure ruling isn't on point. It is a well-established
principle that when a normally tax-exempt entity
conducts unrelated business activities, the profits
from that venture are taxable, and all related
records must be produced if subpoenaed by the
IRS.

"It isn't necessary for the Court to determine
whether that same principle might, or should,
apply to unrelated profit-oriented activities of a
bona fide church," he emphasized "bona fide" to
impress on the Court the distinction between
Church of Scientology and the American Catholic
Church "and I contend it would not, because in the
case before this Court, neither deceased priest was
or ever had been engaged in any profit-oriented activity. The narrow exception previously carved out
by the Scientology Court couldn't apply, nor does
the State enjoy the power to delve into private activities of *legitimate* churches, whether those activities are profit-oriented or not."

"I'm inclined to agree, Ms. Mackay," Woods said.

"I've only asked to see two sets of personnel records for the sole purpose of determining what, if any, common background these two priests might share, that could have set them up as targets for murder. Thompson and Benedetti have been employed by the Catholic Church all their adult lives. Without the records we seek, we have no chance of determining the reason—whatever it was—that they were targeted, or apprehending their murderer."

"Mr. Scalisi?"

"Internal Church and Diocese matters are inextricably interwoven with those of its clergy—performance reviews, promotion evaluation, interparish transfers, job assignments. A look at their records is a look at the Church and is therefore unconstitutional."

Woods pondered. "Ms. Mackay, assuming the Diocese agreed, could the records be purged in such a way that your purpose could be served while still meeting the legitimate concerns of the Diocese?"

"No. We can't be sure exactly what we're looking for and the connection might escape a well-meaning but untrained investigative eye. That wouldn't work."

Scalisi stood. "It's a moot point, Judge. The Diocese would not agree to that approach."

Woods removed his reading glasses, clasped his hands, and leaned forward.

"Courts must often decide between two conflicting, Constitutionally protected rights and, oftentimes, elevate one over the other, even when they are both equally defensible. In addition, public protection has always been a paramount, if controversial, consideration in deciding such issues. However, the grave consequences of my decision today—" Woods looked at both lawyers, "and my distaste for being overturned on appeal, convinces me to take this matter under submission. I realize that time is critical, and I won't delay unnecessarily. My clerk will notify you both when I'm prepared to render my decision."

Both Mackay and Scalisi jumped up to object, but Woods cut them off with two big hands held out in a "stop" gesture.

"I've heard your arguments. That's my decision."

Then Woods disappeared through the door behind the jury box.

✝ CHAPTER 16

A LULL IN THE STORMS presented an opportunity for the Reverend Jacques Duvoir to tend his flower garden, in which his justifiable pride was exceeded only by the satisfaction of seeing his article on rose care published in yesterday's *Española Sentinel's* Garden Section.

Bending over the hybrid tea roses that flanked the sidewalk, Duvoir lovingly clipped dormant canes with a bypass pruner that he hand-sharpened and oiled in his private workshop behind the reliquary.

Holy Spirit Catholic Church had originally been built on land that was useless, except to demarcate

Española from the vineyards, apple orchards, and row crops that supported the then-sleepy village and gave it a rural character.

A hundred fifty years later, when Española emerged as a major agra-industrial hub, the value of Holy Spirit's twenty landscaped acres skyrocketed, but the Diocese wasn't interested in selling.

Wedged in among noisy cold-storage and food-processing plants, the spacious parking lot of the sprawling U-shaped church grounds fronted Beach Road across from a gigantic truck terminal that, on weekdays, drew hoards of 18-wheelers that swallowed up local produce and hauled it away like a swarm of hungry ants at a summer picnic.

While Duvoir liked the big rigs' deep-throated rumble, he hated the smelly diesel exhaust. He glanced at the idle terminal and smiled in gratitude, then crossed himself and thanked God for the peace and tranquility of a beautiful, unseasonably warm Saturday afternoon.

Duvoir wiped the sweat off his forehead with a shirt sleeve, pulled a quart bottle of Arrowhead water from a Styrofoam cooler and lifted the frosty bottle to his lips. He drank deeply and replaced the bottle.

The laser rangefinder told him the Leopold Vari-XIII 3.5-10x tactical scope required a slight elevation adjustment, which he dialed in with a quiet click. In the calm air, the windage knob was set perfectly.

Watching the priest chug-a-lug the water, he removed his cell phone, dialed a number and got a busy signal, and replaced his phone in its leather case that hung on his belt.

When Duvoir put the bottle away and stood upright, he twisted the focus ring to sharpen the target in the reticle, and centered the crosshairs two inches above the bridge of the priest's nose.

Then he changed his mind. "No, that's too easy."

He steadied the rifle on its bipod, then lowered the barrel of the .308-caliber Remington Model 700P-TWS rifle slowly so the crosshairs intersected on the priest's left kneecap.

He drew in a breath, held it, pressed his cheek against the matte-black, semi-beaver-tail composite stock, and squeezed the trigger.

At first, Duvoir thought he'd torn a ligament—until his left knee flopped backward into an inside-out ninety-degree angle and disintegrated. He toppled sideways and came to rest sitting upright, legs splayed out before him, against a pillar that supported the reliquary's terra-cotta roof overhang, staring at the pool of blood that seeped through his pants leg.

A wisp of powder residue leaked out of the barrel tip through the quick-detach TPR-S sound suppressor. He pulled the bolt back to eject the spent cartridge, slid it forward to load a fresh copper-jacketed bullet into the breach, drew a bead on Father Duvoir's right kneecap, and fired again. He watched Reverend Duvoir stare in dumb disbelief as his right leg separated.

"Now," he whispered.

He centered the crosshairs on Father Duvoir's sternum. The third bullet blasted into the chest, exploded the heart, exited through the spine, and lodged in the thick wooden column behind him.

Satisfied, he unslung the rifle, unscrewed the bipod, flipped down the scope end caps, and replaced everything in the Pelican hard case.

Finally, he retrieved the two empty brass casings and dropped them in his pants pocket along with his latex gloves.

He stole a final look at his victim's mutilated, lifeless body, then checked to be sure he'd left no evidence behind. Satisfied that he hadn't, he hustled across the flat tar-and-gravel roof, swung over the edge, and climbed down the fire escape at the back of the California Produce Express truck terminal.

✝ CHAPTER 17

LIEUTENANT MILLER TURNED his VW Passat into the driveway of Holy Spirit Catholic Church and flipped his Camel butt out the open driver's window. Inspector Escalante fanned leftover smoke out the passenger window but didn't complain, figuring it wouldn't do any good.

"What's up?" Miller asked the deputy guarding the crime scene.

"I caught the call from County Comm," Deputy Jensen told them, leaning into the driver's window. "Soon as I saw what I had, I called it in. Backup got here, we checked for a perp, came up empty and secured the scene."

Miller pointed to CSI Investigator Yamamoto, who stood talking to an obese man in black Adidas sweats. The man looked like a ex-NFL lineman who forgot to reduce his 10,000-calorie-a-day intake after retirement.

"What's going on there?" Miller asked.

"Damn if I know," Jensen answered, raising the yellow tape to let Miller's car pass through. "CSI went to work, then a few minutes ago Yamamoto started jawing at that porker. I think he's a priest."

"We'll check it out."

Miller parked by a coroner wagon that was backed up to the reliquary's portico, double doors hanging open. An empty gurney with a folded black body bag stood idly by the body.

A pretty, blond female CSI Investigator wearing jeans and a REMEMBER 9-11 T-shirt leaned against the van, arms crossed over her ample chest as she watched Yamamoto. Two male deputy coroners watched the front of her shirt and Yamamoto with equal interest.

Reverend Jacques Duvoir's corpse sat with its back against a thick wooden column, head drooped onto its chest, shattered legs bent at the knees in grotesque angles, buttocks in a pool of blood.

"Need consent to search inside," Yamamoto told Miller, spittle bubbling from the corners of his mouth.

"No." The fat priest shook his head. "Sorry."

Miller set his hand on Yamamoto's shoulder, and led him several feet away.

"What's wrong, Charlie?"

"I take photos, examine parking lot and every place outside, now need to get in rectory. Priest say we need search warrant."

"He's right unless he consents to the search."

"Maybe exigent circumstances."

Miller shook his head. "Never fly. Jensen checked for the perp half an hour ago. If we go in without consent or a warrant and turn up evidence, we could lose it in court." He looked around, then asked, "Any idea where the shots were fired from, Charlie?"

Yamamoto nodded. "Bullet lodged in post behind body on steep downward angle—" he pointed across the street toward the truck terminal "came from that direction, probably truck terminal roof—only place high enough."

"Escalante and I'll take over here, Charlie," Miller said. "Get a search team up on that roof right away, see if the shooter left anything behind."

"Okay." Yamamoto started packing his camera. When he finished, he picked it up and glared once more at the priest, then told Miller, "Lotsa priests killed lately, Lieutenant, and there'll be more if we don't catch perp fast." He pointed at the priest and added, "If that dumb shit don't cooperate with investigators, his fault, not mine." Yamamoto mumbled something else under his breath, shook his head and walked away.

"That's as pissed off as Yamamoto gets and sometimes he's not too diplomatic," Miller told Escalante. "Let's see if we can schmooze this priest."

Miller approached and flashed his badge. "What's your name, sir?"

"Father Hector Ramos." His neck folds hung over the sweatshirt collar and the matching pants were stretched to their breaking point. "I'm Associate Pastor here at Holy Spirit Parish. Thanks for taking over, Mr. Yamamoto wouldn't take 'no' for an answer. Who's she?" he asked, jerking his chin toward Escalante.

Escalante showed her ID and introduced herself. "You found the body?" she asked.

"Yes." He crossed himself. "Reverend Duvoir and I share a house in the rear. He likes—liked—me to cook something special on Saturdays nights, so I went grocery shopping at about eleven A.M."

"Where?"

"The Española Safeway."

"Where was Reverend Duvoir when you left?"

"Tending his roses here in front of the reliquary. They're Jack's pride and joy."

"Jack?"

"His name was Jacques Duvoir. Jacques is French for Jack. When I got back and turned off Beach Road into the parking lot, he was leaning against the post exactly as you see him now."

"What time was that?"

"About twelve-thirty. At first, I thought he got tired, sat down and fell asleep. He—" Ramos stuck the knuckles of his chubby hands into his eyes and rubbed. "He did that on warm days. Jack wasn't in good health and was older than I. The Diocese recently relieved him of his Pastor duties."

"He was retired?" Escalante asked.

The corners of Ramos' mouth tugged upward in a rueful smile. "Priests don't retire, the Diocese assigns them easier or less stressful duties. I've been de facto Pastor for the past few months."

"By 'de facto,' you mean you do the work without the pay or the title?" Miller said.

"We don't get a salary, and Jack earned the title."

"Do you know of anyone who might want to hurt Reverend Duvoir?"

"No."

"How did you and he get along?"

"Excuse me?"

"You did Pastor work but he kept the title. That musta sucked."

"Priests don't kill each other, Lieutenant. I've told you where I was when he was killed. Check it out."

"Count on it," Miller assured him.

"Did you touch or move his body?" Escalante asked.

"No. I was going to check his pulse, but when I saw all that blood—" Ramos pointed with a square, stubby finger. Even his cuticle was fat. "It didn't seem necessary." He crossed himself again.

"Sergeant Yamamoto says you won't give him consent to search the rectory."

"That's right, Bishop Davidson ordered me not to."

"Your call," Miller said and walked to the Passat.

"Ramos is pretty cool for someone who just found his colleague and house mate slaughtered in the church parking lot," Escalante said.

"Ain't that the truth, Chiquita. I'll freeze the scene, then call the Sheriff, let him know what's happening. Get hold of Mackay, ask her to roust the on-call judge and get a search warrant."

✝ CHAPTER 18

"JUST OUR LUCK," Granz complained to Mackay as he crept slowly down the Beach Flats street in the unmarked police car.

"What do you mean?" she asked.

"We need a warrant and who's on call—the biggest prick on the Bench."

Granz pulled his car into the driveway and punched a button on the weatherproof, electronic guard station's keypad marked PLEASE ANNOUNCE YOURSELF.

"Keefe's not that bad," Mackay told him.

"Your memory's shorter'n a gnat's antenna.

Keefe tried to send you to death row and almost succeeded."

Judge Reginald Keefe once presided over a trial at which Mackay was wrongly accused of murder, and every ruling came down for the prosecution.

She flipped her hand. "Water under the bridge."

"Very philosophical. You're more forgiving than I am—I still hate the son of a bitch."

"Can't hate everyone who's ever tried to shaft me."

Keefe and his wife, Bonnie, lived in his family's old, passed-down estate, protected from the seedy drug dealers, hookers, pimps, thieves, and thugs who prowled Beach Flats by a tall chain-link fence topped by razor wire.

The squawk box answered: "Identify yourself."

Granz stuck his head out the window. "Sheriff Granz and District Attorney Mackay, Judge."

"What do you want?"

Granz rolled his eyes. *Asshole*, he mouthed to Mackay. Into the speaker, he said, "A search warrant."

"Shit." The gate creaked open. "Park in front of the house. And the driveway's narrow, so be careful of the flowers."

Granz flipped on the high beams. When the headlights lit up the flower bed, he intentionally steered into it and shut off the engine. "Whoops."

The sprawling, single-story, wood-shingled house sat on a half-acre of native shrubs and redwood trees between a detached garage and a swimming pool with two connected tennis courts. They walked up on the porch, but before they could ring the bell, a buzzer sounded and the front door swung open.

"I'm in the living room," a man's voice called out from inside.

Keefe sat on a sofa with his bare feet propped up on a coffee table, a bottle of Corona Light in his right hand. He wore Levi's and a denim shirt, and Mackay wondered how a man who looked so good could be so ornery.

"We'll make this quick, Judge," she said.

"Suits me."

A sixty-inch Mitsubishi HDTV was tuned to San Diego State–Stanford NCAA hoops. Keefe muted the sound without shifting his eyes from the screen. "Get on with it."

"Like Sheriff Granz said, we need a search warrant." She handed him several papers, which he ignored.

"Summarize your probable cause, Sheriff," Keefe said, eyes still on the basketball game.

When Granz didn't answer, Keefe looked up. Granz' eyes had glazed over and he was staring into space.

"Sheriff?"

Granz didn't move.

"Sheriff Granz?"

Granz jumped, startled. "What?"

"You okay?" Keefe asked.

"Yeah, why?"

"Never mind, get on with it. Run your facts and probable cause by me."

When Granz had outlined the situation, Keefe set

his beer on the coffee table, dropped his feet to the floor, and sat up.

"You've passed on it?" he asked Mackay.

"I've signed off, Judge. There's enough PC to search the rectory."

"Three murdered priests in six days." He turned to Mackay. "What happened to the motion the Diocese filed seeking to toss out your subpoenas in Woods' court yesterday?"

"Woods took it under submission," Mackay told him.

Keefe stood and walked quickly to a desk that occupied a prominent corner of the room, opened a drawer, rifled through its contents, pulled out a sheet of paper, and wrote for a couple of minutes. When he finished, he nodded in satisfaction and slammed the desk drawer shut.

Granz whispered to Mackay, "What's he up to?"

She whispered back, "Who knows."

Keefe sat back down on the sofa and scrutinized what he'd just written.

"You gonna sign the search warrant?" Granz asked.

"Absolutely." Keefe picked up a pen, signed the warrant, and handed it to Granz.

"And that's not all I'm going to do." He signed the paper he had drafted with a flourish and passed it to Mackay.

She scanned it and looked up. "A court order dismissing the Monterey Diocese motion to quash my subpoenas?"

"That's right, and I expanded the order to include this most recent priest's personnel records as well. You got a problem with that?"

Mackay placed the order in her handbag. "Definitely not, Judge."

"If Woods had the balls to uphold your subpoenas, this priest—what's his name?"

"Reverend Jacques Duvoir," Granz said.

"Right—Duvoir—he'd still be alive. I'll show everybody who's tough on crime. When one judge fails to protect the public, another judge with guts must step up and make things right."

"Is a handwritten court order drafted in Keefe's living room legal?" Granz asked when he and Mackay slid into his car.

"It's unusual, but not unheard of, and it's perfectly legal."

Granz backed his car into the flower bed on the opposite side of the driveway. "Whoops again," he said. "Just can't seem to keep from running over Keefe's flowers." He waited for the gate to open, then spun the wheels and pulled into the street.

"What motivated Keefe to cooperate?" he asked.

"He's lobbying for an Appellate Court appointment," Mackay told him.

"Say what!" Granz' head jerked toward Mackay.

"His name and Woods' just came down from the Governor's office to fill the Sixth District's vacancy created by Justice Stein's retirement. The governor's a Republican, so's Woods—Keefe's a Democrat— if Woods looks soft on crime, especially since September Eleventh, the Governor might appoint a Democrat."

Granz snorted. "God help us if that jerk-off gets appointed to the Appellate Bench."

"I hope he does."

"You're kidding," Granz said incredulously. "Why?"

"We'd be rid of him," Mackay explained.

"That couldn't be all bad."

"That's for sure. I think I'll write a letter of recommendation to the Governor's Appointment Secretary."

Granz laughed and so did she.

"What did your investigators find on the roof of the truck terminal across from Holy Spirit Church?"

He glanced at her. "The gravel was disturbed at the edge with a direct line of sight to where Duvoir was working on his flowers, so we know that's where the shots came from. But he didn't leave anything useful behind."

"Do you think it was the same shooter that murdered Thompson and Benedetti?"

"I'd say it's a possibility we can't afford to overlook. You wanta help toss Holy Spirit's rectory?"

"No, I'm going to start rounding up the grand jurors to convene at eight o'clock Monday morning, then have Escalante serve the subpoenas before Woods gets wind of this and rescinds Keefe's order."

"You mean before they start a judicial pissing contest."

"You could say that."

He grinned. "I *did* say that."

✝ CHAPTER 19

MONDAY, DECEMBER 30, 8:00 A.M.
SANTA RITA SUPERIOR COURT

"MR. FOREMAN, is the Grand Jury ready to proceed?"

"It is."

District Attorney Mackay wore a black herringbone jacket and straight black skirt with a back slit. She made brief eye contact with each juror.

"On December twenty-second, Reverend John Thompson was murdered in the rectory at Sacred Heart Church. Two days later, Reverend James Benedetti was murdered in the gymnasium at Holy Cross High School, where he was principal; day before yesterday, Reverend Jacques Duvoir was murdered while tending his roses at Holy Spirit Catholic Church.

"The investigation leads Sheriff's detectives to believe all three murders were most likely committed by the same person, whom we fear will kill again unless he is caught quickly. To do that we must know about his victims and what they had in common."

Mackay grasped the sides of the podium. "You were convened to compel testimony of the one witness who possesses that critical information."

She paused. "The People call Bishop Jeffrey Davidson."

Bishop Davidson wore his ordinary walking dress, a red-trimmed black cassock over a starched white shirt with a clerical collar. A pectoral cross hung around his neck on a gold chain and a gold ring with a cross appliqué on top, symbolizing betrothal and conjugal fidelity to the Church, adorned his right ring finger.

The Bishop was lean and gangly with reddish brown hair that stuck stiffly out from under a violet zucchetto, and his wire-rimmed eyeglasses perched lopsidedly on his freckled nose over intense cobalt-blue eyes. His pleasant, youthful face reminded Mackay of Huck Finn.

Davidson took the oath administered by the grand juror who sat at a table beneath the oak platform where Foreman Gilbertson presided from the judge's chair. He acknowledged the seventeen members who sat in the jury box, then sat in the elevated witness chair, clasped his hands on a manila folder in his lap, and watched Mackay expectantly.

"Good morning, Bishop Davidson. Before we

begin, I must advise you that you are appearing before a duly constituted Grand Jury that is investigating the murders of Reverends Jacques Duvoir, James Benedetti, and John Thompson. The oath you swore means your testimony has the same force and effect as in a court of law, and you must tell the truth or subject yourself to perjury prosecution. Do you understand?"

"Yes."

"Your attorney is in the hall, and you will be permitted a reasonable opportunity to step outside the Grand Jury room to consult with counsel if you so desire."

"Thank you."

"State your name and occupation, please."

"Jeffrey Allen Davidson. I've served the priesthood all my adult life. Pope John Paul the Second appointed me Bishop of the Monterey Diocese of the American Catholic Church in nineteen-ninety."

"What is a diocese, and what are your duties there?"

"The Diocese is the Church's basic unit, and each is headed by a bishop who is the chief liturgical figure, and supervisor of all Diocese activities."

Mackay consulted a computer-generated printout she had downloaded from the Internet. "I would like to paraphrase a passage from your Catholic Encyclopedia:

The bishop has the right to admit priests to, or exclude priests from, the ministry in his diocese, and to assign priests to parishes and other duties.

"Is that an accurate description of your authority

as Bishop, as it pertains to priests in your Diocese?"

"Yes."

"The Diocese maintains personnel records for all of your priests?"

He hesitated, then said, "Yes."

"As head of the Diocese, those records are under your supervision and control?"

"That's right."

"The subpoena under which you testify here today required you to produce personnel records for Reverends Duvoir, Benedetti, and Thompson, is that correct?"

"You know it did, you signed it."

"So I did. Let's discuss Reverend Duvoir first. Did you bring his file?"

"Yes, it's right here." He picked the manila folder up for her to see, and replaced it on his lap.

Mackay stepped close to the witness stand. "May I have the file, please?"

He started, pulled it back, then handed it to her.

"Please describe Reverend Duvoir's history of duties with the Diocese."

"Jacques Duvoir came to the Diocese of Monterey upon graduation from University of San Francisco with a Doctor of Divinity degree, in nineteen seventy. He has served in the Diocese continuously since, as Associate Pastor at various parishes before being appointed Pastor at Española's Holy Spirit Parish in nineteen eighty-one."

"Was he Pastor of Holy Spirit Parish at the time he was killed?"

"In title."

"Can you explain that?"

"I relieved Reverend Duvoir of pastoral duties earlier this year. He had a health problem."

"What problem?"

"Type 2 diabetes."

"Did he take medication?"

"Insulin injections were prescribed."

"How old was Reverend Duvoir when he was murdered?"

"Fifty-six."

"A young man." Mackay smiled.

Davidson didn't respond. "Depends on your point of view."

"I suppose it does." Mackay bit her lower lip. "Most people with type 2 diabetes work and live normal lives by eating properly, exercising, and taking their medication, yet Reverend Duvoir was so disabled by the disease that he needed to be relieved of his duties?"

"That was my opinion at the time."

"Did his physician concur?"

"As Bishop, it was my decision."

"The question was whether Reverend Duvoir's physician *concurred* with your opinion."

"I didn't consult his doctor, I consulted God."

"Nevertheless, I can subpoena Reverend Duvoir's doctor and his medical records, if necessary."

Davidson sat upright and rubbed his hands together as if to wash away an especially virulent bacteria. "None of this has anything to do with his death."

"You're so certain?"

His ice-cold eyes bored into Mackay. "I'm certain."

"I remind you that you are under oath and perjury is a serious offense. Earlier, you testified that you relieved him of his duties due to health problems—was there another reason you relieved Reverend Duvoir of his pastoral duties?"

"Yes."

Davidson sucked his lips in, chewed on them while he pondered his answer, and blew them out. "I'd like to consult with my attorney."

Mackay and the jurors waited for several minutes. When Davidson returned, Mackay repeated the question.

"I said Reverend Duvoir *had* health problems, not that I relieved him because of them. You inferred that."

"All right, what was the reason?"

"The Reverend was—ah—the subject of an investigation."

The jurors' heads jerked in unison like marionettes yanked by the same string.

"An investigation conducted by whom?" Mackay asked.

"The Diocese. About a year ago, my Finance Officer's credit-card audit uncovered numerous charges by R-O-L Company, a vendor he didn't recognize. He looked into it and learned that R-O-L stands for 'Roulette-On-Line,' an Internet casino scam."

"Go on."

"The Finance Officer immediately notified me

and our legal department. We learned that for the past couple of years, Reverend Duvoir had been laying down bets with half-a-dozen web-based casinos using his parish computer. He covered the losses with Diocese credit cards."

Mackay flicked her tongue over her lips. "How much money did he lose?"

"Fifty-three thousand dollars so far, but we're still auditing past years. It might be more."

"Has the Diocese paid the bills?"

"Not all of them. I froze payment on all invoices and charges incurred by Reverend Duvoir. Our legal department contacted the casino by e-mail—they have a 'contact us' hot key on their web page—and suggested they forgive current charges and refund prior payments."

"What did they say?"

"They e-mailed our attorney, Mr. Scalisi, back and said that—in their words—'no one welches on a gambling debt and gets away with it.' "

"Sounds ominous. Then what?"

"We disputed the unpaid charges directly with the banks that issued the cards. After some negotiation, they reversed them and refused to tender payment to R-O-L."

"How much was disputed?"

"As I said, more than fifty thousand dollars."

Mackay's right eyebrow lifted involuntarily. "Who eventually sustains the losses?"

"The casino, although I don't see how they've actually lost anything. Then the threats started."

"Threats?"

"A man who never identified himself called repeatedly, at all hours of the day and night. When I wouldn't agree to pay, he threatened to send 'enforcers' to visit."

"Visit whom?"

"He didn't say, but it isn't hard to figure out who he had in mind."

"Did you contact the police for protection?"

"God protects us."

"And Reverend Duvoir?"

Davidson sighed. "We were evaluating treatment programs. Jacques was sick but, aside from his addiction, he was an exemplary and revered priest who was loved by his parishioners. I'm afraid your witch hunt has tainted his memory forever."

"Grand Jury testimony is secret."

"That's what President Clinton thought about his relationship with Monica Lewinski."

"Is there anything else we need to know about Reverend Duvoir, Bishop Davidson?"

His eyes were wet-shiny blue pools. "You already know too much."

"Would you like to take a short break?"

"No, thank you."

"Let's move on then. The subpoena also ordered you to produce personnel records for Reverends Benedetti and Thompson. Did you bring those records with you?"

Davidson straightened his back and cleared his throat. "No."

"Excuse me?"

"And I refuse to answer questions about them."

"Refusing on the grounds that truthful answers to my questions would tend to incriminate you?"

"I didn't say that."

"Well, Bishop Davidson, that is the only grounds for refusing to answer my questions without being held in contempt of court."

"The order Judge Keefe issued isn't enforceable so long as Judge Woods has our motion to quash your subpoenas under submission."

"If that is your attorney's advice, it's bad advice, and following it will cause you trouble," Mackay admonished him. "Why don't you step outside the jury room and consult with legal counsel?"

Davidson hesitated, then stood. "Perhaps I shall."

"That's not what I said." Scalisi's voice rose as he addressed Bishop Davidson. "You told me you were bringing all three files."

Escalante stood at a discreet distance, gazing out the window, trying unsuccessfully not to overhear the confidential attorney-client communication.

"I changed my mind, now calm down before you have a heart attack." Davidson patted Scalisi's arm.

Mackay opened the door and stepped into the hallway, where she saw the two men in a heated discussion.

"With all due respect, Mr. Scalisi, you should reconsider the advice you gave Bishop Davidson," Mackay said. "Keefe's order is valid unless a higher court vacates it."

"I told him that before he testified," Scalisi said. "He only just now told me he refused to answer your questions concerning Reverends Thompson and Benedetti."

Davidson shook his head resolutely. "Neither of you realizes the terrible, unnecessary can of worms you'd open by dredging up those priests' past."

"So they *were* part of the gambling problem?" Mackay asked.

"I would not answer your questions before the Grand Jury, Ms. Mackay," Davidson said with a sigh, "and I'll *not* answer them here in the hall."

Mackay barged ahead as if he hadn't spoken. "Has your Diocese received complaints of sexual misconduct against Thompson, Benedetti, or Duvoir?"

"I can see you aren't one to take 'no' for an answer." Davidson glared, and sat quietly thinking for a moment. "All right, Ms. Mackay, I shall make an exception and answer that one question directly. The—"

"Bishop, I advise you—" Scalisi interrupted, but was silenced by a quick shake of the Bishop's head.

Davidson kept his eyes riveted on Mackay even as he spoke softly to his lawyer. "Gerald, there can be no harm in my answering that question honestly. Perhaps if I do, Ms. Mackay will be satisfied and drop her witch hunt."

Davidson crossed himself. "Ms. Mackay, I give you my sacred word as a Christian and Bishop that neither I nor the Monterey Diocese of the American

Catholic Church has *ever* received a complaint alleging sexual misconduct on the part of Fathers Thompson, Benedetti, or Duvoir."

"I believe you," Mackay said softly, "but I'm still convinced that they have something in common, and if we don't figure out what it is soon, there'll be more dead priests. Are you willing to risk their lives?"

"If necessary."

"You'll go to jail until you decide to cooperate, no matter how long that takes," Mackay promised. "Jail's not a nice place."

Davidson smiled benevolently. "As a divinity student in the sixties, I marched with Martin Luther King and spent a month in a Mississippi jail cell eating cockroaches and hominy grits—I don't know which was worse. In the seventies," he continued with a wry smile, "I boycotted the grape fields beside Cesar Chavez. Valley jails are nicer than Mississippi's but they're no picnic.

"In the eighties, I was arrested a dozen times outside abortion clinics from San Francisco to San Diego. In the nineties, it was Bosnia. I've spent more nights in jail than many felons, and a few more won't hurt me."

Mackay shook her head. "If I recess the Grand Jury now, they'll take off for the New Year's holiday and won't reconvene before next Monday—maybe later."

"I understand," Davidson answered.

"Are you always so stubborn?"

"Yes, he is," Scalisi interjected. "In fact, he's being cooperative today."

"I'll arrange for Sheriff Granz to put you in Q," Mackay said, then explained, "Q is the security unit where a high-risk inmate can be isolated and protected from the jail's general population."

"I don't want to be isolated or protected."

"Our jail's full of criminals who'll slit your throat for the gold in your cross and ring, not to mention gangbangers—there are members of the Hispanic Norteños and Sureños gangs in custody all the time. You might not live till next Monday."

"Hispanic gang members are Catholics, Ms. Mackay. They won't harm a Catholic Bishop, and they'll see to it that no one else hurts me, either. I'll be safer in jail than walking from my rectory to my church."

"See what I mean?" Scalisi asked Mackay.

"You worry too much, Gerald." Davidson stood. "Now, if you lawyers are finished, I'd like to go to jail."

✝ CHAPTER 20

"I BELIEVED BISHOP DAVIDSON when he said none of the three priests were sex offenders," Mackay said.

Escalante made brief eye contact with Granz, Miller, and Mackay. It was cold in Granz' office and she tugged her jacket tight over her chest. "Then, they must all be part of the gambling problem. Every parish has computers with Internet access."

"How do you know that?" Mackay asked.

"Bishop Davidson told me as I was walking him to the jail," Escalante answered. "And to gamble on-line, they would have to download casino software."

"Hard-drive searches would tell us if they did," Mackay observed, checking her wristwatch. "It's two-thirty. I'll catch Keefe in chambers. He wants to be a law 'n' order judge, he'll issue a search warrant to seize all three priests' PCs."

"What do priests use computers for?" Miller asked, then added, "Besides layin' down bets."

"They post mass schedules, current events, parish news," Escalante told him. "Shut-ins can go on-line to request and offer prayer."

"How 'bout absolution?"

"Some parishes heard on-line confessions until the Vatican banned it."

"Pity. You coulda logged on, asked forgiveness, said a few Hail Marys," Miller told her.

"For what?"

"Locking up the Bishop."

"I was just following orders." Escalante's voice rose an octave.

"Lighten up, Chiquita, I was joking."

Miller fingered an unlit Camel, rolled it between his palms, and blew loose tobacco on Granz' office floor. "If three priests have gambling addictions, there's prob'ly more."

"I'm not so sure," Mackay said, turning to her husband. "Why would Davidson give up Duvoir but go to jail to protect Thompson and Benedetti?"

Granz stared out the window.

"Dave?"

"Huh?"

"I asked why Davidson would testify that one priest had a gambling addiction but go to jail rather than admit there are others."

"To avoid acknowledging how widespread it is,"

Granz speculated, gnawing his lower lip until he winced in pain. "One gambling addiction's an illness; two's a cancer; three—call the Centers for Disease Control, you've got an epidemic."

"So, he's buying time to find out how far the disease has spread?"

"And to cure it on the q.t."

"You might be right," Mackay agreed. "At the hearing, Scalisi told Woods the Diocese hired an investigator. That means they want to get to the problem before the cops do."

Miller swiveled his chair back and forth and stopped when it pointed in Escalante's direction. "If they hired a licensed PI, we could lean on him, but that could take a while."

"And he might not know anything yet anyway."

Escalante made a note in her spiral-bound, slid a color printout across Granz' desk, and gave copies to Miller and Mackay.

"Downloaded off the web," she explained. "This on-line casino's run by Cassava Enterprises Limited, an Antigua-Barbuda, West Indies corporation. It looks like an aboveboard gaming operation, but there are dozens more whose web sites don't say where they're located."

Miller checked the printout. "How'd you get it?"

"Easy—I typed *casino* in my laptop's search engine, and got a couple pages of hits. They all had one thing in common."

"What?" Granz asked.

"They accept VISA and MasterCard wagers."

"So?"

"I have a—an old friend who's a VISA-MasterCard fraud investigator."

Years before, the friend had tracked credit-card charges to find escaped murderer Robert Simmons. When Mackay had asked how she got such prompt results, Escalante had said, "I made him a promise I won't mind keeping."

"I'll ask him to find out where R-O-L does its banking," Escalante volunteered now. "Maybe we can track them down that way."

"Do I know this wannabe-cop VISA investigator?" Miller asked.

"I doubt it."

"Then I'll go along as backup."

"Not necessary, I can handle it."

"That's what bothers me, Chiquita." Miller crushed the mutilated Camel and stuffed it back in the pack.

Granz leaned forward in his chair, rested his elbows and forearms on the desk, and squeezed his shaky hands together. "Jazzbo, run an NCIC computer search for similars, and check the Secretary of State's corporate database for R-O-L."

"Will do. Other states, too, in case Escalante's hotshot doesn't come through. If it's a U.S. corporation, it's chartered someplace."

Escalante ignored the pointed comment. "A lot of them are in the Caribbean, like OnLineCasino-dot-com. Not only that, but anybody can operate a web casino out of any place with electricity and a phone line—they can be anything from a one-man scam in a bedroom or garage to a legitimate, tax-paying international consortium at Monte Carlo or Las Vegas."

"Check FBI and Interpol organized crime units," Granz told her.

Mackay was shaking her head. "Casino fraud or not, I still don't buy it's a paid hitter."

"Why not?" Granz challenged.

"MOs are too different."

"Pros adapt."

"Maybe, but why torture Benedetti and Duvoir instead of executing them quick and making a clean getaway?"

"The casino's sending a message—don't welch on bets or you'll get the same. And if they think someone besides Thompson, Benedetti, and Duvoir stiffed them, and if they *did* contract out a hit, there's going to be more dead priests if we don't ID the shooter damn fast."

Escalante agreed. "I'll contact the IFCC."

"The what?" Mackay wanted to know.

"Internet Fraud Complaint Center—the FBI and National White Collar Crime Center—set up a cyber-crime clearinghouse. Victims log on, submit complaint information, IFCC evaluates it and disseminates cases to the proper jurisdiction for investigation and prosecution."

"Why don't the Feds prosecute?"

"Cyber-crooks are several steps ahead of Congress—most Internet offenses aren't federal crimes yet."

"How do they decide whose jurisdiction a crime occurred in?" Mackay asked.

"It isn't easy. The game's web server can be in one state or country, but controlled by a perp at a second location, even from a laptop or cell phone, while the victim's in a third jurisdiction."

"Jesus! I just figured out how to e-mail my kid and wire-transfer child support payments to my ex," Miller complained.

Then he added, "I oughta retire while I'm smart as the bad guys."

"You're too young to retire." The corners of Escalante's mouth lifted a little. "An Internet perp can run the con, pull down the web site in seconds, and vanish without a trace. With IFCC, victims can report crime the same way it occurred—on-line, at the speed of light."

"What good's that do us?"

"IFCC keeps cyber-crime stats and patterns in a central repository available to law enforcement. If similar Internet scams or e-mail threats have been reported, they're most likely in IFCC, not NCIC or Interpol. I'll check it out before you waste time chasing dead ends."

"Anything else?" Mackay asked.

No one spoke up.

"I'll call Menendez, see what DOJ came up with on evidence recovered at the crime scenes. You free to run out to the lab with me tomorrow morning, Dave?"

Granz' vacant, glazed eyes stared out the window. He was chewing furiously on nothing, as if someone had slipped him a piece of old shoe leather instead of a T-bone.

"Dave?" she repeated.

He continued to stare.

She stood and touched him on the shoulder. He jerked, blinked his eyes, and ran the back of a hand over his lips. "Did you say something?"

"Are you all right?"

"What—sure. I was thinking."

"One more thing," Miller said. "In an orange jail jumpsuit Davidson looks like all the other scumbags. Some fudge packer claims him as a punk and he beefs, you'll have a dead Bishop in your jail."

"The Bishop won't fight back." Granz leaned back in his desk chair and pressed the heels of his hands into both temples. "Have him put in Q before lockdown," he ordered Miller.

"You got it."

When Miller and Escalante left, Mackay stood behind her husband's chair, massaged his shoulders, and felt his forehead with her fingers. "No fever. What's wrong?"

"I don't feel well, must've been what I had for lunch."

"What did you eat?"

"Miller, Fields and I went to Sophia's for burritos, beans, rice and chips."

"That'd do it to me."

"I think I'll lie down for a few minutes."

"Good idea, Babe. As soon as I get done with Keefe, I'll stop by."

✝ CHAPTER 21

MILLER POKED ESCALANTE's shoulder playfully as they headed down the elevator. "I'll drive you to San Jose to see that VISA investigator."

"I told you I can handle it."

"And I told you that bothers me."

"You sound jealous."

His ruddy face reddened. "I'm playin' a gig tonight at Bo's Alley Jazz Club, maybe you'd like to stop by and listen."

"Are you asking me for a date, Lieutenant Miller?"

"You ain't heard a trombone till you hear mine."

"I'm not sure it's a good idea."

"Why not?"

"We work together."

"I asked you to listen to me play trombone, not to bump uglies."

"You've got a real way with words." She thought about it. "What time?"

✝ CHAPTER 22

GRANZ WAS ASLEEP when Mackay returned. She sat on the sofa beside him and stroked his head.

His eyes fluttered open and he flashed one of the lopsided smiles she'd fallen in love with years before. "What time is it?"

She checked her watch. "Four-thirty."

"I've been asleep two hours?"

"You needed it."

"Did Keefe sign warrants to grab the computers?"

"Yeah, but I had to listen to his new tough-on-crime speech. Fields and one of your detectives are serving them as we speak."

"What took you so long?"

"I needed to discuss something with Escalante, then I stopped at my office and called a travel agent. How would you like to wake up New Year's Day in a tropical paradise, eat some great food, lie on the beach every day, and make love every night?"

"Sounds great. I could use a few days off."

"I'll say."

He sat up and swung his legs over onto the floor. "But we've gotta go to DOJ tomorrow."

"I asked Miller and Escalante to handle it. By the way, have you noticed they've got a thing going?"

"Yeah. Makes the Odd Couple seem like Ozzie and Harriet by comparison."

"For sure." She dug in her handbag and handed him a Pacific Harbor Travel envelope. "Wendy arranged it—we leave tomorrow."

"Where and for how long?"

"Five nights in Manzanillo, Mexico, at the Las Hadas Beach Resort. It's where the movie 10 was filmed. Remember that?"

"No man could forget Bo Derek in a bikini."

She smiled at his attempt at levity, but told him seriously, "I'm worried about you, Dave. Really worried."

"No need." He sat up. "A few days alone with you is exactly what I need. I feel better already."

✝ CHAPTER 23

"YOU PLAYED GREAT LAST NIGHT. Dinner was good, too. ¡Muchas gracias!" Escalante told Miller.

"De nada, Chiquita." He piloted his VW Passat south on Highway One through light New Year's Eve traffic.

"Please don't call me Chiquita."

"What *should* I call you?"

"'Inspector' when we're around others."

"What if we're alone?"

"Me llama Doña Luisa."

"I thought it was Donna."

"My mother Anglicized it when our family immigrated to the U.S."

"Doña then, if you call me James."

"Me gusta. Diego Es un nombre fuerto."

She touched a bandage on his arm with a slim brown finger. "¿Qué es?"

"Nicoderm patch—I quit smoking."

"¡Excelente! ¿Por que?"

"Why!" He sneaked a peek at her out of the corner of his eye. "Because beautiful women don't go for guys who smell like ashtrays."

"Es verdad."

They rode in self-conscious silence to 46A Research Drive, where the unblinking eyes of fence-top cameras stood silent watch over the DOJ complex that cops called Building 46A.

The lab commanded a breathtaking view to the west, where the collapsing winter sun stretched horizontal orange and purple bands across the afternoon horizon.

They punched an intercom button at the top of a five-step concrete landing. A uniformed Barney Fife look-alike checked their IDs, logged them in, and buzzed Criminalist Roselba Menendez' workstation.

Menendez was a little pudgy with brown skin, white teeth, and a Spanish accent. She wore white Reeboks, blue jeans, and a black Hollister Harley-Davidson T-shirt with a stylized iron horse spitting out smoke in puffy letters that read, RIDE ME HARD, I CAN TAKE IT.

"Nice to see you again, Lieutenant," she told Miller, then acknowledged Escalante. "Inspector."

"Have you scientific whiz kids tied those church

murders together for us good guys yet?" Miller asked her.

"We just analyze the evidence," she retorted. "It's you good guys' job to figure out what it means."

"I was hopin' you'd solved 'em by now."

"If I did, what would they pay you for?" She led them through a vast, open-floor-plan office jammed with desks, filing cabinets, and computers, past a swinging half-gate into a hallway lined with doors, a few of which stood ajar exposing an array of mysterious scientific equipment.

She stopped at a sign that read FIREARMS AND BALLISTICS, punched her ID code into a keypad, swung the door open, escorted them inside, and stopped at a metal workbench with swiveling stools. "Let's review the evidence chronologically," Menendez suggested. "First, the shooter got in and out of Reverend Thompson's rectory clean as a whistle—the Woods Lamp picked up no transfers, and the vacuum bags didn't contain any forensically significant trace evidence."

She picked up a highly magnified black-and-white photograph of a bullet, with a plastic evidence bag containing the bullet stapled to the corner.

"This is the slug Doctor Nelson removed from Thompson's head at autopsy. Rifling twist, lands and grooves confirm it was fired from a .25-caliber Beretta automatic."

Menendez indicated several spots on the picture, surrounded by circles of black ink. "Microscopic manufacturing imperfections gouged these marks into the bullet as it transited the barrel. All gun barrels have unique flaws. I can match this slug to the weapon it was fired from if you can find it."

"Not much help," Miller complained. "Most cops I know, including me, carry Beretta .25s off-duty."

"That's what I carry," Escalante confirmed. "So do half the criminals on the street. They're cheap and easy to conceal."

Menendez picked up a pistol. "This is the Colt Python from Holy Cross." She made a logbook entry to maintain the chain of custody and loaded a cartridge.

"Let's test-fire it."

She stuck the barrel into a rubber sleeve that opened into a tank of water and fired a bullet. Then she laid the pistol aside and fished the slug from the tank. Finally she mounted the slug on a glass slide alongside the bullet from the gymnasium floor.

Sliding them side by side under an optical comparison microscope as she peered into the twin lenses, she twisted the scope's knurled knobs to align the bullets and adjust the focus.

"They match," she declared, looking up and squinting to recapture her distance vision. "You've got the weapon that killed Benedetti but I already examined it—no fingerprints and the serial numbers have been obliterated."

"Raise 'em with acid," Miller suggested.

"I tried, but whoever did it removed too much metal."

"Send it to the FBI." Miller tempered his advice: "No offense intended."

"None taken, but if I can't raise them, they can't be raised. The weapon's untraceable. There *is* some good news."

"We could use it," Escalante commented.

Menendez motioned for them to follow her to a metal rolling cart where a high-tech slide projector was hooked up to a laptop computer through a USB cable.

She flipped on the projector's power switch. Its fan whirred, its lamp flared, and a blurry shoe print, with a twelve-inch ruler laid beside it on the hardwood floor, slowly sharpened into focus on the pull-down wall screen.

"Yamamoto's a pit bull," she said with unabashed admiration. "He photographed every wet shoe print at the Benedetti crime scene with his camera perfectly perpendicular to the gym floor, at exactly the same height."

She scrolled through a series of slides, each of a shoe print with the same twelve-inch ruler alongside to establish size and perspective.

"None of 'em are good enough to ID," Miller said.

"No one print is, that's true. Yamamoto suggested I piece them together, using legible slices from each print. When my software constructed the entire right-shoe print using his technique, I got this."

Menendez punched a computer key. From a single blurry print, the computer program started sliding out indistinguishable sections and replacing them with legible slices from the same locations on other prints. The program sent an "operation completed" message and the screen displayed a perfect right-shoe print.

"I ran the composite through the Idaho State Police shoe outsole tread pattern database. Bingo. Nike Airliners, size ten."

"Pretty impressive for a techie lab rat," Miller told her. "But there must be thousands of Nike Airliners in Santa Rita."

"Not exactly like this one. As shoes wear, rocks, metal, glass, and other surface imperfections erode the tread and change the original design with random cuts, scratches, nicks, and dings—we call them 'individual identifying characteristics.'

"A person's gait also impacts the pattern," she went on. "By the time a shoe's got a few miles on it, the tread pattern's unique. If you find me the shoe soon enough, I'll positively ID it."

"That's a start," Miller said. "Now, all us good guys gotta do is find the one guy in the entire world, wherever he is, who owns that Beretta *and* those Nikes before he wears 'em much more, borrow 'em for comparison, and our job's wrapped up. No big deal."

"Maybe if the 'good guys' turned the investigation over to the 'good gals' you'd get better results."

"Why didn't I think of that?"

She handed each of them a closeup shot of the disassembled dead-bolt lock off the gym's side door, which highlighted a number of tiny scratches and gouges.

"Sheriff Granz had good instincts. These are fresh tool marks on the pins and tumblers," Menendez explained. "This lock was picked recently by someone who knew what he was doing, probably using a professional pick gun."

"Any two-bit burglar can buy one on the Internet usin' a hot credit card," Miller told her, then asked, "If you had the tool, could you ID it?"

"I doubt it, they normally don't leave distinctive tool marks. Pick gun needles and tension tools are interchangeable and disposable."

"Anything helpful come out of the Duvoir crime scene?"

"CSI recovered three slugs—two embedded in the pavement beneath Duvoir's knees. They were badly deformed, although the rifling and lands and grooves are identical to the third—it passed through his chest and lodged in a wooden post, and was in good condition. A high-velocity M-118 full metal jacket fired from a Remington .308 rifle."

"Most police TAC and sniper units use Remington 700s and metal-jacketed ammo. You think our perp's a cop or ex-cop?"

Menendez contemplated, chewing the inside of her cheek. "It's not impossible. The same rifle and ammunition in military configuration are used by Army and Marine Corps snipers. European military forces, too, but they call the rifle the NATO 7.62 millimeter. Add the civilian hunting version, and millions of those rifles are out there. Half the ex-military Rambo sharpshooters probably have one in their closets at home."

"God bless the Second Amendment," Miller said.

"Anything else?" Escalante asked.

"I'm afraid that's it," Menendez said.

"Then we ain't got diddly squat." Miller reached for his shirt pocket, then glanced sheepishly at Escalante and touched the Nicoderm patch. "I forgot I quit the Humps."

"The what?"

"The Humps—Camels."

On the way back to Miller's car, Escalante said, "Sheriff Granz was right."

" 'Bout what?"

"He said the shooter's too smart to leave a calling card."

"Looks like. Speaking of—where'd Granz and Mackay go?"

"Manzanillo, on Mexico's Pacific coast—the Las Hadas Beach Resort."

"We oughta go there someday," he said, staring at her.

She smiled and her face flushed. "Are you leering at me, Lieutenant?"

"Moi?" he said innocently, touching his chest with a forefinger. "So, should we consider it?"

She flushed again. "Stranger things have happened."

"Las Hadas—what's that mean?"

"The fairies. And no wisecracks."

"Hey, I'm a serious guy! What do you suppose they're doing right now?"

She looked at her wristwatch. "Probably taking an evening walk on the beach. At Las Hadas, it's almost seven o'clock."

✝ CHAPTER 24

DAVE WAS SLEEPING in the clothes he'd worn on the plane. He had slid the lounge chair under an umbrella on the deck outside their room, but was now directly in the evening sun, which had started dropping toward the horizon to their west.

Kathryn sat on the edge of his chair and said softly, "It's almost seven o'clock." She looked cool and relaxed with fresh makeup and her curly hair still wet from the shower. She wore a crisp black sleeveless blouse, white shorts, and leather sandals she'd bought at the hotel's Tabaqueria y Boutique Souvenir.

"No!" he shouted, his arms and legs thrashing like he was battling the darkest forces of evil.

She nudged him. "Babe?"

"Huh?" His eyes fluttered open.

"Wake up, I think you were having a bad dream."

"I was." He sat up, rested his elbows on his knees and held his head in his hands.

"What about?"

He blew air out of his puckered lips, looked up, and shook his head side to side. "Someone tried to kill me."

"You got overheated in the sun. Next time I go shopping, lie on the bed to take a nap."

"I didn't plan to fall asleep. Sorry."

"Don't apologize, it's okay. Why don't you take a cool shower, then let's walk on the beach before dinner."

"Sounds good." He sat up, stretched and yawned. "Great view, huh?"

Embodying the lifelong dream of Bolivian Tin King Antenov Patiño, Las Hadas Resort's cobblestone paths twisted and turned past a white-on-white fantasy world of gargoyled turrets, cupolas, minarets, villas, plazas, and archways that clawed their way up the eastern tip of Península Santiago like Moorish apparitions.

Halfway up the hillside, Kathryn and Dave's terra-cotta tiled deck looked out at Bahia de Manzanillo, over the tops of cascading red bougainvillaea and spindly, top-heavy coconut palms with stooped, twisted trunks.

Across the bay, along Playa San Pedrito, container ships waited to be offloaded, while gray Mexican Navy patrol boats with angry-looking deck guns nosed into their berths at Zona Naval.

Beyond Manzanillo Centro, a column of smoke wafted from the power plant, stratified, then hung over Playa El Viejo waiting for a breeze to blow it up and over the hills into the jungles of Colima State.

Kathryn heard the shower start, then the bathroom door opened and Dave stepped out, dripping wet and naked.

"Did you bring Excedrin?" he asked.

She moved close and ran her hand suggestively down his stomach. "Want to shower together?"

"You already took one."

"A woman can never be too clean."

"I've got a splitting headache." He took a step back. "Musta got too much sun while I slept."

"We haven't eaten since we left San Francisco this morning, either."

"Maybe that's it."

"The Excedrin's in my bag by the sink."

Kathryn sat at the table and surveyed their bright, airy, spacious suite. White drapes, white bedding, white marble floors, and white rattan furniture complemented glossy white masonry walls. Except for the screen, even the television was white. She hummed a few bars of "Auld Lang Syne."

After Dave finished showering and changed into shorts, T-shirt, and sandals, they strolled along

Calleja de Maria Christina, through the palm-shaded Plaza de Doña Albina, and down the fragrant, hibiscus-lined stairway onto the smooth golden sand of Playa Las Hadas. It was still warm from the afternoon sun, and a few die-hard tourists lingered under their white-roofed beach tents.

"I'm hungry." Dave chewed unconsciously.

"I can see that," Kathryn told him.

She grabbed his hand and led him to the water's edge, pulled off her sandals, and let the water lap up around her ankles. He did the same.

"Let's walk to the Marina, then back to Los Delfines Restaurant for dinner," she suggested.

Supported by fat wooden pilings that also held up the palm-frond roof, Los Delfines' open-air walls stuck out over a shallow lagoon. Only a few tables were taken when they got there.

The maitre d' held Kathryn's chair, bowed at the waist, seated Dave, then flipped open a pair of linen napkins and placed them on their laps with a flourish.

"Bienvenido a Los Delfines, señor y señora," he greeted them. "¿Cómo estás?"

"Muy bien, gracias," Kathryn answered.

"Excelente. Me llamo Ramon."

"¿Por qué el restaurante no ocupado, Ramon?"

"Cena con baile fiestas para Año Nuevo en Restaurante El Terral y Legazpi Restaurante-Discoteca, señora."

"What was that about?" Dave asked when Ramon left them to study their menus.

"He said the restaurant's not busy because they're having New Year's dinner-dance parties at the other restaurants."

Their corner table looked over a bamboo railing into the lagoon, whose green water was illuminated by submerged piling-mounted lamps. Every few minutes, a school of terrified fish leaped to the surface and frantically skimmed across the water, seeking safety in the man-made rock jetty, pursued by lightning-quick two-foot sharks.

The unlucky fish were caught and consumed in a savage frenzy of roily red foam. Whenever the carnage slowed, diners walked to the rail and dropped table scraps into the water, provoking the sharks, encouraging a repeat of the gruesome ritual.

They tried a bottle of nice Mexican wine, rolls with orange butter, red snapper Vera Cruz, and spicy grilled mahimahi.

Over a dessert of coconut flan, Kathryn asked, "How's your headache?"

"A little better."

"You shouldn't have so many headaches. I'm worried about you."

"I don't have that many. It was a long flight without food, then I was dumb enough to fall asleep in the sun. I'll be fine."

"That's what you said in the hospital, after the accident."

"I was right."

"I'm not so sure. You promised to have an MRI."

"I said after the holidays—if I didn't feel better. But I do. And the holidays aren't over yet."

He placed his hand on hers and squeezed.

After dessert they walked back and forth along the short beach between the mouth of the small-craft harbor and the jetty, past Legazpi Discoteca, where they heard the New Year's revelers gearing up for a midnight climax.

"We could watch the new year come in at a party, if you want," Dave told her.

"I'd rather watch from our room."

By the time Kathryn came out of the bathroom, Dave had stripped and was lying on the bed, reading John Grisham's *A Painted House*.

"Great book," he said. "Best he's written."

She took off her blouse and shorts and hung them in the closet. He tossed the book to the floor and watched. She turned around wearing only a pair of bikini panties. The cold air conditioning had made her nipples taut.

"Would you put on your new nightgown?" he asked.

"How do you know I bought a new gown?"

"Em told me."

She dug through her suitcase and pulled out a Nordstrom bag.

"Is the front low-cut?" He asked.

"Yes, see-through, too, but you said you had a headache."

He glanced down. "What I have isn't a headache."

"So I see." She felt herself grow moist. "Give me five minutes to brush my teeth and wash my face."

The lights were off when Kathryn climbed into

bed, but the glow of the crescent moon bounced off the water and shone through the filmy drapes. Dave lay facing the wall. She snuggled up and slipped her hand around his waist. "I have something to tell you," she whispered.

When he didn't respond she propped herself up on an elbow. His face was relaxed, his eyes closed, and he breathed deep and rhythmically, like only a person in deep sleep can.

Kathryn sighed, then switched on the bedside lamp and picked up the telephone.

"Hi, Mom," Emma finally answered.

"It was nice of Ashley's family to ask you to stay with them for a few days," Kathryn said. Hearing music in the background, she asked, "What are you doing?"

"Having a New Year's party. Me 'n' Ash get to stay up for a couple more hours, until midnight."

"Well, I just wanted you to know we love you and miss you, and to say Happy New Year. Have a good time."

"Thanks, Mom. I've gotta go now."

"Okay, honey. Good night." Kathryn held the receiver to her ear for several seconds, then tugged the covers up around her chest, fluffed up a couple of pillows, leaned back and opened a book, but couldn't concentrate on it. Just before midnight she heard the crowd at El Terral count down the final ten seconds of the year.

✝ CHAPTER 25

"WHAT ARE YOU DOING?" Kathryn's cry came out a gasp, her scream a whimper. Her entire bare body trembled. The naked stranger cupped her tender breast and pressed in tight against her, probing from behind.

A second faceless man slid his hand up her thigh. She felt a finger slip inside, then another.

"You can't do that, you're not my husband."

"So what?" The man behind her thrust, and she wantonly teased him with her buttocks. "You like it."

"Yes." She was hot, wet, and ready. And ashamed. "It shouldn't be like this except with my husband."

"Quiet on the set!" The director was nude, too, except for sunglasses, a Rolex, and motorcycle boots. The porn-movie studio was antiseptically white and too warm.

Sweat trickled down her right breast, collected on her nipple, and dripped onto the sheet.

He leaped from his canvas chair. "Lights, camera, action!" His penis swung back and forth like a grandfather clock's pendulum.

The cameraman switched on a huge carbon-arc stage light and aimed it directly into Kathryn's animal-hungry eyes. She squeezed them shut but it didn't help. The light was as relentless and penetrating as her pornographic tormentors.

When she awoke, the tropical morning sun was streaming through the gauzy curtains, burning through her eyelids, and searing her retinas.

Her gown had been pulled up above her waist, and Dave was spooned tightly behind her. He had inserted two fingers and was stroking her wetness. His erect penis poked at her from the back.

"Is that you, Babe?" she asked.

"Who else would it be?"

She grasped him, then turned onto her back, pulled him close, spread her legs apart and guided him in. He lifted himself, and while she massaged her sweet spot, he nibbled her swelling, darkening nipples, moving in and out slowly but insistently.

She arched her back. "Now!"

His relief came first, hers moments later.

Afterward, they lay together. He propped himself up and looked into her eyes. "I didn't know you had wet dreams."

"I don't."

"Couldn't prove it by me. But whatever, it was fun."

"Don't expect this every New Year's morning."

She fanned her face and pushed him off. "Why is it so hot in here?"

"I turned off the air conditioner during the night."

"Why?"

"Didn't think the morning was gonna heat up so fast."

"Turn it on, please."

When he crawled back into bed, she said, "I have something to tell you."

"If you're still horny, it's my duty to try." He laid his hand on her tummy, but she moved it.

"I'm serious," she said, and paused. "I'm pregnant."

"How can you tell so soon?"

"What do you mean 'so soon'?"

"We just finished making love five minutes ago."

"Don't make jokes. It happened in October."

"You're sure?"

"Absolutely. I went to Doctor Burton last Thursday."

He didn't move or speak for several minutes.

"Are you upset?" she asked.

"Of course I'm not upset." He rolled onto one elbow, and kissed her on the mouth. "But I don't learn I'm going to be a father every day. It'll take a little time to sink in."

"I understand. This will change our lives forever."

"It sure will."

✝ CHAPTER 26

At NINE-THIRTY, Kathryn ordered breakfast from room service. She was tying the belt on her white terrycloth Las Hadas robe when the doorbell rang ten minutes later.

"That was fast."

Instead of a waiter with breakfast trays, a maid stood at the door wearing a starched white uniform and a name tag that read, ME LLAMA LUCINDA. Kathryn guessed she was about fifteen.

"¡Hola, señorita!" Kathryn greeted her.

"¡Buenos dias, señora! ¿Quantos personas en éste habitación, por favor?"

"Dos."

"¡Gracias!" Lucinda made a note on her clipboard, and left.

"Who was at the door?"

"A maid, asking how many people are in our room."

"That's weird—she could've looked it up in the guest register at the front desk."

"This is Mexico, we shouldn't expect American logic."

When the doorbell rang again, the waiter rolled in a stainless steel cart, spread a cloth on the table in front of the window that overlooked La Bahia, and set a plate of sliced watermelon, cantaloupe, guava, banana, and pineapple in the center. He uncovered a basket of rolls and muffins, and finally poured two cups of steaming coffee.

Dave came out of the bathroom with a fresh shave and wet hair, his complimentary robe cinched tight at the waist, looking like a hairy-legged stork in a ghost costume. He checked the table. "Looks terrific."

The waiter handed him a check, which he signed after adding a generous tip.

"Will there be anything else, señor?"

"Gracias, no."

They ate silently for a few minutes.

"Is your age a health problem for you or the baby?" he asked.

"Women over thirty-five should have an amniocentesis test to rule out fetal chromosome disorders, but Burton recommends against it in our case because amniocentesis complicates a potentially more serious risk."

He stopped with a fork full of blood-red guava halfway to his mouth. "What risk?"

"What's your blood type?"

"A-positive." He swallowed the fruit with a bite of muffin and picked up his coffee.

"I'm RH-negative. You've got to take a blood test immediately, unless—"

"Unless what?"

"The possibility of genetic defect due to my age plus the inability to detect it by amniocentesis, added to the RH factor, creates a very high-risk pregnancy. Diedre suggested we discuss abortion."

He set his coffee cup down harder than necessary. Coffee slopped over the rim onto the pristine tablecloth. "What did you tell her?"

"That I'd talk to you. She wants us to understand the risks involved, and consider all possibilities."

"Ultimately, it's your decision, but unless your life's in danger, let's not consider it. I'll go for a blood draw Monday."

"I already made an appointment."

"Shoulda known." He ate two slices of watermelon and a hunk of pineapple. "What next?"

"If you're RH-positive, the baby probably is, too. Once Diedre confirms that, she'll watch us closely. If the pregnancy progresses normally, she'll give me a RhoGam injection during my twenty-eighth week to suppress RH antibody production, for the baby's protection."

"What if things don't go smoothly?"

"We take it a step at a time. Diedre will do

everything possible to see we have a healthy baby."

He ate the remainder of his fruit and rolls hesitantly. "There's something I want to ask you."

"Sounds serious."

"Remember a year or so ago, we discussed the possibility of me adopting Emma?"

"Of course."

"How would you feel about me filing court papers to adopt her now?"

"It'd make me happy."

"What about Emma? I need her approval."

"Ask her when we get home."

"I will. What do you think she'll say?"

"'Yes.' Are you sure that's what you want?"

"Absolutely. Know what else I want?"

"Tell me."

"When everything settles down—after the baby's born healthy, and we nail the SOB that's killing the priests, let's take a honeymoon."

"You've got my vote. Where should we go?"

"The most romantic place I can think of—Paris."

"Sounds great," she told him. "I've never been there."

"Me neither, but I've always wanted to go."

"When we get home, I'll buy a couple of travel guides and talk to our travel agent."

He leaned back in his chair and crossed his right leg over his left knee. Kathryn giggled.

"What's so funny?" he demanded.

"Your robe fell open, you're not wearing underwear, and I can see you're feeling romantic again."

"Amazing what a good night's sleep does for a man. Does it have the same effect on a pregnant woman?"

She stood, untied her robe, let it fall to the marble floor, and tugged him toward the bed. "You woke me up this morning, what do you think?"

✝ CHAPTER 27

IT WAS ALMOST NOON when they smeared themselves with sunscreen beneath the white, Moorish-style beach tent.

"Look," Kathryn said after a few minutes, holding her new sandal. "The sole's coming off. I'm going to exchange them at La Tabaqueria. Do you want anything?"

"Sí, un coco-frío."

Dave dived into *A Painted House*, which spawned a new perspective on the stories his parents told about life in rural Arkansas, reminiscent of the Chandler family, before they gave up and moved west to find work in San Diego's aircraft industry.

When Kathryn came back, he said, "Let's name our kid Luke."

"If it's a boy, I like David."

He sucked the watered-down juice out of the coconut through a peppermint-striped plastic straw. "Me too, but he'd always be 'Junior.' Did you get new sandals?"

"No problem, they exchanged the old ones for a new pair." She held her feet up for him to see. "These fit better, anyway."

"Why didn't you buy the pair that fit best to start with?"

"The other pair went with my swimsuit."

He chose not to pursue her reasoning. "You were gone a long time. What else did you do?"

"I figured we might want to get out of the resort for dinner at least once—the concierge made nine P.M. reservations at a seafood restaurant in Manzanillo Centro. Do you plan to read all day, or would you like to do something healthful?"

"I can read tonight." He inserted a marker and dropped the book in their beach bag. "I don't want to work out at their health club, but I wouldn't mind getting some exercise."

"Good—I reserved a three o'clock tee time to play nine holes at Las Hadas Golf Links."

"I haven't golfed in thirty years and you've been taking lessons—you'll kick my butt."

"Probably. I'll make you feel better if I beat you too badly."

"How?"

"Use your imagination."

The back nine at Las Hadas Golf Links was par thirty-six. Teeing up at hole 12, Kathryn was at eleven strokes, Dave at thirty-two, although she had permitted him numerous free drops to get out of the trees, the sand, and the abundant roughs.

"Problem is, I need left-handed clubs," he told her. They rode the cart back to the clubhouse, where he exchanged clubs with the help of a bemused attendant.

Southpaw clubs didn't help. By the time they finished hole 16, he had stopped counting his strokes at ninety-two, not including the free drops and the swings Kathryn hadn't witnessed.

He was also down to his second-to-last ball, a beat-up orange reject he'd picked up along the way. Long before, he had declared the balls, the clubs, the groundskeeper, the weather, and the putting greens to be at fault.

On 17, Kathryn doubled over in laughter when he plunked his grungy orange ball into a water hazard after digging up half a dozen divots. He reserved his final new ball for 18 by walking up to the 17 pin and dropping the ball in the cup. It took him three tries.

"I'll make up the strokes on the eighteenth," he promised.

Hole 18 at Las Hadas is a short hundred forty yards, but reaching the green requires a straight hundred-yard tee shot over a nasty surf and two riprap sea walls.

Dave teed up and drove a divot thirty yards into the near seawall. "That stroke doesn't count."

"Why not?"

"I didn't lose the ball."

"I don't think that matters." Kathryn's eyes were blurry with tears of laughter.

"I still have the tee, too."

"That's good. If there's ever a worldwide golf tee shortage, you'll be the first link in the supply chain."

"Don't scoff."

She shrieked, and when she finally stopped laughing, took a deep breath. "We need to laugh more often."

He laughed, too. "Easy for you to say, I'm the one being laughed at."

"I'm not laughing *at* you, honey, I'm laughing *with* you."

"Sure."

He wound up with a 3-wood, smacked himself on the back of the head, then connected with his longest drive of the day. His last ball covered ninety of the requisite hundred yards to get on the green before splashing unceremoniously into the unforgiving ocean.

He slammed his clubs into the bag. "Driving the cart's a hoot, and I really enjoy the scenery, but this is a dumb game. I quit."

"I want to play through and finish," Kathryn told him. "Will you caddy for me?"

"Sure, my machismo's shot anyway."

She teed up, rocked back and forth, planted her feet, flexed her knees, and lofted a perfect drive that arched onto the green and landed twenty-five feet from the 18 pin.

They drove across the footbridge, he handed her the club, and she two-putted the treacherous par-three hole.

"What did you shoot for the entire nine?" he asked as he steered the cart past the newly constructed, Mayan-inspired Karmina Palace.

"Fifty," she answered proudly.

"A golfer's only as good as her caddy."

Dave parked, handed his clubs to the attendant, and said enthusiastically, "¡Gracias! The left-handed clubs really improved my game."

"¡Excelente, señor! ¿Cuantos golpes?"

Dave shook his head in disgust, as if he might have shot in the low thirties if he hadn't used the wrong clubs on holes 10 and 11. "Fifty-two."

"¡Muy bueno!" The attendant nodded in admiration. "Y Señora?"

"My wife shot fifty—beat me by two strokes."

✝ CHAPTER 28

"You're such a liar," Kathryn told him.

For an extra twenty dollars, the taxi driver agreed to tour Manzanillo on the way to the restaurant. To the taxi's right, between a dirty brown beach and the highway, cargo cranes loomed over the waterfront like disjointed blue and white hawks, and an overloaded diesel locomotive tugged a mile-long string of car carriers toward the city.

"I'd be surprised if you shot under two hundred," she added.

"Me too."

The driver circled the wrought-iron-fenced plaza and crept through dirty one-way streets lined by throngs of shoppers; open-air clothing, shoe, and appliance stores; auto repair shops; bars and restaurants; portable food carts; and a fleet of rusting, abandoned cars.

When they had seen enough, he headed toward the beach. As the cab neared the plaza's back side, the driver slowed and pointed upward.

"Mira. Muchos pájaros."

Thousands of small-bodied pigeons perched wing to wing on every power line, telephone wire, pole cross arm, fence, and hotel balcony rail. Thick, gooey, smelly guano coated every horizontal surface.

"Nice town," Dave murmured under his breath.

Going into the restaurant he tripped, fell down the stairs, and opened a small gash over his eyebrow.

"Damn loose step." He couldn't tell Kathryn he'd suddenly felt dizzy and lost his balance. The restaurant's owner, a skinny man sipping a Pepsi, gave him a Band-Aid.

An hour later, as they headed back to the resort, Kathryn said, "The food was terrible, wasn't it?"

He stared vacantly and didn't answer.

"Dave?"

He snapped his head around as if jolted from a deep sleep. "Huh?"

"I said the food was terrible."

He was sweating heavily. He wiped his forehead and the bubbles from the corners of his mouth, grateful for the dark interior of the taxi. His stomach churned and his dizzy head pounded with a horrifying, merciless fury he'd never before felt.

"Are you all right?" she asked.

As a cop, he feared for his life at times, but this was different—real fear—an inexplicable terror of an untamed evil deep within that he could neither control nor understand. He dared not admit that he had no memory whatsoever of the time between his fall and that instant.

"I'm fine, just full of food and tired," he lied.

"Let's eat in the resort's restaurants every night, rather than waste time going out."

"Good idea."

He glanced at his wife, who was watching the lights of Manzanillo's suburban strip malls slide past the cab's open window. The nausea and confusion had waned, the headache had subsided to a dull ache. "Kate?"

"Yes?"

He struggled to sweep away the mental cobwebs. "I don't care whether we have a son or a daughter, I just care that Emma's happy and you and the baby come through it healthy and safe."

"I know."

When the cab dropped them off, they strolled through the lobby, around the pool, over the wood-planked rope bridge that Dudley Moore stumbled across while pursuing his Perfect 10, past the piano bar, through Plaza de Doña Albina, and back toward their suite.

"I was wondering," Dave said.

"Wondering what?"

"You promised that if you beat me badly on the links, you'd assuage my bruised and battered male ego. Is a beating of fifty to two hundred bad enough?"

"I thought you were tired."

"I feel fine now. I was wondering what assuagement you came up with."

She slowed her pace and let her hand brush against the front of his trousers, which were stretched taut over his growing lust.

"Trust me," she told him, squeezing gently, then promised, "You'll like it."

✝ CHAPTER 29

THEY SETTLED INTO a lazy routine of sleeping late and making love, with the added indulgences of eating fresh-fruit breakfasts, lounging on the beach, taking warm late-afternoon walks and cool early-evening showers.

Their nights started with beer, pretzels, and intimate conversation in El Palmar Piano Lounge, followed by a leisurely dinner at Los Delfines, where the maitre d' had learned their names, which table they preferred, and their favorite food. He said the chef knew how to cook more than three dishes, but they stuck with red snapper, spicy mahimahi, and coconut flan in a fuzzy coconut shell.

On Sunday morning, they arose early, packed, walked to the beach, and claimed their favorite palapa near the Oasis Bar for their last few hours.

Just before noon, Kathryn said, "I feel sad. It was too short."

"The biggest gifts come in the smallest packages—thanks for the best vacation of my life."

"You're welcome." Kathryn kissed the tip of her finger and leaned over to touch it to his lips. "I'm not ready to go home either, but it's time to check out."

They dropped off their beach towels at the toallero, trudged reluctantly up the hill to their suite, stacked their suitcases by the door, and waited for a bellman's cart to shuttle them to the front desk.

The concierge flagged a cab. "Is your last day at Las Hadas, no?" he asked as he loaded their luggage in the trunk.

"How did you know?" Kathryn asked.

"You look so sorrowful, señora."

Lost in their private thoughts, they rode to the airport without noticing the speed-bump stops; melon, lime, and papaya farms; banana and coconut plantations; green-canopied papaya groves; or the villages with thatch-roofed homes that lined the busy two-lane road.

The Boeing 737 rumbled south on the lone runway, lifted off, and nosed up into a deep blue cloudless sky above a long, skinny stretch of virgin shoreline crowded into the surf by mangrove swamps. After the flaps retracted, the pilot banked inland over dense jungle and continued the slow circle until all they could see below was the shimmering Pacific.

As the plane climbed toward cruising altitude, Kathryn skimmed a month-old *Alaska Airlines Magazine*, a SkyMall catalog, and a *Consumer Reports* that someone had left on the empty center seat. Dave absorbed the final melancholy-sweet pages of *A Painted House*.

When the plane turned north along Baja California's western coastline, he closed it and slipped it into his carry-on.

"Finished?" Kathryn asked.

" 'Fraid so." He adjusted the air vent, switched off the overhead light, reclined the seat, and listened to the big jet engines eat up the miles between paradise and San Francisco.

Eventually, he turned sideways in his seat so he could see his wife's face. Her eyes were closed.

"Are you asleep?" he whispered.

"No, I was thinking what a wonderful time we had."

"We sure did." He paused. "I'm going to be the best husband to you, and the best father to Emma and the baby, for as long as I can."

Kathryn turned to face her husband. "Why would you say such a strange thing?"

"I just wanted to tell you before we get home, in case I don't get another chance."

"Is there something you aren't telling me?" she asked. "Why wouldn't you get a lot more chances?"

"Just covering all the bases—you know how afraid I am of flying." His hands gripped the arm rest tightly.

She reached over and covered his left hand with

hers. "You know it's an irrational fear. Flying's safer than driving a car, especially in the Bay Area."

"Tell that to the people who were aboard those four airplanes that crashed on September Eleventh."

✝ CHAPTER 30

MONDAY, JANUARY 6, 8:30 A.M.

MACKAY WAS SHUFFLING through a lopsided stack of papers when Inspector Escalante carried in two cups from the Starbucks cart in the courthouse atrium, handed a decaf to Mackay, and dropped into a leather chair and crossed one long leg over the other. As usual, she wore impeccably tailored trousers and an expensive jacket.

"Welcome back," she greeted her boss. "How was your trip?"

"Couldn't have been better. Thanks for telling me about Las Hadas, it was perfect."

"Someday I'd like to spend a few days there with a special man."

"You have someone in mind?"

Escalante paused. "Maybe, I'm not sure." Then she emptied a cream container into her cup and asked, "You told Sheriff Granz you're pregnant?"

"Yes, he was waiting when the lab opened at seven o'clock this morning, to have blood drawn."

Mackay patted the pile of newspapers, memos, mail, and reports on her desk. "No priest murders while he and I were in Mexico. Maybe we've seen the last of them."

Escalante blew on her coffee and sipped cautiously.

"Don't bet on it. We'd better catch this wacko fast, or there'll be more."

"Unfortunately, I agree. Did DOJ come up with anything helpful?"

"The slug in Thompson's head can be matched to the Beretta .25 that fired it, if we can find it. Same with Duvoir—the bullets can be matched if we can find the rifle."

"What kind of rifle?"

"A .308 Remington."

"That narrows it down."

"A little. A hundred thousand of that model have been manufactured for civilian hunting, and thousands more in a modified version for worldwide military and police sniper duty."

"So, it's as common as the Beretta?"

"Not quite, but finding either weapon would be like—how do you say looking for a small thing?"

"Searching for a needle in a haystack."

"That's it. We could start by test-firing weapons belonging to all licensed hunters in the county."

"It'd be a waste of time unless we did the same for members of the military. What else?"

"The shoe prints at Holy Cross gymnasium are men's Nike Airliners, also identifiable. But we have the same problem—locating the shoes for comparison."

"Dave wears old Nike Airs on weekends, just like thousands of other men."

"James too."

Mackay froze, cup halfway to her lips. "James?"

"I meant Lieutenant Miller."

"Fess up."

"What do you mean, Ms. Mackay?"

"Kathryn," she corrected. "When *you* call a man by his first name, something's going on besides work."

"No big deal, we went out a few times while you were in Mexico." A hint of color crept into her bronze cheeks and climbed to her ears. "We worked, too," she tacked on unnecessarily.

It sounded feeble to Mackay. "You're blushing."

"I'm not!" The purple flush spread to her neck and chest. "He's a gifted musician and an even better cook."

"A man doesn't cook for a woman unless—"

"It was just a couple of dinners." She unconsciously flicked her tongue over her lips.

Escalante swallowed the last of her coffee, squished the empty cup, tossed it into the wastebasket, and changed the subject. "I should drink it without cream—fewer calories."

"As if you need to worry. Did you get over the hill to see your credit-card-investigator friend?"

"We figured a phone call would be faster."

"Uh-huh," Mackay said skeptically. "What did you find out?"

"R-O-L deposits its credit card receipts at Silver State Bank on Plumb Lane in Reno. I phoned the bank's branch manager. Deposits come by mail, never over the counter."

"Are they ever made at an ATM?"

"I didn't ask, why?"

"Deposits are date-and-time stamped and ATMs have cameras. Federal law requires banks to archive their tapes."

"¡Maldita sea! I should have thought of that. We might catch a glimpse of the person who made the deposit." Escalante jotted a reminder in her notebook.

"Whose name's on the account and signature cards?" Mackay asked.

"The bank manager told me it's in the name of Howard Ira Roller—H.I. Roller—I don't think she got it."

"High Roller—cute. Where does the bank send the monthly statements?"

"Mail Boxes Etc on Smithridge Lane in Reno."

"Did you check it out?"

"One of my old Police Academy friend's a Washoe County homicide detective. She interviewed the mail drop's owner—High Roller's address is a vacant lot on Rock Boulevard in Sparks."

"Figures," Mackay commented. "Who picks up from Mail Boxes Etc?"

"Nobody. Once a week they package the mail up and ship it to another drop in Carson City."

"Sneaky. How did High Roller pay for the boxes?"

"Cash up front for a full year rental plus weekly shipping charges. The Carson City drop's behind a dildo display at a dirty-book and sex-toy shop. My friend said the floor was sticky. The owner never sees the clients pick up, because boxes are intentionally tucked away so mail can be retrieved any time of the day or night anonymously."

Mackay laughed. "Get mailed and nailed in one stop. More dead ends."

"Es verdad, lo sciento. We have no idea if it's just a simple mom-and-pop cash cow, an organized offshore scam, or the underground arm of a major Nevada casino."

"Much less whether they hired a professional hit man and if so, how to track him down."

Escalante shook her head and raised an eyebrow. "NCIC computers turned up nothing on R-O-L or Roulette-On-Line, neither did the Sec-State corporate database. We haven't contacted other states yet."

"FBI and Interpol?"

"No recently reported contract hits. And no known mechanics whose whereabouts they can't account for."

"That's a profession with a lot of turnover," Mackay speculated. "There are hundreds of paid hitters they don't know about. How about IFCC?"

"No similar complaints."

"Did you check the e-mail address on R-O-L's web site?"

"The web site's been rolled up. I got the address off the letter they sent Scalisi, but the e-mail account's closed, too."

"I had to give a credit card number to my ISP to open an account."

"Me too," Escalante agreed, "but there are dozens of free ISPs that don't keep records and most pay ISPs wouldn't cooperate with cops if we found them. They're like on-line casinos, lots of them are run out of garages, spare bedrooms or anyplace big enough to house the server. They come and go faster than an eighteen-year-old sailor on shore leave."

Mackay shot Escalante a look but didn't comment on the unusual off-color remark. "The credit card they paid monthly fees with would probably be in H.I. Roller's name anyway—same address, same dead end."

"That's how we saw it."

Mackay slurped her coffee and made a face. "Cold coffee would gag a maggot. Just what I don't need, I'm already queasy in the morning." She didn't mention that her barely swelling tummy and breasts forced her to wear what she considered her loosest, dowdiest wool suit.

She set the cup on the corner of her desk. "You seized Benedetti and Duvoir's computers?"

"We searched the hard drives the night you left for Manzanillo," Escalante told her.

"That was New Year's Eve."

"We worked on the computers, then ate dinner at James' house."

"Did you get anywhere?" Mackay asked, then quickly explained, "I meant with the computers."

The corners of Escalante's mouth tugged upward. "En ninguna parte—con ordenadores."

"I don't speak Spanish well enough to know what you just said."

"It's just as well. If anyone was gambling on-line using those computers, they removed the casino software."

"Can't erased files be recovered?"

"Sometimes. I dragged the County's computer guru, Ellie Nottingham, down here on New Year's Day. She was ticked off and hungover."

"She shouldn't've drunk so much on New Year's Eve."

"Exactamente. She found CyberScrub on both computers."

"Found what?"

"CyberScrub," Escalante repeated. "It's a first-rate, over-the-counter security software program that scrambles and removes web-browser tracks, and eliminates all traces of old e-mails and other deleted files."

"Sounds suspicious."

"That was my first reaction, but Nottingham said it's a common security measure. Most organizations, including the County, use similar programs to foil hackers or other unauthorized users who might try to retrieve sensitive data after it's been trashed."

Mackay asked if a computer-forensics lab might be able to recover them.

"No," Escalante told her. "CyberScrub exceeds U.S. Defense Department standards for permanent removal of digital data—the church's computers are dead ends."

"What isn't—besides your relationship with Lieutenant Miller."

"It's not a relationship yet."

"Yet?"

"Ms. Mackay!"

"Call me Kathryn, and—" The phone buzzed and she punched the speaker button.

"It's your gynecologist, Doctor Burton," Mackay's secretary announced. "She said it's urgent."

Mackay placed a hand over the mouthpiece and turned to the inspector. "I need to take this."

"Should I leave?"

"Not necessary."

Mackay switched off the phone's speaker and picked up the handset. "Good morning, Diedre."

"The lab called with your husband's blood test results. He's RH-positive."

"That's not necessarily a problem, right?"

"In your case it is. Your blood screen came back O-negative, with a significant RH-antibody presence."

"How significant?"

"Enough to escalate very quickly into a life-threatening condition for the baby. I want you to see an RH-disease specialist right away."

"Of course, if you think it's important."

"It's not important, it's critical. The doctor I want to refer you to is at the Cleveland Clinic in Ohio. Is that a problem?"

"Nothing I can't work out."

"Good. His name is Satish Singh. I spoke with him this morning. He agreed to consult with me as I monitor your pregnancy, but only if he can examine you immediately and call the shots."

There was a short silence on the line, then Burton said, "Kathryn, Singh's a bit eccentric, but in my opinion he's the best high-risk pregnancy OB-GYN in the United States. After he examines you and evaluates your amniocentesis, we'll work together to deliver a healthy baby. How soon can you get away?"

"I'll try to make airline reservations on tonight's red-eye out of San Francisco, then call Cleveland Clinic to firm up an appointment time. Thank you, Diedre."

Mackay dragged in a breath, blew it out loudly, then set the handset into the cradle as gingerly as if it were a priceless five-hundred-year-old porcelain Ming vase.

"I have to fly to Ohio for prenatal testing. Let's wrap up this briefing."

"There's nothing that can't wait until you get back. I'll bring Chief Fields up-to-date and keep him posted."

"I'd better book a flight before it gets any later and there are no empty seats."

Escalante stood, then bent over the desk and put her hand on Mackay's arm. "Kathryn, as I said before, whenever you need another woman to talk to—"

"Thank you, Donna, that means a lot to me."

✝ CHAPTER 31

"I'M DUE IN COURT at nine o'clock." Judge Reginald Keefe tugged impatiently on the sleeves of his judicial robe and indicated a chair. "You might as well sit."

Keefe's utilitarian office lacked style, warmth, character, and substance, which, in Sheriff Granz' opinion, matched the man behind the desk perfectly.

Granz perched on the edge of the uncomfortable straight-backed chair and leaned his briefcase against the legs. "You'll find what I have to say worth your time."

"Doubtful. Make it fast."

"I know Governor Graham sent your name down along with Woods' for possible appointment to the Appellate Court."

"So?"

Granz fingered a bandage inside his left elbow and sat back. "Graham's a conservative, ex-prosecutor Republican."

"He's goddamn card-carrying John Bircher."

"So is Woods. And you're a left-wing Democrat bleeding-heart liberal from the civil bar."

"I wouldn't put it that way."

"Graham will."

"If you plan to insult me, get out of my chambers."

"I was stating facts. If you were insulted I apologize."

Keefe looked at Granz through suspicion-squinted eyes. "Apology accepted. Go on."

"Your name came down because Graham's making a run for President. He needs to consider a token liberal to prove he's open-minded and convince voters that's the kind of president he'll be if they elect him."

"He'll appoint me if he wants a judge who's tough on crime."

"Compared to you, John Gotti and the Gambino Family were tough on crime. When Graham finishes paying lip service to the knee-jerk liberal far left, he'll appoint Woods unless someone runs interference for you."

"You forget it was Woods who tossed out Mackay's subpoena and got that priest killed— what was his name again?"

"Duvoir. I didn't forget."

"I ordered the Bishop to testify."

"And he didn't give us jack—he's still in jail. How does that make you look?"

"Nevertheless, it was a good order."

"I agree, but one pro-law-enforcement order in fifteen years doesn't line you up to the right of center. Graham will appoint the man his appointment secretary, Ronald DeWitt, says works best politically, and since the World Trade Center and Pentagon, that means someone backed by law enforcement."

Keefe glanced at the clock. "What's all this got to do with you?"

"I can get you appointed."

"How?"

"The Governor's—"

Granz' jaw started working like he was chewing a hunk of jerky, spit bubbled at the corners of his mouth, his eyes glazed over, and the veins in his neck bulged as if they might split the skin.

Keefe leaned forward. "Granz?"

Drool puddled on Granz' chin. His arms quivered.

"Sheriff!" Keefe's voice rose in alarm.

Granz suddenly blinked several times, licked his lips, and wiped his chin on his sleeve. "What?"

"You scared the shit out of me, Granz. What happened?"

"Nothing."

Granz yanked a paper cup from the dispenser on the side of the water cooler by Keefe's desk and held it under the blue spigot. "Mind if I have a drink of water?"

"Help yourself."

He pulled a bottle from his briefcase and washed down a handful of pills. "Thanks."

"No problem. You sure you're okay?"

"Just a sudden stress headache."

Keefe steepled his fingers. "Where were we?"

Granz pinched the bridge of his nose between his thumb and forefinger. "Unless somebody does some heavy lifting on your behalf, you've got less chance than a popcorn fart in a hurricane."

"Is that an offer?"

"That's right. You've got to have law enforcement's support."

"You're only one cop."

"I'm *top* cop."

"The police chiefs will never support me."

"I can neutralize their opposition."

"It'd still take some serious juice."

"Twenty-five years ago, Ron DeWitt and I were young Sheriff's deputies together. Partners, in fact. DeWitt was good-looking and smart—a rising star with a future, a foxy wife, and a house behind a white picket fence."

"I'm listening."

"He went home one day and learned his wife, Rose, had hauled ass with a butch dyke from San Francisco. Rosie didn't leave anything behind except her wedding ring, a get-lost note, and a stack of credit card bills bigger than the equity in his house."

"Why would I care about this?"

Granz continued as if Keefe hadn't interrupted. "DeWitt loved Rose more than anything in the world. For two years he turned into a belligerent, out-of-control, falling-down drunk. I covered for him, saved his ass more times than I can remember. When he climbed out of the bottle, he no longer wanted to be a cop, and enrolled in Santa Clara Law School."

"Go on."

"That was almost twenty years ago. I've got a lot of bad memories from those days. DeWitt wants to ride Graham's coattails all the way to the White House. He owes me big, and I'm willing to call in the markers."

"Why would you do that for me?"

"I want something in return."

Keefe furrowed his brows, but his eyes widened with interest. "Try to bribe me, I'll toss you in your own jail and flush the key."

Keefe paused, but when Granz didn't respond, he asked, "What's the quid pro quo?"

"Nothing illegal, just a little help cutting through some bureaucratic red tape."

"What kind of red tape?"

"Jam an adoption through for me as fast as possible and I'll write your letter of recommendation, drive it to Sacramento, chat with DeWitt about the good old days, and hand-deliver my letter supporting your appointment to the appellate court."

Keefe leaned back and crossed his arms over his chest. "Adoptions take time."

"Bull. Social worker interview, background check, verification of birth parents' status. All unnecessary bureaucratic crap in this case."

"Who's the kid?"

"Emma Mackay."

"Let me think." Keefe tugged on an earlobe and pretended he needed to be convinced.

"This is a one-time offer, Keefe. Take too long, I walk out and deliver a different letter to the Governor's office. Catch my drift?"

The Judge ignored the not-so-subtle threat. "I remember when Emma Mackay's father was killed in that Los Angeles courtroom shooting a few years back. A terrible tragedy. Young girls need fathers."

"You're all heart, Keefe."

"Since she's over twelve, I need her consent."

"I spoke to her about it last night."

"What did she say?"

" 'Of course, Dave, it was inevitable. Do I get a raise in my allowance?' "

Keefe's face cracked into a smile that looked more like a triumphant smirk. "I could get it done in a week if you deliver all the necessary papers immediately."

"I'll have them on your desk before you go home this afternoon."

"Tomorrow morning's fine. Meanwhile, run rap

sheets on yourself and Mackay. Shouldn't take more than a few hours. By the way, there's a two-hundred-dollar adoption fee."

"Jesus Christ!" Granz reached inside his coat.

"Put your checkbook away, I wouldn't want anyone to get the wrong idea. I'll waive the fee. Have you filed a petition with the court clerk?"

"It's filled out, in my briefcase."

"Give it to me, I'll file for you then intercept it, so it doesn't fall into a bureaucratic black hole at Social Services."

"We've got a deal?"

"Call it a mutual favor."

Granz slid the petition across the desk. "Whatever."

"One thing—send me several sheets of Sheriff's letterhead stationery. I'll draft the letter to the Governor personally, for your signature."

"Knock yourself out, I don't give a damn what it says. Next Monday morning, we'll exchange signatures—yours on the adoption order, mine on your letter."

Keefe grinned. "Was there anything else on your mind?"

Granz stood. "Nope. If you need me for anything in the next hour or so, I'll be in my wife's office."

"Don't worry about a thing, Dave, I've got it under control." Keefe stuck out his hand. "It's nice to swap favors with a friend."

Granz ignored Keefe's extended hand. "Don't push it, Reggie. I'd sooner have a rabid skunk for a friend."

✝ CHAPTER 32

GRANZ HANDED HIS WIFE a cup of coffee and plopped into a chair.

"I must look like a charity case," Mackay said. "Maybe it's my outfit."

"Whadaya mean?"

"Escalante brought coffee when she briefed me this morning, too. But pregnant women shouldn't drink regular coffee, so please make it decaf next time, okay?"

"I'll try to remember." He grabbed her cup. "I'll drink yours, too. What'd she have to report?"

"Nothing breaking. Why don't you check with Miller later?"

"Will do."

"Diedre Burton called a few minutes ago. You're blood test came back RH-positive."

"That's what we expected, right?"

"Yes, but my prenatal blood test shows a significant level of RH antibodies."

He clamped his fingers around the cups in his lap, then jerked them away. "Damn, that's hot! Is everything okay?"

"We don't know yet. She referred me to a specialist. I already set up an appointment."

"Tell me when and where so I can go with you."

"Tomorrow morning at Cleveland Clinic."

"Isn't there someone closer than Ohio?"

"Diedre says he's the best."

"Then I'll make flight reservations for us."

"Already did—I fly Continental out of SFO an hour before midnight."

"Just you?"

"It's only a couple of days, three at the most. I'd rather you stay with Emma."

He thought about it. "If you're sure you don't need me there, I'll take Em shopping for a new dress."

"Why?"

A lopsided smile creased his boyish face. "Keefe's going to sign the adoption order next Monday."

"Impossible."

"That's what he said at first, but I convinced him otherwise."

"You talked to Keefe? I didn't even know you'd filed the petition."

"I filled it out this morning while I waited for the blood draw. Keefe will complete it, and file for us after you stop by his clerk's desk and sign it."

"What about the Social Services report, background checks, all that other paperwork?"

"He's got authority to short-circuit most of it, and I promised to run our raps for him, and drop off a complete package tomorrow."

"Why would Keefe do this for you? You hate each other worse than a mongoose and a cobra."

"We declared a temporary, mutually beneficial truce."

"Dave, you didn't—"

"I made Keefe an offer he couldn't refuse but kept you out of it. It's strictly between Keefe and me—"

Suddenly, he felt a monster grab his eyeballs, roll them back, and try to claw its way up from his soul, in another evil attempt to commandeer his brain.

"No!" he told it.

"No what?" Mackay asked.

He sucked up his resolve, willed himself to look at her, then swallowed the black monster down with a mouthful of steaming coffee, followed by another, and a third.

"I said 'no,' there's nothing improper about what Keefe and I agreed to, just a gentlemen's agreement. Don't worry about it."

"I'm not worried. How can you down hot coffee like that?" Mackay asked.

"It's not that hot."

Mackay walked around the desk and tugged him to his feet. "I'll go sign the petition."

She hooked her arm through his and walked him to the door, head on his shoulder. He twisted the knob but she stopped him before he swung the door open.

"Dave?"

"Yeah?"

"All of a sudden I feel like I waddle instead of walk."

"It's your imagination. No one else will notice unless you confide in them. Does Escalante know?"

"Yes, I told her."

"Did she say you waddle?"

"No, but I'm her boss. I had to wear this old suit today because my others feel too tight."

"I like it."

"No you don't. Do I look dowdy?"

"You look more beautiful than ever."

"Maybe you'll get lucky before I take off for the airport, sweet talker."

"How 'bout right now?" He glanced meaningfully at her leather sofa.

"Tempting, but I need to wrap up a few things now that I'm going to be gone again."

"I can wait until after work."

"It'll be worth the wait, you'll like me better than ever."

"Not possible—how come?"

"My other suits were too tight in the tummy."

"Yeah?"

"The good news is they're tighter in the chest now, too."

"Doesn't matter to me." He licked his lips. "Anything more'n a mouthful's wasted, anyway."

"Get out of here, Granz."

✝ CHAPTER 33

THE CONTINENTAL AGENT was a black woman about ten years Kathryn's senior with a BETTY—SUPERVISOR nametag, a generous figure, and a toothy smile. She scrutinized Kathryn's driver's license, keyed Mackay's ticket into the computer, and handed it back with a boarding pass.

"Seat thirty-six-B."

"That's a center seat. Is there anything on the window? I'd like to sleep."

"Sorry, coach is full and there are standbys." Betty shook her head. "Are you sick?"

"Just tired." She leaned against the ticket counter. "And pregnant."

"Been there my own self. Flying's no picnic in your condition, 'specially early when your stomach's churning all the time. How many kids you got?"

"This'll be my second."

"I got four boys. How long you been in line?"

"Almost an hour."

"Back's killing you, huh?"

"And how! Feet, too."

"I hear that! Don't know what kinda work you do but if you're on your feet all day like me, you don't wanta be squished between two fat guys on no airplane. Gimme that ticket and boarding pass."

Kathryn hesitated, then handed them back. Betty ripped them up and dropped them in the wastebasket, punched a few computer keys, printed out new documents, and handed them to Mackay.

"I moved you to seat two-A. Two-B's empty. First class boards 'bout ten-thirty."

Kathryn slid her credit card across the counter. Betty pushed it back. "Forget it."

"I'm not sure I can accept it without paying."

"Sure you can. We fly empty first-class seats almost every flight, and give away plenty of upgrades—handicapped folks, angry folks, pushy folks, you name it. As shift supervisor it's part of my job."

Betty checked her computer. " 'Sides, they gave away seat thirty-six-B while we were talking. You take this plane to Cleveland tonight, it's in first class. Have a nice flight."

Kathryn stuffed the ticket into her handbag. "Thank you very much, I can't tell you—"

"Next!" Betty had turned her attention to another passenger.

The security line was short and they didn't search her, so Kathryn rolled her carry-on to the gate, collapsed into a seat, kicked off her shoes, propped her feet on the bag, and dialed her cell phone.

"Granz."

"You said to call and let you know everything's okay before we took off."

"How come you called my cell phone instead of our house line?"

"I didn't want to wake Emma."

"Your flight on time?"

"They said it'll leave at eleven. If I'd known the security checkpoint lines would be so short, I could have left home an hour later."

"Then the lines would've been out the door. Post-September Eleven air travel—always an adventure."

"I was upgraded to first class, so now I can sleep."

"Good. Whatcha gonna do for the next hour?"

"I brought a book."

"Well, relax and don't worry about Emma and me, we'll be fine. Call tomorrow after you see the doctor."

"I will. I'd better go."

"Me, too. I'll miss you."

"I love you, Dave."

He didn't answer.

"Dave?"

He didn't answer, but the line stayed open.

She increased the volume. "Dave?"

She heard something hit the floor, then the line clicked and went dead. She punched the End button. "Bad reception inside the building," she muttered.

She leaned back, glanced around to be sure no one she knew was watching her as she slipped on her secreted Dr. Dean Edell reading half-glasses, and opened her book. It was *RH Disease and You— Delivering a Healthy Baby.*

✝ CHAPTER 34

EVERY JANUARY THE MID-WINTER Fifties Jubilee drew Woodies, Street Rods, and Cruisers to a two-day bash at the Wharf-Boardwalk. Car owners showed off, checked out paint jobs, ogled chrome flathead V-8s, sat on tuck 'n' roll upholstery, and swapped lies. Sunday night they cruised up Ocean Street, around the Town Clock, and down the mall to the beach where Boss Rod was crowned. The owner got a trophy and a check for a thousand dollars.

The Monday, January 6, *Santa Rita Centennial* headline reported PRIEST HOT-RODS FOR GOD above a color photo of Reverend Jason Ryan beside his red Deuce Coupe holding the Boss Rod trophy. It said Ryan donated the thousand dollars to his parish's youth ministry.

• • •

An SUV swung into the alley behind Blessed Mother Catholic Church, Reverend Jason Ryan's parish. Wipers slapping, it idled along, fat tires crunching wet pea gravel. When the headlights lit up the red Coupe nosing into the carport behind Reverend Ryan's tiny bungalow tucked into a corner of the church grounds, it pulled in.

The driver climbed out, unsheathed a Buck BUD110 automatic lock-back knife, stuck the four-inch blade into the Hot Rod's tires, then returned to the SUV and punched a number into his cell phone.

"Hello?" *He could see Jason Ryan answer the phone through the kitchen window.*

"Reverend, this is California Highway Patrol Dispatcher Allison. Officer Stanfield reported a red Deuce Coupe in Grovers Alley behind your house with four flat tires. DMV shows it's registered to you. Probably vandalism. Your insurance will want a police report. Could you meet Stanfield by your carport? He'll shine his patrol car's red light in your window so you know it's him."

He slipped a red lens over the portable spotlight and shone it over the redwood fence.

"I see the red light but—"

"I understand you're nervous. Here's the CHP number. Hang up and call me back."

Ryan jotted down the number, pressed the Disconnect button, released it, and dialed.

● ● ●

His cell phone chirped. "California Highway Patrol, Allison speaking."

"Sorry for being such a pain." Ryan apologized.
  "Better safe than sorry, Father."
  "I'll be right out."

The stun gun dropped the priest instantly to the damp concrete floor. He dragged the body into the shadowy space between the car and the fence and leaned against the Deuce's radiator.

When Ryan stirred, he slapped the priest's face. "Stay awake. Are you afraid?"
  "God, yes."
  "I know the feeling. Open your mouth."

He stuck the pistol barrel between the priest's teeth and pulled the trigger, splattering jagged skull fragments and shredded brain on the award-winning, candy-apple-red Deuce Coupe.

He rolled the priest's head to the side, picked up the mutilated bullet carefully, swished it around in a puddle of rain water to wash off the blood, and dropped it into his pants pocket.

Then he attached the portable voice changer to his cell phone and punched in a number. The line was busy. When the answering service came on, he dialed in a deep male voice and said, "I tried to call but your phone's busy. Answer next time, if you want to stop me."

✠ CHAPTER 35

STANDING OUTSIDE THE CARPORT in Grovers Alley, Miller stomped his feet so he wouldn't track water and mud into Escalante's new Toyota. "After stumbling across this mess, I bet that jogger runs someplace else in the mornings from now on," he told her.

Escalante unlocked the passenger door for him. "Dead bodies aren't pretty," she agreed coolly.

"I meant the mess on the Coupe's candy-apple-red paint job."

"Must you joke about everything?"

"Homicide dicks who don't joke, worry. Homicide dicks who worry, screw up. Homicide dicks who screw up set murderers free and look for another line of work."

"You're so cynical, James."

"Not cynical, experienced."

"You're cynical, *Lieutenant*." She spat the word out like a mouthful of curdled milk.

Escalante slammed the Camry's driver door and snapped her shoulder harness into the lap belt while Miller climbed into the passenger seat. She started the engine and waited, not looking at him.

He stared at her but she didn't react. "What?" he finally asked in his most innocent voice.

"Buckle up."

"I'm flattered that you care." He clicked the buckle together. "Scared this pretty face'll get messed up if we have an accident, huh?"

"I don't want to get a ticket."

She threw the shifter into drive, threaded her way down Grovers Alley past soggy clumps of dead weeds and dirty brown puddles, turned west on Morrissey, and accelerated toward the East Side.

Miller broke the silence first.

"Waste of time." He watched her from the corner of his eye. "Didn't turn up diddly squat at that crime scene."

"We can't find evidence that isn't there."

"I suppose."

She lapsed into another silence.

"No witnesses, the alley's under a foot of water so there's no tire tracks, and the shooter's cool enough to scoop up the slug he wasted Ryan with and haul it away," he went on. "What's up with that?"

He peeked at her but her expression revealed nothing.

"If I had my choice," he went on, "the shooter woulda left the bullet in a plastic bag along with his name, address, Social Security number, and sexual preference, but I guess he forgot to ask what makes me a happy camper."

"Are you going to chatter all the way back to your house?"

"Probably."

She pursed her lips. "He *is* very cautious—doesn't give up much of himself."

"Yeah, he's a lot like you that way."

"According to Yamamoto," she said, ignoring his comment, "shoe prints in the carport are similar to those at the Holy Cross gym."

"Close only counts in horseshoes. Even if they were made by the same shoe, every step changes its individual identifying characteristics—you heard Menendez. Benedetti got whacked two weeks ago. If the shoes've been worn since, it's too late for a match."

"I hope you're wrong, but I think you're right."

"Whoever this nut is, he's smart—cancels Ryan's ticket, and floats off like a fuckin' ghost."

"If you insist on being profane, I can drop you at a bus stop."

"Sorry."

She offered no absolution, so he said, "We're assuming the same perp whacked 'em all. Maybe we ought to consider the possibility of a copycat."

"Or worse—copycats."

"Spooky thought. While Nelson was bagging Ryan's body he told me he'll do the autopsy tomorrow. I doubt he'll turn up anything useful."

"Should we go to the morgue and observe?"

"I'll wait for the movie to come out."

"What?"

"It's a cute way of saying I'll read the protocol when Nelson releases it."

"Oh. American slang is strange."

Escalante turned into Miller's Prospect Heights driveway and pushed the shifter into park.

The awakening morning sun tumbled through puffy gray clouds, slicing opportunistically through the leafless cottonwood trees to paint wet-yellow stripes on the side of his house.

She left the engine running. "See you later."

He didn't budge.

"Are you going to get out?"

"In a minute. I'm very sorry, Doña."

"You embarrassed me in front of Sergeant Yamamoto. I asked you to not call me Chiquita."

"I know. It slipped."

"You hurt my feelings."

"What's it mean that's so bad?"

" 'Tiny' like a Chihuahua dog. When you call a woman Chiquita, it's condescending, demeaning, and sexist."

"That's not how I meant it."

"How *did* you mean it?"

"The same way as Francis Bret Harte."

"What's a 'Bret Harte'?"

"Not a *what*, a *who*. An American poet. During the California Gold Rush he was living in Tuolumne County when he wrote a poem called 'Chiquita.' One of the lines goes, 'Chiquita, my darling, my beauty.' "

"You read poetry?"

"I love poetry. It's music in words."

She shook her head slowly. "Everything about you surprises me, Diego."

"That good or bad?"

"Depends."

A sudden hint of a smile creased her cheeks but disappeared as quickly. "Mostly good. The poem is very pretty."

He grinned, displaying newly laser-whitened teeth. "I think Harte might've been talking about his horse, but you get the idea."

She squeezed her lips together, pressed a fist tightly against her mouth, but lost the battle and laughed aloud. "You're digging yourself into a hole, James."

"I love the way you laugh."

"Don't change the subject."

"I meant Chiquita like *plátano*."

"A banana?"

"No, bananas are ordinary, Doña. *You're like a 'plátano'*—exotic, beautiful to look at, and sweet to eat."

Color crept up her neck, across her olive face,

and settled on her cheekbones. "How can you say
such dumb things half the time, and beautiful
things the other?"

She reached across the seat and ran her fingers
through his beard, which he had mowed to a digni-
fied professorial length and trimmed neatly. It
glowed ruddy red, like his face.

"Tú estás muy guapo." Her voice was deep and
throaty.

"No one ever called me handsome before."

"Then, no one has looked close enough before."

He cleared a lump from his throat. "Would you
like to eat before we go back to work?"

"Okay, but I need to shower first. Messy crime
scenes make me feel sucia y fea."

"You could never look dirty and ugly to me."
There was an embarrassed pause before he said,
"We're in uncharted water here, Doña. I'm afraid
we've set something in motion that I don't want to
stop, but you might be sorry about after."

"I do not do things I will be sorry for, and I still
want to shower."

"My bathroom door locks, I won't bother you."

"No preocuparso por usted." Escalante switched
off the ignition as she translated and opened the
driver door. "It is not you I worry about, it is myself."

✝ CHAPTER 36

THE SKINNY CONCRETE driveway beside Miller's 1950s house ended at a detached garage where a wooden gate opened into a large, grassy backyard. Dormant apple, plum, and pear trees stood among the rose and hydrangea bushes, waiting for the warmth of spring to arouse their reproductive urges and give birth to another crop of sweet summer fruit.

Miller opened the gate and unlocked the back door, and he and Escalante kicked off their wet shoes, peeled off their socks, and draped their jackets over twin brass claw hooks in the utility room. The winter-morning cold clung wetly to the walls so he cranked the thermostat up to seventy-two degrees, gave her a thick white Turkish towel and washcloth, and shut the bathroom door behind her.

In his bedroom, he stripped off his damp clothes, slipped on Levi's and a black T-shirt with dolphins on the chest over the letters DSFD, and padded barefoot into the kitchen.

The shower started as he was grinding aged Sumatran beans in a Krups, and he was whisking minced onion, chopped cilantro, and ground cumin into a Pyrex bowl full of beaten eggs when his wall phone chirped.

He considered ignoring it but couldn't. "Miller."

"Soy yo." She stood on a rug outside the shower, the pounding water almost drowning out her voice.

"Why are you phoning the kitchen from the bathroom, Doña?"

"You said to call you if I need anything. I'm on my cell phone."

"I meant 'call' like in 'shout.' "

"Oh. You speak in English colloquialisms or slang that I sometimes don't understand."

He laughed. "¿Qué necesitas?"

"Champú."

Hot, wet bathroom air slapped him in the face when he cracked the door, but through the fogged-up shower glass he could make out a vague female form that slipped tantalizingly in and out of focus, like a swimmer at the bottom of a deep pool.

"Hand me the shampoo, please." She stuck a hand over the shower door. When she did, her body pressed against the glass and swept away the fog like a squeegee.

He handed the shampoo over the top. "Anything else you need?" He sucked in a deep breath and blew it out hard, stirring up eddies that rippled visibly through the steam-impregnated air.

"Sí." She slid the shower door open. "You."

She shimmered and glowed like a nymph in an impressionist watercolor under the running water. It splashed over her jet-black hair and dripped from her nose and chin, then sheeted over her chest, finally gathering at her hips and tumbling down her slender legs.

She leaned out and kissed him, then pulled his shirt over his head, and tugged off his Levi's.

He stepped into the shower.

"Do you really think I am sweet to eat like a plátano?" she asked.

"Yes."

"Prove it."

Soon, she pushed him against the back of the tub, kneeled over him so her breasts brushed his face, and lowered herself, slowly consuming him. He watched her for a moment, then shut his eyes.

"Why did you stop looking at me?"

"Because you're like a sunset—too beautiful to look at for very long without hurting."

"You are a poet."

"I haven't been with a woman for a long time," he told her, his voice hoarse. "I can't wait any longer."

"It's all right, come with me now."

Afterward, they lay together under the water. When she felt it start to run cool, she suggested they get up.

"Ice-cold water *would* ruin the mood," he agreed. "Besides, I'm famished."

When the omelets, toast and jam were gone, they sat back in their chairs and sipped coffee.

"What does the DSFD on your shirt mean?" she asked.

"'Deep, silent, fast, and deadly.' A long time ago, when I was young and foolish, I served in the U.S. Navy Submarine Service. It's our motto. Silly, huh?"

"Not at all." She finished her coffee, set her cup down reluctantly, and said, "I should go."

"I know. Are you going to call Mackay in Cleveland and fill her in?" he asked.

"I cannot tell her about us yet."

"I meant last night's murder."

"Oh. No, there's nothing she can do about it, and she has plenty on her mind right now." She checked her watch. "It's eleven o'clock in Cleveland. She's probably at her doctor's office."

✝ CHAPTER 37

"HOW LONG HAVE I kept you waiting?" Doctor Satish Singh dropped into a high-backed swivel chair and placed several sheets of fax paper carefully in the center of his desk, aligning the edges with his fingertips. His office walls were festooned with diplomas and awards, among which was a Doctor of Medicine from Princeton University that Kathryn Mackay had carefully scrutinized while she paced his empty office.

"Half an hour." She sat on edge of a leather recliner.

"Sorry. I hoped to review your medical history earlier, but I was called out on an emergency."

Singh wore a starched white lab coat that accentuated his smooth coffee-with-cream skin, jet-black hair, and droopy mustache. He was short and extremely thin with a small, triangular face, pointy too-big ears that stuck out like bat wings, and eyelids that drooped lazily over chocolate-colored eyes.

"No problem. Thanks for seeing me on such short notice." Despite herself, she did a double take at his appearance.

"I see you agree," he said with a smile.

"Agree?"

"That I look like a middle-aged Mahatma Gandhi. Everyone thinks so except me. As an amateur college thespian, I rather thought I resembled Ben Kingsley, whose real name was Krishna Bhanji. I should be so lucky.

"But now I want to talk about you." His easy smile was warm and fatherly. "May I call you Kathryn?"

"Please."

He leaned forward, twiglike hands folded one inside the other. "The medical file Doctor Burton faxed to me shows no weight, heart, diabetes, hypertension, or other disorder. But, as she advised, your RH-antibody screen is positive. If the fetus is RH-positive—which it almost certainly is—your antibodies can pass through the placenta, attack its red blood cells, and cause erythroblastosis fetalis. It's called hemolytic disease of the newborn, or HDN."

"We didn't discuss how bad it is, or what should be done about it," she told him.

"That's why she referred you to me. Ultrasound will tell us if fluid has accumulated in the baby's belly, head, chest, or heart, indicating severe anemia. I'll extract amniotic fluid that our laboratory will evaluate using delta-OD 450 for the presence of bilirubin, a by-product of red-blood-cell breakdown. The bilirubin is stated as a 'titer ratio.' If that ratio were to reach one-to-sixteen, I would consider your baby to be at serious risk.

"Assuming yours is now below that, our lab will establish a baseline. Burton will draw blood each week, air ship it to Cleveland Clinic, and our techs will plot each measurement against your baseline on a Liley Graph. If I see a rapid, significant upward trend, other measures should be taken at once."

"Such as?"

"Cordocentesis—percutaneous umbilical blood sampling, or PUBS. Blood is drawn from the umbilical cord to directly measure the baby's actual antibody levels, so we know how severe the anemia is and how well, or poorly, the baby's system is compensating for the destruction of its red blood cells. I would recommend you return to Cleveland Clinic if that's necessary."

"Couldn't Doctor Burton do it?"

"I want to be diplomatic here." He hesitated. "She referred you to me for a reason, Kathryn. PUBS is complex even for a highly skilled perinatologist who performs them regularly. But ultimately it'll be your decision."

"What do you do if the anemia *is* severe?"

"Intrauterine fetal blood transfusions—to provide the baby with fresh, oxygen-carrying red blood cells."

"More than one?" she asked.

"Maybe several. They should be done at a high-risk-pregnancy specialty hospital like Cleveland Clinic's tertiary care center, in case a cesarean section is necessary."

"How likely is that to occur?"

"In a fraction of cases, the procedure triggers premature uterine contractions."

"Doctor Burton is qualified to perform a cesarean section, right?"

"The transfusions require a great deal of skill, Kathryn. Under these circumstances, even if the cesarean goes flawlessly, the baby might require specialized care. Why not make a decision later, in consultation with Doctor Burton, when and if it's necessary."

He stood. "My nurse will prep you. She's a Registered Diagnostic Medical Sonographer who's performed thousands of ultrasounds. Almost as many as I have amniocenteses—you're in very good hands."

Kathryn lay on the table watching a color monitor mounted atop the Hitachi 6000 Digital Doppler Ultrasound. In addition to the monitor, the PC-based system recorded the images on a hard drive for later review and printout.

The sonographer slid the transducer over her gelled belly while Singh recorded a detailed anatomic survey and fetal measurements. When he finished, he selected an amniocentesis site, which he marked with a strawlike tube that left a small indentation in the skin.

"There's no fluid buildup," he said. "The fetus is developing perfectly."

She crossed herself. "Thank you."

"Do you want to know your baby's sex?" Singh asked.

"Absolutely," she said.

"You're carrying a boy."

She closed her eyes and smiled.

"Do you want a local anesthetic to deaden the skin where the amnio needle will be inserted?"

"No, I'd rather be stuck once than twice."

Singh swabbed the insertion site marked by the tube, and his nurse maneuvered the ultrasound probe until the monitor displayed the chosen path for the needle.

"You'll feel a slight pinch," he told her, then inserted the needle. He watched its path on the monitor and guided it into a pocket of amniotic fluid.

"Are you all right, Kathryn?" he asked.

"I think so."

He drew a little liquid, removed the syringe and squirted it down the sink drain, then attached a fresh syringe.

"The first half-cc is discarded because it might contain your skin cells from the needle," he explained. "That would contaminate the fluid and perhaps cause the lab to analyze your chromosomes instead of the baby's."

When the 30-cc syringe filled he pulled out the needle, drained the pale yellow fluid into sterile tubes, and asked her to verify her name on the labels. After she initialed them he applied a Band-Aid over the needle insertion site.

"That's it," he said.

While Mackay dressed, Singh wrote notes in her medical file. He stopped and looked up when she entered.

"Please sit down," he said. "How are you feeling?"

"I'm a little crampy."

"Slight cramping like gas pain is normal. If you experience vaginal leakage, extremely severe cramps, fever, or bleeding, call my answering service immediately. Don't lift anything heavy for the next couple of days."

"Trust me, I won't."

"More than seventy-five chromosomal abnormalities can be diagnosed from fetal skin cells in the amniotic fluid, including Edward's or Down's syndrome trisomies. But the cells must be cultured and stimulated to grow, which takes a couple of weeks."

"How will I find out?"

"I'll fax the results to Doctor Burton. The delta-OD 450 bilirubin analysis will be completed tonight. Where are you staying?"

"Right here at the InterContinental Hotel."

"Go to your hotel, have a nice dinner, then get a good night's sleep. Call me after lunch tomorrow, and I'll tell you when you can go home."

✝ CHAPTER 38

"SORRY TO CALL YOU SO LATE," Kathryn said into the phone, checking her watch. "I know it's almost midnight, but by the time I finished at Cleveland Clinic and checked into the hotel this evening, I was exhausted. I sat on the bed to take off my shoes and next thing I knew I was waking up a few minutes ago. I didn't even eat dinner."

"When I didn't hear from you by five o'clock California time, I was worried something went wrong," Dave Granz told his wife over the phone. "Are you and the baby okay?"

She lay on her bed still fully dressed, TV tuned to the Classic Movie Channel. In H.G. Wells' *The War of the Worlds*, terrified Londoners were fleeing the city, two days after the Martian cylinder landed.

"Ultrasound showed no fluid accumulation or other abnormalities they can detect visually."

"I don't pray often, but I guess God heard me this time."

"Let's hope He keeps listening. Doctor Singh drew amniotic fluid for testing. I'm supposed to call him after lunch tomorrow to learn the results. If everything checks out, my return flight leaves Cleveland-Hopkins at five."

"Call me as soon as you know."

"I will—promise."

She punched the TV remote's Off button, sat up and yawned. "Are you interested in knowing whether we're going to have a son or daughter?"

"It's a boy—right?"

"Yes."

"I kept my fingers crossed. Toes too."

"That must've made you walk funny." She laughed. "Is there anything going on there that I should know about?"

"I shouldn't worry you with it."

"You just did. Tell me."

"Another priest got snuffed last night. Father Jason Ryan. A jogger found the body early this morning."

"Same shooter?"

"Hard to say, he got away clean."

"Just like the others."

"Right. Escalante and Miller think we ought to consider a copycat, but I'm not sure I agree."

"I don't think we can afford to overlook the possibility," she replied. "Has Doc Nelson determined time and cause of death?"

"Cause was obvious—the top of his head was blown away, brains were scattered all over the carport and the front of his car that was parked there. Nelson hasn't determined exact time of death yet, he's gonna do the autopsy tonight."

"I'll call him tomorrow. Anything else?"

"One thing—maybe good news."

"It's about time."

"Bishop Davidson sent over a message. He's ready to testify. I guess jail wasn't such fun after all."

"I'd better get him on the stand ASAP. Would you tell Escalante to round up the grand jurors, and convene them for eight o'clock Thursday morning, please."

"Consider it done."

"How are *you* feeling?" she asked.

The was a brief silence on the other end. "Fine, why?"

"Those headaches."

"Forget it, they're nothing. It's you and our son I care about."

"What's Emma doing?"

"Homework. Want me to call her?"

"No, let her study." She stretched and yawned again. "I'm sooo tired—and I still have cramps from the amnio. As soon as we get off the phone, I'm going to wash my face, brush my teeth, and go back to sleep."

"Good idea. You're sure you're all right?"

"No, I miss my family."

"I love you, Kate."

"Me, too. Talk to you tomorrow."

Wednesday morning dawned cold and clear. After watching the morning news and taking a long, luxurious shower, Kathryn ate lunch at The Watermark restaurant on the Cuyahoga River's East Bank. Afterward, she strolled through the narrow, vertical-sided streets of Cleveland's Entertainment District, where she stopped at an imported-foods store to buy Dave and Emma a three-jar box of Swiss fudge ice-cream topping and French raspberry preserves for herself. At the bookstore next door she picked up a baby-care book. Down the street she found an exclusive maternity boutique and bought a beautiful but pricey Italian wool business suit.

At three-thirty P.M. she walked to a small park near the water. She chose a bench that was off by itself, under a naked sycamore tree on a knoll looking over the rippling, intensely blue Cuyahoga. She recalled reading that the river had once been so polluted that it caught fire.

She thought of her husband and the intricacies of life, crossed her fingers, drew in a deep breath, and dialed Doctor Singh's office to find out whether later this afternoon she would be catching a cab back to Building M at the Cleveland Clinic, or to Cleveland-Hopkins International Airport.

✝ CHAPTER 39

CONTINENTAL AIRLINES FLIGHT 755 angled steeply up off the Cleveland-Hopkins tarmac at exactly five P.M. The icy blue water of Lake Michigan was giving way to the Chicago, Illinois–Gary, Indiana megalopolis when Mackay pulled the in-flight phone out of its holder on the seat back in front of her and slid her credit card through the magnetic reader.

Doctor Morgan Nelson answered from his morgue office and asked if she was still in Cleveland.

"I'm on my way home. How did you know where I was?"

"Your husband observed Ryan's autopsy last night."

"That's what I called about."

"First I want to know what Singh told you."

"You know Singh?"

"I know *of* him."

"The fetus has no fluid accumulation or abnormalities, but my titer ratio's one-to-sixteen."

"You really piss me off, Kate."

"And you make me feel so glad I called."

"With a titer ratio that high you had no business leaving Cleveland Clinic."

"That's exactly what Singh said, and exactly how impolitely he said it. Based on your subtle diplomacy, I take it you agree that one-to-sixteen's critical?"

"Of course—not that it matters whether my unexpert opinion concurs with the country's preeminent perinatologist."

"It matters to me. You're my friend, and I trust your opinion."

"Yeah? Then take my advice, based on that opinion."

"Which is?"

"When your plane lands at San Francisco, catch a return flight and get your butt back to Cleveland. Odds are high you'll lose your baby without continual oversight by the best doctor available."

"Diedre Burton's good."

"She's not a specialist."

"She knows what she's doing though, right?"

"I judge a doctor's competence by how many screw-ups come under my knife. I've never autopsied one of hers, but a good doctor calls in greater expertise when she's over her head. She called in Singh. What does that tell you?"

"That she's cautious."

"No, it tells you she's a good enough doctor to know she might not be able to handle it, ethical enough to admit it, and a good enough friend to refer you to the best."

"I can't move to Cleveland for six months."

"I specialize in dead people, Katie, not live pregnant patients. But if I did, and one of them didn't follow my advice to stay where I could give her the benefit of my expertise, I'd refuse to treat her."

"That's exactly what Singh did," she said with a sigh. "When I told him I had to return home he said he couldn't accept me as a patient, and faxed the ultrasound, amnio, and lab results to Burton."

"Why did you ask my advice?"

"I guess I hoped you might say something to make me feel better."

"A friend doesn't tell you what you want to hear just to be touchy-feely—if he does, he's not your friend."

"Morgan—"

"A friend tells you the truth, and the truth is your baby's life is at risk. Like I said before, you piss me off sometimes."

"But you still love me?"

"Once in a while." He paused. "Goddamn stubbornness must be the quality that you and Dave found so appealing in each other. He won't follow my advice either."

"What do you mean?"

"I told him to have an MRI after he smashed his head in that Thanksgiving accident. Last night he said he hasn't gotten around to it yet. What does *'hasn't gotten around to it yet'* mean?"

"He says he feels fine."

"My aching ass!"

"I take it you don't believe him?"

"Last night he had a skull-splitting headache. I asked how often he has 'em, but he shined me on. I had to remind him to pay attention to the autopsy. It was as if his body was parked at the curb while his mind was racing around the track. And he kept staring off into nowhere with a vacant look in his eyes, like a nineteen-sixties drugged-out, space-cadet hippie. He was drooling, too, and said 'huh?' whenever I talked to him."

"You're exaggerating. Besides, there's a lot going on right now, Doc—my pregnancy, these damn murder investigations. He was preoccupied."

"You might be right. My concern's based on a couple hours' casual, nonclinical observation, under less than ideal conditions. But when I asked if he's been suffering memory lapses, he said, 'Yeah, now you mention it. I can't figure out where my off-duty weapon is. It's a Beretta .25. I must've lost it.' "

"Seriously?"

"Yep. I asked when was the last time he saw it. He said he unholstered it the night of the shootout and accident, and hasn't seen it since. I asked if he reported it missing, and he says, 'Yeah, but I bought a new one—cost enough to pay for an infant car seat, a year's supply of baby food, and a truckload of disposable diapers.' "

Nelson paused. Mackay waited to see if he was

finished. He wasn't. "Have you noticed any unusual behavior on Dave's part?" he asked.

"Some."

"He might be epileptic, Kate."

"There's no epilepsy in his family."

"Epilepsy's a sort of medical black hole, but we know it's more likely to result from severe head trauma or brain tumor than genetics. Since he's reluctant to take an MRI, you've got to insist."

"What if the MRI determines he *is* epileptic?"

"Then we know. There's no cure, but seizures can be mitigated with antiseizure medicine. Most epileptics lead relatively normal lives as long as they're diligent about taking their meds. When they get forgetful, the seizures increase in frequency and intensity, and they could eventually kill him."

"What should I look for to know if he's having a seizure?" she asked.

"Involuntary, repetitive muscle movement—twitching, jerking, lipsmacking, chewing, excessive saliva production. As the episodes increase in severity, he might lose consciousness."

"For how long?"

"Usually a few seconds, two to three minutes at most. You'll think he's daydreaming, or not paying attention."

"As you did last night."

"Exactly. But in rare cases, episodes might last hours. During prolonged *status epilepticus* episodes he might function without knowing what he's doing, and he won't be able to recall afterward what he did. Like I say, rare but not unheard of."

"You're frightening me very badly, Morgan."

"Imagine how he feels—something's wrong but he doesn't know what it is, or how serious it might be."

"He might realize he's sick?"

"He's a smart man. Even if he doesn't *know*, he probably *senses* it."

"Then why would he refuse treatment?"

"Denial—pride—fear of losing his job if anyone finds out he's sick."

"How would someone find out, even if it were true?"

"Don't be naive, there are ways. As a physician I must tell you that epilepsy might render him incapable of being sheriff. If I've come to that conclusion as his friend, imagine what a nasty political opponent could make out of it. Watch him closely, Katie, and get your husband and the father of your unborn child in for an MRI. That's my advice as a doctor *and* a friend."

"I'll try," she promised.

"You'd better do more than try."

"Dammit, Doc, what more can I do? I've hassled him until he's on the verge of rebellion. You know Dave almost as well as I do. The harder I push, the more he resists. If I push much harder, he'll dig his heels in and *never* see a doctor, just to prove he doesn't need me or anyone else telling him what to do."

"You're probably right," Nelson conceded.

She hesitated. "Besides, your advice is based on just one bad night." She hesitated. "I'm hoping nothing's wrong with Dave except lack of sleep and stress."

"I'd like to believe that, but I don't," Nelson answered.

She punched the button on the arm rest, leaned the seat back as far as possible, and squeezed her eyes shut. "Sorta makes Ryan's autopsy seem unimportant, but why don't you tell me what you turned up."

"Time of death was about ten P.M. Cause was a single gunshot, but it was no routine head shot."

"Explain."

"The shooter stuck the barrel in Ryan's mouth. I found gunpowder stippling and muzzle-gas burns in the throat. Entry wound was in the soft palate. The slug penetrated the medulla oblongata on the brain stem, took a chunk out of the anterior cerebellum, transited the posterior cerebrum, exploded the skull before exiting the back of the skull, and lodged in the carport's concrete floor. Trajectory indicates Ryan was lying on his back."

"They recover the slug?"

"No, and that's interesting. The concrete had a hole in it under the exit wound but there were gouge marks around it. The shooter dug the bullet out with a knife and took it with him."

"Smart."

"Yes, and cruel." The line was silent for a few seconds before Nelson added, "When the cops catch whoever's murdering these men they'd better shoot first and ask questions second."

CHAPTER 40

"Do you swear the testimony you are about to give is the truth, the whole truth and nothing but the truth?"

In a rumpled orange jumpsuit, with uncombed hair and two days' stubble, Jeffrey Davidson looked like the inmate he had become.

He raised his right hand. "I do."

"Be seated." The Grand Jury Secretary took her place at a desk beneath the Bench while Davidson perched on the edge of the witness chair.

District Attorney Mackay stood at the podium, determined not to show how badly her back ached.

"Restate your name and occupation for the record," she instructed.

"Jeffrey James Davidson, Bishop of the Monterey Diocese of the American Catholic Church."

"I remind you that you are appearing before a duly constituted Grand Jury, convened to investigate the murders of Reverends Jacques Duvoir, James Benedetti, John Thompson, and now Jason Ryan. You must testify truthfully or subject yourself to a perjury prosecution."

"I understand."

"On December thirtieth of last year, you went to jail rather than answer my questions about Reverends Thompson and Benedetti, correct?"

"Yes."

"What changed your mind?"

"Another of my priests is now dead, and because of my stubbornness I'm probably to blame. I can't risk further tragedy."

"Did you bring Thompson's and Benedetti's personnel records as required by the subpoena?"

"I was brought here directly from your jail. The records, including those of Father Ryan, are in the custody of my attorney. I have instructed him to have them in your hands by noon today."

"That's acceptable, thank you."

Mackay pushed her fists into her lower back and twisted slightly to relieve the pain, pretending to consult a yellow legal pad before continuing.

"You previously testified that Reverend Duvoir was under investigation by the Diocese for gambling on the Internet and covering his losses with Diocese credit cards to the extent of some fifty thousand dollars, is that right?"

"Yes."

"The police investigation indicates that all four priests might have been murdered by the same person. If so, they might have been killed for the same reason as well. Did the Diocese suspect Reverends Thompson, Benedetti, and/or Ryan of gambling and embezzlement?"

"Father Ryan was the finest man I ever knew. He never did anything wrong in his life."

"All right, then let's concentrate on Thompson and Benedetti. Were either of them involved in gambling or embezzlement?"

"It's possible, but we don't think so."

"Were they under investigation for *any* wrongdoing whatsoever?"

Davidson looked at his lap, then back at Mackay and cleared his throat. "Not at the time when they were murdered."

"Explain that, please."

"I shall." He cleared his throat again, sat ramrod straight in the chair, and looked into Mackay's eyes.

"John Thompson and James Benedetti were childhood friends," Davidson began, falteringly at first. "They grew up and attended the University of San Diego together, where they remained best buddies, roommates, teammates on the basketball and football teams. Father Thompson was athletically gifted. Father Benedetti was only mediocre but he was much brighter. There was no jealousy between them, though. They earned simultaneous graduate degrees in theology, after which the Bishop of the San Diego Diocese ordained them into the priesthood the same year."

"When was that?"

"Nineteen-sixty-eight."

"What were their Church duties after ordination?"

"Father Benedetti was a parish priest. Father Thompson taught at Saint Sebastian, a boys' high school in San Diego. They were only blocks apart."

"Go on."

"John Thompson's athletic prowess and love of sports led him into coaching. A few years after taking over the athletic department, Saint Sebastian became a sports powerhouse." He hesitated. "It also became the site of the worst crisis in Diocese history. He was responsible for both."

"Please continue."

"A few years after he arrived at Saint Sebastian, a member of the football team told his parents that Father Thompson watched him in the shower with what he called 'unusual interest.' When pressed, the boy revealed that Coach Thompson had engaged him repeatedly in sexually explicit conversations and showered him with unwanted physical affection. He told his parents some of the other football players had the same experience. They thought Father Thompson was 'funny.' "

"Funny?"

" 'Gay' wasn't part of the lexicon in those days, Ms. Mackay. The boy's father was a lawyer. He told

Monsignor Winfield something had better be done. The Bishop confronted Father Thompson. He denied all the allegations, of course. Then more boys and their parents came forward with similar stories."

"How many boys?"

He shrugged. "A dozen, maybe more—the Diocese never counted."

"What did those boys say?"

"There were charges of improper touching and worse."

"How much worse?"

"Forced mutual masturbation, oral copulation, and anal penetration."

Mackay sighed deeply. "What did the Church do?"

For the first time, a crack split open Davidson's facade of composure. He looked at Mackay, then the jurors, beseeching them with his eyes to understand.

"Please keep in mind that this was many years ago, before the, uh, the unbelievable extent of sexual misconduct in the Catholic Church became fully apparent."

"Go ahead," Mackay encouraged.

"Bishop Krewzinski, God rest his soul," Davidson crossed himself, "appointed a special liaison to conduct a quiet investigation and report back. It's obvious in retrospect that the Bishop was more interested in avoiding a scandal and not destroying his reputation, or one of his priest's, than he was in protecting the children in his Diocese."

"I'd say so," Mackay agreed.

"Bishop Krewzinski used horrible judgment but as I said, things were different thirty years ago."

"You're saying that excused what he did?"

"Don't put words in my mouth, I can speak for myself," Davidson retorted, his face flushing. "I'm simply establishing the context in which those events occurred. At that time, no one could have imagined the insidiousness of the cancer that had already invaded the body of our Church, or how pervasive it would eventually become. Given the power of hindsight, it's fair to say the Church didn't behave so responsibly in those days."

Mackay resisted the urge to say, *That's the understatement of the century!* Instead she asked, "So, the Diocese covered up Thompson's pedophilia and the boys' molestations and shipped him out so he became someone else's problem, just like they did in Boston?"

"Yes, but that couldn't happen today. Because of men like Bernard Cardinal Law and Bishop Krewzinski, who swept the disgrace under the rug, U.S. bishops adopted the Charter for the Protection of Children and Young People, in November 2002. Under the Charter, a priest who molests a child in the future will be defrocked and turned over to civil authorities and the Diocese will assist in any criminal prosecution. For past offenses, a priest is permanently removed from the ministry."

"Why wasn't Thompson defrocked?"

"His case fell through the bureaucratic cracks. The San Diego Diocese no longer had authority over him. The records had been destroyed, so no notification of his—uh—his *transgressions* was officially forwarded to the Monterey Diocese. We had no evidence to support any action against him, even under the new Charter."

"Sounds like a catch-twenty-two," Mackay told him.

"It was, unfortunately," Davidson conceded. "From now on when a priest is transferred, his personnel record must be forwarded to the new diocese or parish and it must include any information that might reflect on his fitness for the ministry."

"That's reassuring," Mackay said, her sarcasm more obvious than intended.

Davidson paused, thinking, then murmured, "If only these policies had been in place thirty years ago—"

Davidson didn't finish his thought and Mackay didn't pursue it, but his meaning was clear.

"Bishop Davidson, why did you refuse to answer questions before this Grand Jury on December thirtieth?" Mackay asked.

"The Catholic Church's intent is to protect victims of papal criminal behavior, not vice versa. In this case, it was the priests themselves—Reverends Thompson and Benedetti—who were the victims. After they were murdered, they were no longer able to hurt anyone. I saw no point to it."

"Now you see it differently?"

"Yes. Jail gave me time to think and I came to realize that the relationship between the Church and society as a whole—indeed the credibility and the very viability of the Church—requires that we adopt a more open, responsible, and cooperative relationship with civil authorities. In other words, we've got to get our heads out of our—out of the sand—become a better neighbor and partner to the secular community as well as our nonsecular constituency.

"I was wrong refusing to answer your questions and I apologize. To the extent my bad decision contributed to Father Ryan's death, God will see I am punished."

No one in the room moved or made a sound.

"You said the San Diego Bishop appointed a special liaison. Whom did he appoint?" Mackay asked.

"The one person Father Thompson trusted implicitly."

"Father James Benedetti," she surmised.

"Correct. He went into the investigation with a distinct bias, but after interviewing the athletes and their parents he became convinced beyond any doubt that the complaints were justified. Father Thompson continued to deny culpability, even to his closest friend."

"What was the ultimate outcome of the Diocese inquiry?"

"Father Benedetti was pressured to wrap it up quietly and quickly by whatever means necessary."

"What means were necessary?"

"Monetary settlements, record destruction, and Father Thompson's immediate transfer to the Monterey Diocese."

"Was Father Benedetti transferred to Monterey as part of the deal?"

"Not at the time. A few years later a new Bishop took over and transferred Father Benedetti out of his Diocese, ostensibly for engineering the cover-up—I think it was because the new Bishop feared it would eventually become public. Father Benedetti was just following orders."

"He was the fall guy for the Diocese."

"An ugly characterization, but accurate. It's not unheard of even today, as everyone now knows."

"Was Father Benedetti ever accused of sexual improprieties?"

"Absolutely not. His sin was a noble excess of love and loyalty for his friend that manifested itself in unfortunate ways."

"Were there any complaints about Father Thompson after he transferred to Monterey?"

"No, as I told you in the hall after my first Grand Jury appearance, the Monterey Diocese never received any complaints."

"A half-truth at best," Mackay reprimanded.

"I answered your question exactly as you asked it, and I answered truthfully. If you had phrased your question differently—"

"It no longer matters," Mackay interrupted.

"No, I suppose not. The reason might, however. Among the conditions of Thompson's transfer from San Diego to Monterey was that he not teach or coach boys' athletics."

"How about Benedetti?"

"There were no restrictions on Father Benedetti. In an ironic turn of fate, he became coach of the Holy Cross High School basketball team—universally loved by his players, none of whom ever say a bad word about him."

"Bishop Davidson, do you know of your own knowledge that Reverend Thompson was a pedophile?"

Davidson hesitated. "Since he's now deceased, I suppose I wouldn't be violating my sacred vow by admitting that many years later, I heard Father Thompson's confession. He confessed to molesting many boys and begged absolution. Father Benedetti sought absolution for his role in the cover-up, as well."

"Did you grant them absolution?"

"Of course, they repented and atoned with a lifetime of exemplary work. I granted them both absolution. That's what I meant by there being nothing to gain, especially after they were dead."

He paused again. "Now, I'm afraid the scabs have been—albeit rightfully and necessarily—scraped off those old sores. Let's hope, Ms. Mackay, that when they finally heal and the cancer is gone, our tiny part of the Body of the Catholic Church is healthier and wiser for the additional pain and injury you and I have inflicted upon it today."

✝ CHAPTER 41

IMMEDIATELY AFTER ADJOURNING the Grand Jury, Mackay set up an emergency briefing in her office with Granz, Miller, and Escalante and spent fifteen minutes filling them in on Davidson's testimony.

She summed up by saying, "We're wasting our time and resources hunting for a hired gun. I don't think these murders have anything to do with Internet gambling or embezzlement."

"You're certain?" Miller asked.

"The only things I know that are certain are death and taxes."

"Trite but true," Miller said, pushing his lower lip up over his upper as he thought. "But I'm not sure you're right about the gambling connection."

"What's your thinking?" Mackay asked him.

"Right after Duvoir stiffs a casino Davidson gets

several telephone threats and tells the caller to get lost. Immediately after, Duvoir gets snuffed. Casino owners aren't choirboys and they don't take kindly to being ripped off. And Davidson didn't deny they might've been involved in the gambling mess."

Escalante picked absently at a thumb nail as she thought. "I agree with Ms. Mackay," she argued. "The notion that a professional contractor did the dirty work bothered me from the start, even though we didn't have any other leads at the time."

"Contract killers are creatures of habit," Mackay added. "A professional develops a style and sticks with it because it works. The less deviation, the less chance of getting caught. These MOs aren't remotely similar."

"Four firearms, four murder victims, four priests, four clean getaways," Miller said. "They sound pretty damn similar to me."

Escalante turned to face Miller. "That's where the similarity ends."

"Convince me."

"Three carried handguns: one small-caliber; one a cannon; and one who-knows-what. One perp hauls the gun away and leaves the slug behind; one leaves both the gun and the slug behind alongside the victim's body; one doesn't just haul the gun away, he digs the slug out of the concrete floor and takes it too. One of the perps shoots his victim three times with a sniper rifle."

"Just playin' devil's advocate," Miller answered slowly. "Like you said, a pro does the job and gets out, he doesn't torture or get in the victim's face.

Murder's a business, and whackin' someone by surprise or from a distance is the safest, most businesslike technique."

Escalante sat back in her chair. "If the shooter's not a pro, who is he?"

"What makes you think it's a 'he'?" Mackay wanted to know.

"Because you can count the known female serial killers and professional shooters on both hands and have fingers left over," Miller told her.

"According to Bishop Davidson, Thompson was a pedophile priest," Granz interjected, his gaze shifting around at the other three. "My gut tells me the killer's a molest victim."

Miller stroked his neatly trimmed red beard. "Davidson said Thompson walked the straight and narrow for the past thirty years. Besides, the other priests weren't pedophiles."

"All we know is Davidson says they didn't get any complaints about them. The Catholic Church is full of perverts."

Miller nodded. "You got a point."

"So we can't dismiss the possibility," Granz insisted.

"If it *was* one of Thompson's victims, why'd he wait almost thirty years to get torqued enough to snuff Thompson's candle?"

Granz crossed one leg over the other. "Because a pedophile's victim is usually grown before he realizes how ugly and permanent the scars are. When he *does*, and finally comes to grips with who trashed his life, it doesn't matter how many years went by. He's pissed off and looking for revenge."

"No question," Mackay agreed. "I see it all the time in women who were raped as children or teens."

"Well, if you're right, trackin' him down's gonna be a big job," Miller observed. "Trails get cold after a couple of months. This one's cold enough to turn the snot on a bloodhound's nose into slimy icicles."

"We've got to start someplace," Granz replied, ignoring the sarcasm. "My instincts tell me that we ought to go on the assumption Thompson *was* taken out by one of his victims."

"I doubt the Church kept a neat little list of molest victims, in case the cops decided they wanted it later." Miller said, then asked, "How do we find Thompson's victims after all these years?"

Granz tugged his earlobe. "Ideas?"

Escalante sat up in her chair and crossed her ankles. "Thompson's victims had to attend Saint Sebastian High School while he taught there, from sixty-eight to seventy-four. We get the school's enrollment records for those years."

"You think they still exist?" Miller said.

"They might."

"I'll issue a subpoena duces tecum for school documents including historical enrollment records," Mackay said.

Miller looked at Granz. "You grew up in San Diego, what high school did you go to?"

Granz uncrossed his legs and stretched them

stiffly out in front of him as if he had just awakened from a deep sleep, but his eyelids fluttered rapidly and he stared out the window without answering.

"I can see the light's on in the house but doesn't look like anybody's home," Miller said. "You listenin', boss?"

"I—I—yeah, I was thinking. What'd you say?"

"What high school did you go to?"

"I graduated from Mira Mesa High School, class of seventy-three."

"How big was Saint Sebastian in those days?"

"Big—maybe four thousand students, why?"

Miller puckered his lips and exhaled slow and loud. "In seven years that's twenty-eight thousand middle-aged men we gotta locate."

"Not if we narrow it down by concentrating on the men who live in or near Santa Rita County," Escalante told him.

"What if Saint Sebastian's old enrollment records have been tossed?"

"Bank records," Mackay said. "There should be a pattern of checks to individuals at about the time the Diocese cut its deal to pay off the victims' parents. I'll add them to the subpoena."

Miller shook his head. "Banks don't keep records that long and it's unlikely the Church did, either. Even if they did, let's hope Saint Sebastian doesn't have the same auditor as Enron, because if they do, when we drop the subpoena on the desk we'll have to rummage through the shredder."

"Do you have a better idea?" Mackay asked.

"Nope." Miller stood up and straightened his

suit coat. "I better gas my car up, swing by my house, grab some clothes and make tracks for sunny San Diego."

"Stop here on your way. I'll complete the subpoena and leave it with my secretary for you to pick up." Mackay looked at her husband and raised her eyebrows in a silent question. He nodded and held up two fingers.

"If we're going to head off another murder, we've got to act fast," she told Escalante. "Go with Lieutenant Miller. Two investigators get more accomplished, and faster than one."

Escalante stood. "Exactly what I was thinking."

When Escalante and Miller left, Granz asked, "You suppose Miller and Escalante will rent one motel room or two in San Diego?"

"I hope one. My budget can't handle much more."

Mackay glanced at her watch. "I've got just enough time to make my appointment with Doctor Burton."

"What are you seeing her about?"

"She's my OB-GYN. I'm pregnant, remember?"

"I meant was there anything specific?"

"No, Babe, I just saw Singh yesterday. But since he refused to keep me as a patient, I need to make sure Diedre will keep me on, even without Singh's consultation."

✝ CHAPTER 42

"YOU SHOULD HAVE TURNED left, back there on Martin Luther King Freeway." Escalante alternated between studying the rumpled AAA map and peering through the rain-streaked windshield watching road signs.

"That's the way to Lemon Grove." He continued south on the San Diego Freeway.

"And the direction of Saint Sebastian High School."

"No point going there now, Doña, it's almost eight o'clock. School's closed for the night."

"I know, but if we want to be close to the school

tomorrow morning we're too far south. Whoops, now you passed the Seventeenth Street exit."

"So?"

"I spotted a couple of decent-looking motels."

"I don't want a decent-looking motel."

"We have to stay someplace."

"No foolin'?"

The VW's headlights slashed through the dark slanted rain and when they lit up the HWY 75 WEST sign, he eased into the right lane and veered off.

"You're lost," she teased.

"Nope."

He merged onto the Coronado Bay Bridge and accelerated to seventy miles per hour to keep up with the late beach-bound traffic.

"Men are never lost, they're *temporarily displaced*."

"Very funny!"

"I don't want your machismo to suffer when you stop at a gas station to ask directions."

"I know where I'm going."

To their right as they crossed the bridge, Coronado's lights sprouted like flowers out of the black ocean, against a twinkling backdrop of bobbing navigation buoys, slow-moving Navy warships and civilian freighters, runway lights of North Island Naval Air Station and beyond that, Lindbergh Field.

Escalante stuck the map in the door pocket, reclined the leather seat, brushed the hair off her forehead, leaned her head against the restraint, and gazed out the passenger window.

He watched from the corner of his eye. "Beautiful."

"It sure is."

"I meant you."

She didn't answer for several seconds. "I wish we could stay near the beach."

"We are." He followed Orange Avenue to the water's edge, pulled into the Hotel del Coronado's main entrance, and shut off the engine.

"We don't have reservations."

He walked around the car and opened her door. "I made reservations when I went home to pick up my clothes."

The bellman loaded their two small bags onto a cart, and they followed him into the lobby.

"How many rooms did you reserve?" she asked.

"How many would *you* have reserved?"

"One."

"Then we'd better release the second." He didn't wait for her to ask. "I didn't want to presume."

"That was sweet." She pointed at the Babcock and Storey Bar off the lobby. "Let's check in to our room, have a glass of wine in that lounge, then find a restaurant."

They ate dinner at the Sheerwater, overlooking the Pacific. The rain had stopped, and a full moon shone brightly through ragged gaps in the cloud cover. The ocean had turned in to a boiling black cauldron crowned by whitecaps whose tips the wind ripped off and blew away like luminescent wisps of smoke.

They spotted the silhouette of a sleek Navy ship

steaming toward the horizon, churning up a frothy green wake behind her fantail.

Escalante took a bite of broiled swordfish and pointed. "Is that a submarine like you were on?"

He chuckled. "No, subs're stealthy. It would've submerged at the three-mile marker so you wouldn't see it."

"What kind of ship is that?"

"Missile cruiser—a nuke."

"Nuke?"

"Nuclear-powered."

After dinner, they lingered over coffee and dessert, then strolled through the Victorian building and grounds, then went to their room. For the second time in three days they made love under a stream of hot water in the shower.

✝ CHAPTER 43

AFTER AN EARLY BREAKFAST at the Palm Court, Miller and Escalante checked out of the hotel and drove to Saint Sebastian High School, which sprawled over several acres of prime real estate east of Balboa Park.

An overweight woman rose from her desk and waddled to the front counter of the old, ornate administration office. In her midsixties with hennared beehived hair and a sour round face, her drab pea-green dress draped over her rotund body like an army tent.

Miller checked the embossed nameplate on her

cluttered desk that identified her as Mrs. Beverly Grundy, Executive Assistant.

Miller flashed a smile. "Good morning, Mrs. Grundy. We'd like to speak with the school principal."

"Are you parents?"

Miller glanced at Escalante. "Not yet."

They presented their IDs. Grundy held the photo cases at arm's length next to their faces, inspected them, and handed them back. "I guess this is you."

"I hope so," Miller said. "Like I said, we'd like to see your principal."

"What about?"

"Is he here?"

"Certainly, we open at eight o'clock." She sniffed. "I'm his right-hand person."

"I'm sure you're indispensable."

"Wait over there," she ordered, pointing at a row of old wood chairs that looked like instruments of torture for recalcitrant students. "I'll see if he's busy." She tossed them a dirty look and disappeared through a burnished oak door with a rectangular frosted-glass window, slamming it hard enough to rattle the glass on which gold-leaf letters spelled out:

MONSIGNOR ALOYSIUS XAVIER WILLOUGHBY, PH.D.
PRINCIPAL

"What's her problem?" Miller whispered to Escalante.

"You challenged her authority and status."

"String me up with a dirty rope."

Momentarily, Grundy returned. "Follow me."

Monsignor Willoughby was about the same age as his assistant but was her antithesis in every other way: short, thin, and bald, with wire-rimmed eyeglasses that rode low on his nose, a warm smile, and sparkling green eyes. He rose from his chair behind an oak desk that had been polished over the years to a whiskey-colored sheen that matched the door.

He shook their hands and motioned to his chairs. "Welcome to Saint Sebastian. Please sit."

The office was small but comfortable with deeply cushioned chairs and a small matching sofa surrounded by walls lined with leather-bound books, diplomas, awards, and dozens of photos of the Monsignor with his teachers and students. In every photo he was smiling, as were his companions.

Escalante took in the surroundings with quiet appreciation. "This doesn't look like the principal's office where I went to school."

"A Catholic school?" Willoughby asked.

"Yes, Father."

"Some parochial schools take discipline to extremes. I try to make my students feel welcome when they visit me, no matter the reason. In my experience, kindness works better than intimidation."

He clasped his hands on the desk. "Mrs. Grundy said you're police officers."

"We are," Miller said. "I'm afraid I insulted her. If so, I apologize, it wasn't intentional."

Willoughby flipped his hand as if to shoo away a mosquito. "She's an institution. I was transferred here in seventy-five and she predates me by several years. I'd be lost without her, though. How may I help you?"

Escalante handed him the subpoena duces tecum. He read it and looked up, frowning. "If I knew exactly why you need these records, maybe I could save you some time."

"All I can say is we're conducting murder investigations. Does the high school maintain its own financial and accounting records, or are they centralized at the Diocese?"

"We maintain financial-transaction records here, but I'm afraid thirty-year-old bank records are out of the question. We keep them for six years in case the IRS audits one of our benefactor's charitable contributions. After that we destroy them."

"We were afraid of that. Are student records for those years available?"

He pinched his nose together with his right thumb and forefinger, pushed his glasses up, and thought for a few seconds. "In a manner of speaking, but I doubt you'll be able to find what you need."

"Why not?"

"I'll show you." He rose and motioned for Miller and Granz to follow. Halfway down a wide corridor flanked by teachers' offices, he unlocked an ancient padlock, flipped on a light switch, and swung open two massive doors. Old unoiled hinges protested loudly, and the pungent odor of mildewed paper, stale damp air, and decaying insect carcasses floated up.

Willoughby crinkled his nose and led them down two flights of rickety stairs before turning on more lights. They stood at the entrance of what looked more like a medieval castle's dungeon than a repository of academic records.

About 150 feet square, the archives had a 30-foot-high ceiling with massive beams that supported the floor above. Old-fashioned wire-caged incandescent light fixtures hung from the beams, but their feeble yellow light barely reached the room's walls, which were defined by the old building's outer foundation.

Thousands of old, sagging, built-in wooden shelves around the perimeter were propped up in spots by rotting 2-by-4s and stuffed with moldy, cobwebbed cardboard boxes. Dozens of empty, rusty bug-fogger cans littered the waterlogged cement floor.

"We have a serious black widow spider problem," Willoughby explained.

Floor-to-ceiling metal shelving units crisscrossed the room's interior, creating shadowy dark tunnels barely wide enough for a person to pass through.

Willoughby waved his hand in a sweeping gesture. "This is our record-storage room. It's a bit disorganized, but contains individual student records all the way from the inception of the school in nineteen-twenty-two until fifteen years ago when we built a new storage facility across campus."

Miller tried to do some mental math, but failed

and told Escalante, "I'm not good at math without a calculator."

"Sixty-five years plus," she said.

Somewhere nearby they heard a pack of rats squeal angrily at the disturbance, and scurry off. Escalante shuddered and took an involuntary step closer to Miller.

He leaned over and whispered, "Don't look to me for protection, I was gonna hide behind you."

"How many student records are in here?" she asked.

"More than a hundred thousand," Willoughby told her. "One student per file, about three dozen files per box—almost three thousand boxes."

Miller whistled softly. "There any sort of indexing system?"

Willoughby shook his head.

"They grouped by year?"

Willoughby shook his head. "I'm afraid not."

"Alphabetically?"

Willoughby shook his head. "Sorry."

"I give up—is there *any* system or logic to the way they're filed?"

"No. We keep them upstairs for five years after a student graduates, then transfer them to the archives. Like I said, now they go to a new unit, but this wasn't a user-friendly work environment— when a class's records came to these archives, they were shoved into whatever space was available, and may have been moved about since."

"The years aren't kept together?" Escalante asked hopefully. "If they were, once we found a box for one year we're interested in, the others would be close-by."

Willoughby shook his head again. "Sorry, there's no rhyme or reason to where they end up."

"Is there a master list of enrolled students by year or any other logical grouping?"

"I wish there were, but no. The State Education Code calls those 'directories.' We keep them during the academic year, for use by college and military recruiters or others who might need a listing of graduating seniors. By law, the amount of information the directories can contain, and that can be divulged, is limited. After students graduate, that year's directory is useless. State law doesn't require us to keep them, so we don't."

"So, what do these records contain?"

"Grades, attendance history, test results, disciplinary actions, et cetera."

Miller looked at Willoughby. "What we're looking for, Father, is a way to locate the names and addresses of students enrolled at Saint Sebastian from nineteen-sixty-eight to seventy-four. We don't care about their grades or any of that stuff. Can you think of any way we can do that using the records here in the archives?"

Willoughby pursed his lips. "The only way would be to read every file in every box."

"That'd take a team of investigators several weeks."

"Months," Willoughby corrected. "And you still might not find them."

"Why not?"

"In eighty-five, heavy rains flooded this room and saturated everything within two feet from the floor. Those files were hauled to the dump. The files that weren't totally ruined are the ones you see here."

"And smell," Miller said.

"Unfortunately. It takes me weeks to purge my system of mold and mildew spores after I come down here." Willoughby sneezed three times in rapid succession.

Miller did, too, and so did Escalante.

"This is a dead end," he told her. "Let's get back to Santa Rita where we might do some good without ruining our health."

Miller headed his car north on I-805. Miramar Naval Air Station was sliding by the right side of the car and four F/A-18 Hornets were taxiing toward the runway when Escalante punched Miller's arm.

"Huh?"

"Turn around and go back to the school."

"What for?"

"I know how to get the information we're after."

"So do I, but I don't want to breathe mold spores or wear a gas mask and fight off basement rats for two months."

"If I'm right, it'll only take five minutes. Turn around."

He flipped a U at Highway 274. "You gonna share your revolutionary investigative strategy with me?"

"Patience."

• • •

"You're back already?" Willoughby asked. "Did you forget something?

"Do you have old yearbooks for the sixties and seventies?"

"Sure."

"There's one published each year, with names and pictures of all the students, right?"

Willoughby's face broke into a grin. "Very clever. Follow me to the school library."

They were arranged on a dusty shelf in a room behind the library's office, along with hundreds of out-of-date textbooks. "Take them—we keep the excess copies that aren't sold—I've got dozens."

They were passing Miramar NAS again when Miller said, "That was good thinking. It would've never occurred to me. You're a natural investigator."

He strummed his fingers on the steering wheel in time to imaginary music as he thought. "We concentrate on football players. Fifty guys per team for seven years is three-fifty. Allowing for boys who played several years, it's no more than a couple hundred."

"I thought there were eleven players on a football team."

"Eleven on the field at once, but there are different positions and substitutes. If we run those two hundred players through DMV for Santa Rita, San Benito, Monterey, and Santa Clara County residents, we'll prune it to a dozen or two."

"Manageable," Escalante agreed, then added, "Speaking of teams—we make a good one."

"Not good, great." He watched her for a reaction.

"If you don't keep your eyes on the road you'll kill us both."

✝ CHAPTER 44

REVEREND ANTONIO GARCIA was, as usual, running late. At 4:40 P.M. he grabbed a supply of communion wafers from behind the altar, and charged across Sacred Virgin Church's parking lot. *He dropped his keys, bent and picked them up, dropped them again, then forced himself to stop and drag in several deep breaths.*

"What'll happen if I'm a few minutes late?" he asked himself aloud rhetorically. "Nothing, so calm down," he answered.

When he sensed his heart rate had slowed, he inserted the key in the door lock of his new Saturn.

He slipped on latex gloves, then removed the Remington .308 from its case, attached the Leopold tactical scope and jacked a high-velocity M-118 full-metal-jacket cartridge into the chamber.

The rifle rested on its bipod atop a six-inch-high scupper that confined and channeled rain to down spouts in the flat roof. He pressed his cheek against the matte-black stock, moved his eye close to the lens opening, then, swinging the rifle's barrel tip left to the right very slowly, found the blue Saturn. He twisted the focus ring until the driver's door handle was sharp and clear in the reticle, then lowered the rifle, popped a handful of pills, and waited.

The crosshairs lowered slowly until the intersection centered on the back of Garcia's head. He adjusted the elevation up one click to compensate for the distance from which he was firing, which he knew was at the outer limit of the weapon's accuracy range.

He was ready. He breathed—exhaled—breathed again—held it—and squeezed the trigger. A tiny puff of gray smoke blew out through the unsilenced barrel tip. In the chilly, late-afternoon air the smoke disappeared almost immediately.

Father Antonio Garcia would have heard the sharp crack of the rifle's report a few nanoseconds after he felt the massive impact, had he still been alive.

But he wasn't—the pointed bullet had slammed into his skull at more than twenty-five hundred feet per second—about twice the speed of sound. It came out through his left eye socket, ripping out hair, skin, bone, brain, blood, and gelatinous eye tissue, splattering them on the side of the car before passing through the window and lodging in the driver's headrest.

By the time he hit the ground, the top of his head

was gone and great spurts of bright red blood gushed from where it had once been.

He watched for a moment to be sure his victim was dead. Leaving the spent cartridge brass in the chamber, he flipped shut the end caps and removed the scope, unscrewed the rifle from the bipod, and stowed everything in the Pelican hard case.

Without looking back he tugged off the gloves and stuck them in his pants pocket, swung over the side of the old warehouse roof, and walked away as casually as a man with no place to go, and plenty of time to get there.

✝ CHAPTER 45

"THAT YOUR PHONE CHIRPING, or mine?" Miller asked Escalante, turning the volume down on the Volkswagen's stereo, which was playing a digitally remastered Ramsey Lewis Trio CD.

He and Escalante had set their cell phones on the console between their seats when they left San Diego the second time, Saint Sebastian High School Bulldog yearbooks stacked on the backseat.

"Yours," she said. "When mine rings, it plays music."

"What music?"

"The first four notes of Beethoven's Fifth Symphony."

"Pretty classy."

He grabbed his phone and punched the Send button. "Miller."

"Where are you?"

"Moss Landing, Sheriff."

"Escalante with you?"

"Yeah, I was gonna drop her off at her place on my way home."

"Don't," Granz told him.

"Lemme guess why." Miller tossed Escalante a look and mouthed, *Son of a bitch!* "Another murder, right?"

"Yeah," Granz confirmed.

"Where and who?"

"Sacred Virgin Church in The Flats—another priest."

"God damn! The church should've moved outta that dung-heap neighborhood years ago. Yamamoto's CSI team been called out?"

"He's at the scene with Doc Nelson. Kate and I are headed there now."

Escalante pulled a portable magnet-based red light from the glove box, handed it to him, and plugged it into the cigarette lighter.

"We'll meet you in thirty minutes, boss." He rolled the window down and dropped it on the roof.

Two blocks from Judge Keefe's fortified estate, Sacred Virgin Church sat fifty feet back from the street behind a skinny parking lot sandwiched between a pair of adjacent derelict warehouses—remnants of better days when both they and the Church played vital roles in Santa Rita's bustling beach, boardwalk, and fishing industries.

Transients, drug dealers, and INS dodgers now called the buildings home, and Hispanic gangbangers scrawled graffiti on them like flea-bitten, mongrel dogs urinate on fence posts to mark their territory. Reverend Garcia couldn't paint over it as fast as it appeared.

Miller swung onto Second Street and pulled in behind Granz's M-class Mercedes between a green coroner wagon and a CSI van. He and Escalante clipped badges on their jackets and ducked under the yellow crime-scene tape stretched across the parking lot entry, between the ancient adjacent buildings.

They spotted Yamamoto supervising a man who was cable-winching a blue Saturn up his tow truck's tilted bed. The truck's headlights lit up a group of people huddled together with their backs to the street, kneeling by a man's body. He wore a priest's black cassock and lay on his side, legs tucked up in his tummy, bloody head resting on an extended arm as if he'd fallen asleep.

The group stood and moved aside when two deputy coroners picked up a heavy plastic body bag from a chrome gurney, unrolled it, and laid it out on the asphalt.

Miller and Escalante walked up behind them and inspected the pool of shiny red, coagulating blood. Miller cleared his throat loudly so he didn't startle them and touched his boss on the shoulder.

Nelson, Mackay, and Granz turned.

"Fill us in," Miller said.

"Reverend Antonio Garcia, Sacred Virgin's parish priest," Granz told him grimly.

"Who found the body?"

"Anonymous passerby called it in."

"How long's he been dead?"

"No more than an hour," Nelson told them.

The deputies slid the corpse into the bag, zipped it, and wrestled it onto the gurney, which they rolled to the van, slid in, then slammed the doors. One of them caught Nelson's eye, flipped his thumb toward town and raised his eyebrows questioningly.

Nelson picked up his medical bag and nodded permission to transport the body to the morgue. "You want to observe?" he asked.

Mackay declined.

"Me neither," Granz echoed.

Nelson shrugged. "I'll autopsy him tonight, give you a buzz if anything unusual turns up. Don't bet that I'll learn much we don't already know."

"Did they recover the slug?" Escalante asked after Nelson and his deputies drove away.

"Yamamoto dug it out of the headrest." Granz handed her a sealed clear-plastic evidence bag.

She held it up toward a streetlight and inspected the bullet inside. "It's a rifle slug similar to the one that killed Duvoir."

"That's what I thought, too," Mackay told her.

"Yamamoto's having Garcia's car towed to DOJ," Granz added. "If the shooter rode in it or ransacked it afterward, maybe he left behind trace evidence—hair, skin, fiber transfers—something—anything."

Miller shook his head. "Worth a try but they won't find anything in the car."

"Why not?"

"The shooter wasn't within a quarter of a mile of Garcia *or* his car."

"Explain that," Mackay urged.

"M-118 metal-jacket rifle bullets hit quiet, hit fast, hit hard, and penetrate deep. An M-118 woulda shattered Garcia's skull without slowing down, then passed through the window and bottom of the car unless—"

Escalante finished his thought: "Unless fired from so far away that by the time it reached the target, it lost so much velocity that something soft as a headrest would stop it."

"Exactly."

"How far away?" Mackay asked.

Miller sucked his lips in and squeezed one eye shut while he thought. "Five hundred yards at the closest, probably a thousand, maybe farther."

"Anyone determine the bullet's trajectory?" Escalante asked.

"It entered the car window higher than the headrest, Mackay said. "According to Yamamoto, the path in the headrest was definitely downward."

Escalante looked around for a rooftop or other vantage point. Behind her, the sun was releasing the day's final energy into a roiling thick layer of ugly black clouds. "My guess is it was fired from a rooftop, but there are dozens, and if the shooter's consistent, he didn't leave anything behind to work with."

"There's no such thing as a perfect getaway," Granz observed. He turned and pointed. "Jazzbo, tomorrow morning get CSI on the roofs to the west. If he left behind so much as a smudged shoe track, crushed cigarette butt, or crusty old lunger, I want it collected, taken to DOJ, analyzed, and traced to a suspect."

"Will do."

"Maybe he got careless and left a cartridge casing."

"Maybe he wrote his name and address in the gravel."

Granz shot his detective a dirty look.

Escalante frowned and poked Miller discreetly. "Why west, Sheriff?"

"Bullet entered the back of his head, exited the front. His car was parked headed north, key ring still hanging from the driver's door when Yamamoto got to the scene. Looks like he was shot while unlocking it. If so, he was facing east with his back to the west. The shot had to come from that general direction."

He studied the sky. "Weather forecast is for no rain until tomorrow night. There are only three or four roofs the shot could've come from. Search them with a fine-toothed comb at first light."

"Got it."

"Even if we find the roof, there won't be much left if it rains awhile," Escalante pointed out. "Let's hope the weather forecast's right, at least until morning."

"It's a risk," Granz conceded. "But in the dark we might miss something or, worse, step on it. Better wait until daylight."

"I'll have Fields send some of his inspectors to help Miller's crew," Mackay volunteered.

"Thanks," Miller said. "We got one break—a car headrest is soft, so the bullet ought to be in good shape."

"Get it to ballistics ASAP," Granz ordered.

"Will do. I'll roust Menendez, have her meet me and Donna at DOJ tonight, put the slug under a comparison scope with the one that killed Duvoir. If it matches, at least we know we're looking for the same shooter in two murders."

"Supervise the unloading of Garcia's car," Granz told him. "No need to send Yamamoto if you're there."

"Right. You want me to call out DOJ's automotive inspection team tonight?"

"They can get to it tomorrow," Granz told him. "Speaking of tomorrow, be in my conference room at eight o'clock."

"We'll be there."

"You do any good in San Diego?" Granz wanted to know.

"Don't know for sure yet."

"What does that mean?"

"We seized all the yearbooks from the early seventies. If our shooter was a Saint Sebastian High

School student while Thompson taught there, his name and picture are gonna be there—just a matter of time till we find him."

Granz stared at Miller without comment.

"Whadaya think, boss?" Miller urged.

"That'll work. You look through them yet?"

Miller shook his head. "We came straight here."

"Where are the yearbooks?"

"Backseat of my car, why?"

"I could look through them to speed things up."

"Thanks, Sheriff. But you've got plenty on your hands. My investigative aide's standing by at the SO to pick them up when we're done here," Escalante said, referring to the Sheriff's office. "He gets paid to do grunt work—let him do it."

"How long?"

"Three days—four, max."

Granz thought about it. "Get on it. I want answers before every Catholic priest in Santa Rita gets whacked."

✝ CHAPTER 46

SATURDAY, JANUARY 11, 8:00 A.M.
SANTA RITA SHERIFF'S CONFERENCE ROOM

GRANZ AND MACKAY picked up scones, muffins,
bear claws, and dark roast at Surf City Java Shop on
their way to the briefing, laid them out on the conference room table with napkins and paper cups,
then helped themselves while they waited for
everyone else to show.

When Miller arrived with Escalante, he went
straight for the coffee, pumped two paper cups full,
plopped into a chair facing the window, and heaved
a deep sigh. Escalante put a scone on her napkin, a
muffin and frosting-covered bear claw on his, then
sat beside him and started eating.

"Good thing somebody brought food." Miller's mouth was full of bran muffin.

"You look like crap," Granz told him. "Been awake all night?"

"Damn straight."

"Accomplish anything?"

"Escalante and I went to the morgue after you left the crime scene to observe Garcia's autopsy—waste of time, Nelson didn't turn up anything new. Soon as he finished, we grabbed a bite to eat and—"

Granz made a face. "Takes a ghoul to eat after watching him hack up a dead body."

Miller stuck a hunk of bear claw into his mouth and washed it down with a swig of coffee. "No different than watching a butcher slice up a—"

Granz held his hands out in a "stop" signal and interrupted again. "Sorry I mentioned it. Go on."

"After we left the morgue we tried to get Menendez on the horn."

"Tried?"

"It was Friday night. She had a date, finally answered her cell phone at about one A.M. as she was drivin' home."

"From where?"

Miller kept his face pointed toward his boss, but checked Escalante out of the corner of his eye. She frowned. "We didn't ask where she was, what she was doin', who she was doin' it with, or what position they used. We didn't figure it was any of our business."

"It is when she's on call."

"But she wasn't, some new kid had the duty. I

sweet-talked Menendez into driving down to the lab in the middle of the night on her weekend off, as a favor."

"Actually," Escalante corrected, "I promised I'd fix her up with a great-looking guy I know."

Granz set his coffee cup down harder than necessary, slopped coffee on the table, and tossed a handful of napkins onto the brown puddle. "I don't care why she did it—what'd she come up with?"

Escalante dug a stack of black-and-white glossies out of her handbag and laid them on the table just as James Fields rushed in.

"Sorry I'm late." He grabbed a blueberry muffin and a cup of coffee and pulled a chair up to the table beside Mackay, across the table from Miller and Escalante.

Fields picked up the photos, studied them, and dropped them on the table. "A match."

He bit a hunk off the muffin. "I assume one of these slugs was dug out of Garcia's car headrest last night. What's the other?"

Escalante walked to the pot, pumped herself and Miller more coffee, then sat back down. "The slug that killed Father Duvoir."

Granz rocked his chair back on the rear legs and clasped his hands behind his head. "What else?"

"We drove around The Flats, checked out which buildings west of Second Street have accessible roofs and direct lines of sight to Sacred Virgin's parking lot. Then Fields and I rounded up cops for the search teams," Miller told him.

"How many teams?"

"Twelve—six roofs, two teams per roof, each with one CSI criminalist, one SO dick, and one DA Inspector."

"Why two teams per roof?"

Miller pointed at the window. Thick black rain-pregnant clouds hung ominously over the western section of Santa Rita, threatening to dump a deluge any minute. "Check outside."

"Jesus Christ, just tell me, will you?"

Miller's eyebrows flicked up and his jaws clamped momentarily, rippling his jaw muscles. "Sure. National Weather Service moved their rain forecast up to midmorning. We need those roofs searched before it starts raining."

"Good." Granz' eyes shot toward the window, then back. "Excellent."

"Gonna cost a shitload of overtime."

Mackay flipped her hand. "Let the bean counters worry about it."

Everyone was dressed in weekend casuals except Fields, who wore a suit, right sleeve tucked neatly back into itself.

"About an hour before daybreak," Fields said, "Yamamoto, Miller, Escalante, and I set up teams and had them standing by when the sun came up at seven twenty-six. They're on the roofs as we speak."

Escalante shook her head. "I won't hold my breath."

"Me neither," Miller agreed. "The shooter hasn't made a mistake yet."

"Everybody makes mistakes, Lieutenant," Granz

reprimanded, "you just haven't spotted his yet. You're paid to be Chief of Detectives—start detecting."

Granz dropped his chair back on all fours and drained his coffee. "I'm going to the restroom."

"I need to use the ladies' room," Mackay said and followed him out.

Miller started to draw his third cup of coffee. The stainless steel insulated pump pot was almost empty, and he was tilting it to drain the last few drops when the conference-room phone rang.

He pulled his eyebrows together. "I thought we told the search team leaders to call my cell phone."

"We did," Fields confirmed.

"Lieutenant Miller," he said, punching the phone's Speaker button.

"I have a message for Sheriff Granz and District Attorney Mackay."

The caller spoke in a slow, high-pitched, electronically altered monotone female voice.

Escalante pointed and whispered, "Tape it."

Miller depressed the Record button. "Who's this?"

"You're wasting time. My message is for Granz and Mackay."

"They stepped out."

Miller flipped a thumb toward the door.

Escalante and Fields jumped up and ran out the door.

The line was silent for a second.

"Tell Mackay and Granz if they don't stop me, there'll be more—a lot more."

The line clicked and the phone went dead.

✝ CHAPTER 47

MACKAY WAS STANDING outside the men's room door, arms crossed over her chest, tapping her right foot.

"Get the Sheriff and come back to the conference room, quick!" Fields shouted.

Granz slammed the door open. "What's the damn commotion about?"

She hooked her arm through his and tugged him toward the conference room. "C'mon, we've got to get back."

"Jesus Christ, can't Miller handle things for five minutes while I take a leak?"

"Take it easy, Dave. Jazzbo's one of the good guys—he's on our side. Don't be so hard on him."

"You're right—sorry."

"Don't apologize to *me*."

When they got back to the conference room,

Miller was staring at the phone and listening to the dial tone. "Damn!" Granz punched the Speaker button. "I walk away for one minute—"

Miller switched on the phone's speaker, then pressed the Play button. "Let's see if the recorder got it."

The county's central phone system controller hissed, clicked, hummed, rewound the tape, paused, and played back the message.

Mackay immediately recognized the machine-changed voice. She told them about the call she and Emma had taken at home on Christmas Eve. "I told Dave," she said.

"First I heard about it," Miller commented, watching Escalante for a reaction.

He didn't get one. "Me too," she confirmed.

"The caller didn't mention a killing," Granz said. "I figured it meant nothing."

"Benedetti got shot that night, boss." Miller was shaking his head. "You shoulda told us about the call."

"I know." Granz cleared his throat and gave his detective a feeble smile. "I'm sorry."

"Forget it, prob'ly wouldn't've mattered," Miller lied, his face flushing. The tension was broken by the chirp of his cell phone.

"Miller," he answered.

He listened and said "uh-huh" several times. "Okay, send everyone home, roust Menendez, and get it to the lab. Tell her we need results yesterday."

He listened, stroked his beard, and said into the phone, "I *know* Menendez isn't on call, Charlie. Tell her Escalante threatened to renege on her promise if she doesn't come down personally. She'll know what you mean."

He folded the StarTac. "Shooter cleared a spot, propped his rifle up against a rainwater scupper on the old Pacific Seafood Cannery roof. Yamamoto found an empty Advil bottle. He bagged it and is taking it to DOJ."

Granz slid his chair back from the table and crossed one leg over the other. "That's something. Maybe Menendez can lift a usable print off it."

"Prob'ly not—Yamamoto says the pill bottle had a powder residue on it like they put on the inside of disposable gloves."

"Figures. We better figure out how to catch the son of a bitch—he's a mad dog." Granz leaned back in his chair. "To do that, we've got to think outside the box. Any ideas?"

"We're attacking from the wrong end," Escalante suggested. "We can't catch him *after* a murder, so let's catch him *before*."

"How?" Mackay asked.

"Figure out how he picks a target, then get there before he does."

"He's after priests," Miller observed, "but there are dozens in Santa Rita County. Why'd he zero in on these five?"

"I think I've figured it out," Escalante answered.

Granz uncrossed his legs. "I'm listening."

"Their pictures were in the newspaper just before they were murdered."

"I didn't see 'em in the paper," Miller told her,

then added, "but I usually just skim the front section of the *Centennial* to see what kinda bad press they're givin' us that day."

"Me too, but I logged in to the archives of all the local papers, including the weekly tabloids. Thompson's fund-raising raffle appeared just once, and only in the *City Post* and—"

"Nobody but left-wing radicals read their crap," Miller interrupted.

"Exactly," Escalante agreed. "That's why none of *us* saw it. Benedetti's Afghanistan trip with his basketball players was announced in the *Centennial's* Teen Beat Section; Duvoir's guest rose-care column was in the pull-out gardening section of the Española paper—a throwaway for most people. I'll bet you don't even scan either of them."

"Never."

Granz glanced at Miller and Escalante, then looked at Mackay. "I rarely read anything from South County—how about you?"

"No." Mackay shook her head. "I don't look at Teen Beat, either. From now on maybe I should make time to scan every newspaper."

"That makes two of us," Escalante said, then continued. "Ryan's picture was published on the front page of the *Centennial* with his hot rod the morning after the Mid-Winter Fifties Jubilee wrapped up. That's probably the only one we all saw."

Everyone fell silent, thinking. Finally, Granz asked, "How about Garcia?"

"He's the exception," Escalante admitted. "I haven't made the connection to him yet."

"Television," Mackay said. "Thursday night, channel seven news covered Davidson's release from county jail. While Garcia was waiting outside the jail to give him a ride home, a reporter hassled Garcia into a sound bite."

"What'd he say?"

"He refused to talk about the Bishop, all he told the reporter was he would be late getting to Community Hospital. He offers communion there every weekday at five P.M."

Granz thought it over. "Father Garcia's live on TV one night, dead the next afternoon."

"Killed unlocking his car at about the time he'd be leaving for the hospital," Mackay added. "Where's the Coroner's inventory?"

Escalante slid a paper across the table.

Mackay read it quickly, passed it to Granz, and said, "He was carrying communion wafers."

"I say we set up a sting," Miller proposed.

"Lay one out," Granz directed.

"Simple—you and the DA make up a phony story and plant it with the media—make sure it's got a picture of our decoy standing out in front of the church."

"What church?"

"The church where we're gonna take the sumbitch down."

"A church he hasn't hit before," Escalante added, "and one he sees an easy way into and out of—the closer to the freeway, the better."

Granz nodded thoughtfully. "Might work."

"I know the one," Mackay told them. "But we

can't risk an innocent bystander getting hurt. I'll contact Bishop Davidson, ask him to evacuate the church on the q.t. for a day. If we're right, and the pattern holds, that's all it'll take."

"I agree," Granz told her. "Park a few cars in the parking lot, make it look as normal as possible."

"I'll take care of that," Miller volunteered. "Get 'em from the impound yard."

"One thing," Granz added. "The decoy stays inside at all times or he'll get wasted from a distance with a rifle. The shooter's got to get close to the undercover officer or it won't work. Next question— who's the decoy?"

Fields looked around and made eye contact with the other four. "Me."

"Why you?" Granz asked.

"Less likely to be recognized—I've been off the street for the past few years as Chief of Inspectors."

Granz contemplated. "Our shooter's smart, efficient, and vicious. You get sloppy, you get dead."

Fields unconsciously ran a finger over his tucked-in coat sleeve. "I looked death in the face once and didn't like it—I won't get sloppy."

Granz looked around the table. "This is our best chance. Everyone go along?"

No one dissented.

"We need today and Sunday to set up everything."

"That works," Escalante agreed. "Masses are scheduled throughout Saturdays and Sundays, but Monday's a quiet day."

"Soon as everything's in place, I'll hole up inside the church," Fields confirmed.

"Good, let's get to work. Fields?"

"Yeah?"

"Remember—the nut we're looking for wasted five men—don't be number six. No one's going to second-guess you, so when he shows up, take him out."

"Count on it."

Granz stood. "I promised Emma I'd buy her a new dress for Monday morning."

"Special occasion?" Miller asked.

"You might say that."

✝ CHAPTER 48

"HOW DO I LOOK?" Emma turned around slowly twice, arms out, so Dave and Kathryn could admire her new dress.

"Beautiful, sweetie," Kathryn told her.

"What do you think, Dave?"

"You're a fox."

For the first time in weeks, Monday morning broke bright, warm, and clear, the cloudless sky a deep sapphire blue. They waited outside Judge Reginald Keefe's chambers where, through the Court Building windows, they watched the sun heat up the lawn, sending a layer of steam into the air like smoke from countless tiny grass fires.

Kathryn checked the morning newspaper, folded it, and stuck it her handbag. A shoulders-up photo of James Fields in a black suit coat, clerical shirt with Roman collar, glasses and a mustache accompanied a Living Section story introducing the new priest at Holy Ascension Catholic Church.

"Exactly what we wanted," she told her husband. "Let's hope he takes the bait."

"He'll take it," he assured her.

Emma sniffed one of the pink buds in her bouquet. "Mmm, the roses smell great. Thanks, Dave."

"You're welcome."

"Where's the camera?"

He pointed at his briefcase. "With a new roll of film."

"Mine's in my handbag," Kathryn told them.

At eight-thirty, Keefe's clerk came out and summoned them into chambers. Judge Keefe was wearing suit trousers and white shirt with bright red braces and matching tie. He introduced himself to Emma, said good morning to Kathryn, and turned to Dave with a smile.

"Morning, Sheriff." He pointed at a manila folder on his desk. "The adoption order is ready. Have you signed that final document I sent to your office?"

"Yes."

Dave pulled a single-page letter from his briefcase and handed it to Keefe, who checked the letterhead and Sheriff David Granz' signature, then read the letter carefully.

"This is my copy?" Keefe asked.

"That's right."

He put it in his desk and locked the drawer. "When will you deliver the original to the party we discussed in Sacramento?"

"Tomorrow."

"Excellent. Let's get started. You look very pretty, Emma. Did you bring a camera?"

"My mom and Dave did."

Keefe slipped into his judicial robe, buttoned it, and straightened his tie. "Then why don't we take a couple of pictures."

Dave and Emma posed with Keefe, then with Kathryn, then Emma posed with her mother, holding her roses. When Keefe's clerk had shot a dozen photos, Keefe opened the manila folder and pulled out a Superior Court adoption order.

He leaned over his desk and twisted the top off a maroon Mont Blanc pen. "You have consented to the adoption, Emma. Once I sign this order, neither of you can change your minds."

She put her hand in Dave's. "We won't change our minds."

"All right, then."

Keefe signed the order and handed it to his clerk. "Record this and have certified originals sent to Ms. Mackay's and Sheriff Granz' offices."

Keefe shook Kathryn's and Emma's hands, then held his hand out to Dave. "Congratulations."

Dave ignored it. "Thank you, Judge."

"Thank *you*, Sheriff."

"That's it?" Emma asked when they were back in the hallway.

"Yep," Dave told her. "Sorta anticlimactic, huh?"

"I guess—whatever that means. Are we gonna celebrate?"

"I made seven o'clock reservations at The Shadowbrook," Kathryn told them.

"I meant something like ditching school and going to the boardwalk."

"Fat chance." Dave grabbed her hand. "C'mon, I'll drive you to school."

"Aww, Dave!"

When they pulled up to her school, Dave leaned over and kissed his daughter on the cheek. "I love you."

"I love you, too, Dave."

"Think you might ever feel comfortable calling me Dad?"

"Sure, but I'm used to calling you Dave."

"I know. It'll take time."

He was driving past Holy Ascension Church when his cell phone chirped. "Granz."

"How does it feel to be a father?"

"Hi, Kate. Terrific."

"I have to work a little late," Kathryn told him. "I'll meet you at home so we can all go to the restaurant together."

"I have a five o'clock meeting. How 'bout you take Emma and I'll meet you there."

"No problem, see you later."

He punched the End button and dropped his cell phone onto the console. "Yeah—later."

✝ CHAPTER 49

THE OLDEST NORTH MONTEREY Diocese parish, Holy Ascension sat on a knoll overlooking the ocean in one direction and a freeway in the other. Dormant flower gardens flanked the parking lot that connected a frontage road to the small, meticulous, historic chapel built entirely from rough-hewn coastal redwood.

Inside, at the back of an elevated altar platform that resembled a theater stage, a door opened into an add-on rectory. Besides the chapel's main entry, the only exterior door led from a rear corner of the platform to a detached shed that stored garden tools and trash cans.

Fields got there before dawn on Monday, parked the police-impound Ford near the chapel's front steps, unlocked one of the double doors, crossed himself, and shut the door behind him. He had on the same black cassock, clerical shirt, glue-on mustache, and fake horn-rimmed glasses he'd worn for the photo in that morning's newspaper.

He switched his cell phone to vibrate and hooked it inside his belt, under the cassock, beside his pistol holster. After checking the exterior door's lock, he switched off the chapel's interior lights and settled in.

Twelve uneventful hours later the cell phone buzzed against his hip.

"Yeah, Fields."

Although alone, he spoke in a hushed voice that the hardwood floors, raw plank walls, and varnished oak pews amplified and bounced back and forth like a Ping-Pong ball in an echo chamber.

"How's it going?" Granz asked.

"No problems, except all I found to read during the day was an old *National Geographic*."

"What, you don't read the Bible?"

"*National Geographic* has better pictures."

"Funny," Granz said. "The building secure?"

Fields sat at a hinged drop-down wooden table built into the wall beside the open rectory door, in the glow of a video monitor that cast shadows across his face.

"Lights are off except a couple of lamps in the rectory to make it look like the priest's at home. The shooter'll have to walk in the front door and down the aisle in the chapel to reach the rectory. The key is for me to spot him before he gets inside."

"How do you know he won't come directly into the rectory?"

"Can't—windows are too high, and there's no door from the rectory to outside. It was built before building codes required two exit routes."

"Is the front floodlight bright enough for Yamamoto's surveillance camera to pick up any movement in the parking lot and approach to the main door?"

He glanced at the glowing green and white still-life of the parking lot. "Yeah, the feed's bright and clear as a bell. I saw a deer in the monitor a few minutes ago, damn near had a heart attack."

"Good—keep a close eye on it."

"It's the only edge I've got—I'm watching that screen like Victoria's Secret Fashion Show was playing in full color."

"The element of surprise'll work for you if you sit tight and make the shooter come to you when he shows."

"*If* he shows." Fields looked around nervously, then grinned in self-conscious embarrassment.

"Not *if*, Jim—*when*."

"What makes you so certain?"

Granz hesitated. "Instinct."

"My instincts say the same thing."

Fields tugged at the collar of his clerical shirt. "Tell Kate next time I dress up like a priest, to get me a bigger outfit if I've got to wear it over body armor."

"There won't be a next time, he'll come after dark."

Granz glanced to the west, where the sun's flaming orange corona was melting into the deep blue liquid horizon. "Sunset was half an hour ago."

"I'm ready." Fields hoped he sounded more confident than he felt.

"You better be. If he spots you first, you're dead."

"I'm inspired by your optimism."

Granz ignored the sarcastic anxiety. "Make absolutely sure the only way the shooter can get in's through the front door. Go check the exterior door lock one last time, get your ass in a shadow, and stay alert."

Fields disconnected, walked to the platform's back corner, twisted the dead bolt, rattled the door, strode back to his chair, pulled it close to the table, and stared into the monitor.

It took him sixty seconds—long enough that he didn't see the black-clad man drop a device into his jacket pocket and dash across the parking lot toward the church's main door.

One final check—he ejected the pistol's magazine, made sure it was full, and jammed it back into the weapon's handle.

A Glock-19 and fifteen rounds of ammunition weighs more than two pounds. With its reassuring weight in the right front pocket of his black chinos, he bent his knees and sprinted across the dimly lit parking lot, ducking behind each parked car along the way like a soldier zigzagging through a mine field.

It took just seconds to cross the lot, climb the stairs, move to the corner of the landing, squat, and lean back against the wall to catch his breath, in the blind spot directly beneath the surveillance camera.

Fields saw the monitor's picture shudder. He rocked back in his chair and rubbed his eyes—the picture was rock solid now—probably an electrical surge or gust of wind.

He gulped in cold damp air and held his right hand out in front of his face. Steady—it was time.

He pulled out a tiny can of WD-40, sprayed the door handles and hinges, tugged on a pair of black lambskin gloves, zipped up his black jacket, rolled the black ski mask down over his face and neck, and released the Glock's safety.

Fields wondered if this would turn out to be a waste of time like most stakeouts. But it was a fleeting doubt because, like Granz, every cop instinct he'd developed over thirty years told him the killer would show, and soon.

He checked his pistol one more time, set it on the table, and forced his eyes back to the glowing monitor.

He depressed the latch cautiously and swung the door open slowly. It creaked almost inaudibly. He ducked into the vestibule of Holy Ascension Catholic Church.

Fields tilted his head, listened, tiptoed to the edge of the platform and listened again.

• • •

It was at least a hundred feet from the door to where the priest stood; too far to aim the Glock in the dim, flickering light and guarantee a hit. He knew he'd get only one shot and it must be perfect.

Fields listened for a few more seconds. Heart racing, he shrugged and said aloud, "Musta been my imagination."

He closed the door, took a quick step to the left, and stood motionless.

Fields sat back down at the monitor table and, with shaking hands, slipped on a Bushnell night-vision goggle headset, buckled the chin strap, and pivoted the infrared illuminator lenses down in front of his eyes, locking them in place.

When the priest turned away, he crept down the aisle between the pews and lay on the floor, back against the vertical edge of the platform where he couldn't be seen from above. He heard nothing—he hadn't been detected.

Fields watched the shooter sneak toward the altar. Coughing loudly to mask any sound that might betray him, he dropped to his knees and crawled several feet to the side of the table. Hoping the shooter's first move would be toward the monitor's glow where he'd last been, he thumbed off the safety of the SW99 Smith & Wesson automatic and pointed the pistol at the spot he estimated the man's masked head would appear over the platform's edge.

When the priest coughed, he gripped the Glock in both hands, sucked in a breath, jumped to his feet, and spun toward the glow of the video monitor in a hunched-over shooter's stance, Glock at arm's length, sighting down the barrel.

Fields guessed right.

In the infrared goggles the assassin popped up in the exact spot he'd figured, a fluorescent pea-green silhouette against a black background in his gun sight. Fields lowered the front ramp to the intruder's chest.

"Shit."

The priest had moved and he could no longer see him. He knew of only one way to find his target in the dark—by sound—get his adversary to talk.

"I know you're there." His voice was muffled by the mask.

He spoke loudly, swinging the Glock left to right and back again, frantically searching for the bulk of a man's body.

He turned his head sideways and listened. "Are you a cop?" he said.

"That's right."

Fields' voice was calm, belying a pounding heart

that hammered thunderously in his ears. His left hand tightened on the big Smith & Wesson's Melonite grips.

"I've got you lined up in my sights," Fields said. "Do what I tell you or I'll blow your head off."

"No you won't. Cops're trained to shoot second, never first—it's their biggest weakness."

He stepped to his right and kept talking. "I figured you'd set me up sooner or later."

"You're so fucking smart, why did you show up?"

He moved a couple of steps to the left, to change the angle of the cop's voice. He thought he knew where it came from.

"Does it matter?"

"Not to me."

Fields fought to stay calm. "Drop your weapon and put your hands behind your head."

"I don't think so." He moved back to his right and listened again.

Fields knew he should shoot but figured that as long as he controlled the situation he might force an outcome other than a shootout—it could be a fatal mistake, but despite the talk about shooting first and asking questions later, the assassin was right— he couldn't simply gun the man down.

They were fifteen feet apart.

"Last warning—you don't have to die," Fields said.

Blind in the dark, he triangulated on the voice, pointed the Glock toward the cop's calculated position, and flipped off the safety.
"One of us does."

"Bad choice."

"On your part."

Fields realized he had waited too long—the shooter had drawn a bead on him.

He could have shot first, but hesitated an instant before squeezing the trigger.

"Oh, shit." Fields fired.

The Glock's recoil jerked his arm upward a split second after he saw the Smith & Wesson's muzzle blast.

A ten-thousandth of a second later Fields felt the impact knock the air out of his lungs, fling him back, and slam him to the floor. It probably saved his life—the Glock's second slug whistled over his head, smashed into an urn of holy water, and showered him with liquid.

The Smith & Wesson's huge, 10-millimeter hollow point magnum slug smashed into his chest just right of the sternum, ripped through his internal organs, blew a hole in his back, and took out two ribs as it exited.

Before he collapsed he heard the cop struggle to his feet. He tried to lift his arm, but it refused. The Glock fell to the floor.

Fields felt wet but not sticky, and all his parts seemed to work—as near as he could tell, the Kevlar vest had caught the first bullet and the second had missed. Wheezing to catch his breath, he climbed to his knees and crawled to the edge of the platform.

Rising up on his elbows, he peeked over and spotted the assassin sitting upright against the front row pew, head flopped onto one shoulder, legs stretched out in front, arms dangling uselessly at his sides. The man's knuckles were immersed in black shiny blood that had pooled under his buttocks, and was spreading across the hardwood floor.

Fields raised the S&W, then decided a second shot wasn't needed. He climbed to his feet and kicked the shooter's Glock as far as possible.

Suddenly his legs gave out and he began to tremble violently, as his body stopped consuming the massive doses of adrenaline it was still pumping into his bloodstream.

He collapsed, more than squatted, over the injured man.

He tried to speak but nothing came out except a soft moan and stringy globs of bloody, foamy spit.

• • •

Fields peeled off the ski mask, aimed a Mini-Maglite in the assassin's face, then lurched back.

"Oh God! Oh Jesus! Oh my God!" His voice was hoarse with tension, anger, fear, and shock.

"Goddammit, why?" Fields demanded.

Frothy red oxygenated air spilled out of his destroyed lung, gurgled past his lips, and dripped off his chin. He felt cold.

Summoning one last burst of strength, he laid his hand on the cop's arm.

The cop stared back wordlessly.

He fought back the insidious blackness long enough to whisper, "I'm sorry."

Fields grabbed the man's shoulders and shook him hard, flopping the head on the limp neck like a rag doll.

"Don't die, goddammit!" Fields screamed and shook his attacker again. "Tell me why, damn you!"

It was too late. Sheriff David Granz was dead.

✝ CHAPTER 50

MONDAY, JANUARY 13, 10:30 P.M.
SANTA RITA COUNTY MORGUE

"YOU DON'T HAVE TO BE HERE." Morgan Nelson turned his gaunt face toward James Fields, removed his skull cap, and ran a hand over his buzz cut.

He, Fields, and Miller stood in the hallway, backs toward the open door to the autopsy suite where Granz' sheet-draped body lay on a stainless steel table.

"Sure I do, Doc."

Fields' jaws clinched, rippling the muscles under his pockmarked cheeks. He still had on the slacks and clerical shirt he'd worn under the cassock, cell phone hooked to his belt by an empty holster, his pistol having been seized as evidence.

"And you know why—he was my friend."

"Ours too." Nelson was dressed in green surgical scrubs and rubber-soled shoes with plastic booties pulled up over the tops.

"And his wife, the *best* friend I've ever had, is in a goddamn hospital bed four floors above us, in shock."

Nelson fought back a tear. "Autopsies are my job, not yours. You don't look like you're up to it."

"I'm all right."

Nelson stared at him. "It's your call, but you don't look all right."

"I have to be." Fields' voice trembled. "I put him on that table."

Nelson shook his head. "From what I learned at the crime scene, Jim, I'd say he put himself on the table."

"Either way, Doc, observing his autopsy might help me make sense of it."

"I wouldn't count on it."

Nelson removed his bifocals, knotted his hands into fists, and with his knuckles massaged his eyes, already bloodshot from grief and exhaustion.

He pulled paper scrub suits and booties, masks, and latex gloves from a drawer and handed them to the two cops. Backs still toward the autopsy suite, they wordlessly slipped into them.

Nelson led them into the autopsy suite. He switched on a bright overhead halogen light fixture with built-in video and audio recorders. When the tapes started winding he keyed the headset microphone, hesitated briefly, then slid off the sheet.

Granz' eyes were closed, his face relaxed in what looked like a smile. Except for the bullet hole in his chest, whose ragged edges had begun to crust over with coagulating blood, he might have been asleep.

Nelson exhaled loudly, then started dictating his external examination.

"The body is that of a well-developed, well-nourished, forty-seven-year-old white male, seventy-two inches in length, weighing one hundred eighty pounds."

He rolled the body from side to side to examine the torso, lifted the arms and legs, checked the underlying tissue, then inspected inside the ears, nose, mouth, eyes, and other body orifices.

"Rigor and livor mortis onset is absent—hair is short and brownish blond, irises are green, nose and ears normal, teeth natural. The chest is symmetrical, abdomen flat, external genitalia unremarkable. Upper and lower extremities exhibit no tattoos, scars, or deformities."

Nelson stopped and yanked a paper towel from a dispenser, wiped his brow and face dry, then wadded up the towel and threw it hard at the wastebasket, but missed.

"Son of a bitch!"

He picked up the towel and kicked the wastebasket across the room. It smashed into a cabinet on the opposite side of the room with a metallic *clunk* and landed upright, its sides caved in, lid hanging lopsidedly from the broken hinge.

"Dirty rotten goddamn son of a bitch!"

He snatched up the wastebasket with both hands

and slammed it back down on the floor. The lid flew off. He ripped the towel into shreds and dropped them into the mutilated receptacle, then stormed back to the autopsy table.

He took several deep breaths and wiped his face with another towel, which he set on the bench behind him.

"Sorry," he said.

"You gonna be okay, Doc?" Miller asked.

"Absolutely—I feel much better now."

Without waiting for a response, he turned his attention back to the body.

"The only apparent injury is a single gunshot wound, the center of which is forty-five centimeters from the top of the head and three centimeters to the right of the anterior midline of the chest."

He leaned over the body and adjusted his bifocals.

"The entrance wound is approximately one-point-five centimeters in diameter with a slightly ovoid entry defect, surrounded by eccentric abrasion."

He rolled the body to its left. "Exit wound is through the posterior skeletal muscle of the right subclavian region. The projectile tracks front to back and slightly downward."

Nelson slid two black plastic body-blocks under Granz' back, then sliced deep V incisions that started at each shoulder and met at the bottom of the sternum.

A second cut connected the V to the pubis, diverting slightly around the navel. A third ran from hipbone to hipbone, intersecting the leg of the Y.

He laid back the abdominal skin, exposing a layer of pebbly yellow subcutaneous fat that looked like shiny, blood-streaked marbles, then peeled skin, fat, and soft tissue off the chest wall to reveal the rib cage.

Finally, he ran two cuts up the outer sides of the rib cage with the Stryker saw, lifted out the breastplate, and laid it on the table.

Visually examining the internal organs, he cut the pericardial sac and pulmonary artery.

After removing the heart he tied strings to the carotid and subclavian arteries, snipped out the larynx and esophagus, cut the pelvic ligaments, bladder and rectal tubes, and lifted out the organ block, which he inspected and laid aside.

"Preliminary cause of death," he dictated, "is massive hemorrhage due to penetration of the bullet through the right heart auricle and right lung—"

Everyone looked up as Escalante rushed in carrying a paper scrub suit, mask, booties, and latex gloves.

"How's Kathryn?" Nelson switched off the recorders, removed his headset, and hung it around the back of his neck.

Fields and Miller watched her expectantly.

"Kathryn's conscious and stable."

Escalante struggled into the gown, then leaned against Miller while she pulled the boots over her shoes. He patted her affectionately on the shoulder and she leaned her head against his big hand for a moment.

"What happened?" Nelson asked.

"After Lieutenant Miller and I secured the crime scene, I drove to The Shadowbrook, where she and Emma were meeting Sheriff Granz to celebrate the adoption."

"Adoption?"

"He adopted Emma. Judge Keefe signed the adoption order, and his clerk filed it at nine o'clock this morning."

"I had no idea," Nelson said softly.

"I didn't either, until Emma told me on the way to the hospital."

"How little we know even about our closest friends." Nelson spoke more to himself than to the others. "I'm going to change from now on, pay more attention to the things that really matter."

Escalante laid her hand on Nelson's shoulder.

"Tell me about Kate," he said.

"When I first told her about the shooting, she didn't believe me, just sat there without saying anything, like it was some sort of sick joke. When she saw I was serious, she grabbed her head, started to stand up, but passed out."

"Shit. Her blood pressure fell dangerously low. How long before paramedics arrived?"

"A couple of minutes—they were dispatched from Central Fire, three blocks from the restaurant."

"What'd they do?"

"Started a saline IV drip and transported her to the ER immediately."

"Damn lucky. If her blood pressure stayed that low for more than about five minutes, she could've suffered permanent brain damage—not to mention the damage it might've done to the baby in a hell of a lot less time than that. Did she fall?"

"Yes, unfortunately."

Escalante pushed the paper mask up onto her forehead. "Her stomach hit the corner of the table, then her head hit the floor."

"Damn! Has she miscarried?"

"Not yet. When I left to come here, they were monitoring her."

"What about Emma?"

Escalante managed a tiny smile. "Bravest kid I ever saw—stayed calm, directed traffic in the restaurant to keep people out of the way, kept telling paramedics to be careful, that her mother was carrying her baby brother."

"She's a hell of a kid. Where is she?"

"Sitting in a chair holding her mother's hand. I can take her home with me tonight if you think that's a good idea."

"No." Nelson shook his head. "I'll arrange for hospital staff to set up a bed in Kate's room so she can spend the night with her mother. I'll drop in from time to time."

He looked around. "Let's finish up."

Escalante slid on the latex gloves.

"Put on your face masks, too," Nelson advised. "Some aerosolization is unavoidable when I open the cranial cavity."

He pulled the body-blocks from under Granz' back, set one aside, and slid the other under the head. With a scalpel he cut a deep, straight incision through the scalp, over the crown of the head from the top of one ear to the other, peeled the front skin flap down over the face, and the rear flap over the nape of the neck.

He ran the Stryker saw around the perimeter of the skull, creating an upside-down bowl that, using both hands, he twisted back and forth. When the calvarium was loose, he lifted it off.

He set aside the skull and inspected the brain.

And gasped.

"Oh, Jesus!"

Fields and Escalante crowded close.

With a gloved fingertip, Nelson pushed against a hard, white, puffy, dense mass that clung to the front of Granz' brain. Like an anemic crab, its spiny, claw-tipped legs dug tenaciously into the soft, pinkish gray brain tissue. The brain had swollen and turned an angry red where it tried unsuccessfully to fight off the intruder's invasive roots.

"My God that's ugly," Miller said. "What is it?"

"Brain tumor—the biggest I've ever seen."

"What caused it?"

Nelson shook his head. "No way to say—medical science hasn't discovered the cause of brain tumors yet—we think most result from environmental factors."

"Such as?"

"Low-frequency electromagnetic fields, radiation, chemicals, viruses—severe head injury."

"What caused his?"

"Impossible to say, but he's suffered two life-threatening head injuries—the first at the hands of the Gingerbread Man behind the Seacliff Hotel a few years ago—that one damn near killed him. Could've caused a tumor that the second head injury compounded."

"What was the second?" Escalante asked.

"The car accident the night before Thanksgiving."

Miller cleared his throat. Fields shuffled his feet. Escalante squeezed her lower lip between a thumb and index finger.

Nelson snipped the brain stem, carefully lifted out the brain, and set it on a tray.

Fields sighed. "Now what?"

"I take a biopsy and send it for testing."

"Cancer?"

"Yes, but it doesn't really matter. A brain tumor does its damage through the pressure it exerts on the brain, disrupting the nerve-cell activity. Eventually I'll dissect and analyze it."

He rolled off his latex gloves and motioned for the others to do the same, then led them into the hallway.

"You three get out of here. I've got research to do. Let's debrief tomorrow morning—say, eight o'clock in the Sheriff's conference room."

As Fields, Miller, and Escalante stripped off their paper gowns, Nelson told them, "You might want to grab some sleep tonight and get back to work looking for your priest killer tomorrow."

Fields frowned. "I'm confused. Are you telling us that Granz *wasn't* the shooter?"

"Possibly." He leaned against the wall and started to go on, but his voice caught.

"If Granz had any idea how sick he was—and given the size of that tumor, it's inconceivable to me that he didn't—he might not have gone to that church tonight to kill anyone else."

"Why, then?" Fields asked, not sure he wanted to hear the answer.

"Maybe to commit suicide."

"Cop-assisted suicide." Fields squeezed his eyes shut tight, and recalled Granz' last words: *I'm sorry*.

"Our priest killer might still be out there," he added.

"Get some sleep," Nelson said. "Let's hope I have a better answer for you tomorrow morning after I do my research."

✝ CHAPTER 51

TUESDAY, JANUARY 14, 8:00 A.M.
SHERIFF'S CONFERENCE ROOM

AN ARCTIC COLD FRONT moved into Santa Rita overnight, dusting San Lorenzo Park with a rare blanket of ice that twinkled in the brilliant morning sun like a Tiffany's display case loaded with backlit diamonds.

Two dozen kids stopped on their way to school to scoop it up and roll rock-hard ice balls that they threw at passersby, then ran away, screaming with the carefree delight that graces only the young and innocent.

Inside the Sheriff's conference room the mood was grim.

Inspector Donna Escalante and Sheriff's Chief of Detectives James Miller sat close together, gazing out the fogged-up window, quietly lost in their separate, private thoughts.

Escalante was halfheartedly picking at a blueberry scone and Miller was sipping a cup of coffee when DA Chief Inspector James Fields trudged in. He head-jerked a nonverbal "hello" and collapsed into a chair with his back to the window, as if to deny that the world could ever be bright and cheerful again.

"Morning." Escalante watched him, worry clouding her usually stoic face. She wore neither lipstick nor eye makeup, and her jet-black hair was still shiny-damp from the shower.

He exhaled through pursed lips like a child blows out the candles on a birthday cake.

"I'm beat," he told them.

Miller set down his paper cup to study his long-time friend and professional counterpart from the DA's office. "Ain't my business, Jim, but you look like shit."

"You're being overly generous."

"You get any sleep last night?"

Fields yawned, covering his mouth with his left hand. He was clean-shaven and wore a fresh white shirt, tie, and meticulously pressed wool business suit, but his face was drawn and haggard.

"Not a damn wink. How about you two, were you able to sleep?"

Miller glanced at Escalante, who shrugged as if to say, *He already knows.*

"Not much," Miller told him. "We tossed and turned all night."

Miller didn't mention that he and Escalante had made love before they fell asleep. Afterward, he'd confessed to an overwhelming guilt. She'd told him that death can awaken a hunger for closeness that often translates into sexual arousal, that he shouldn't feel he betrayed his friend.

He had slipped out of bed and into the shower still feeling guilty. She had found him there crying, climbed in with him, and held him until he stopped.

Fields clenched his fist. "I replayed that damn shooting a thousand times. Maybe Nelson's right. Dave had me cold—could've easily killed me, but he hesitated long enough to shift the advantage my way. I should've seen it. Maybe I lost my nerve when the chips were down, I don't know."

Miller couldn't find his voice, so Escalante leaned across the ancient, Formica-covered table and placed her hand over Fields'.

"I'd have been too pumped to do anything but shoot first and worry about the consequences later," Escalante told him. "It took clear thinking and courage to give him the chance you did."

Miller nodded. "She's right. Last time someone pointed a gun at me I had to go home and change skivvies. Granz shot at you, don't forget that."

Fields tapped his chest with a finger. "I was wearing body armor."

"He didn't know."

"Yes he did; I told him."

"All the same," Escalante said, "you cut him a hell of a lot more slack in that church than most cops would have. Don't beat up on yourself." She squeezed Fields' hand and sat back.

Miller thought she'd never looked so beautiful, and appropriate or not, decided life was too short not to ask her to marry him soon. He hoped Dave would understand the timing.

The door swung open and Morgan Nelson entered wearing last night's bloodstained scrubs, face shadowed in salt-and-pepper stubble, purple bags dragging down his lower eyelids like a bloodhound. He glanced around, set his coffee on the table, and fell into the chair beside Fields'.

"How's Kathryn?" Escalante asked.

"Sleeping. I spent the night riding the elevator between the basement and fourth floor. Soon as I determined she hadn't suffered a concussion from the fall at the restaurant, I sedated her."

"The baby?"

Nelson raised his eyebrows. "Touch and go. Once paramedics stabilized her, the shock was no longer life-threatening, but a rapid drop in blood pressure, of that magnitude, even for a short time, could still kill the baby. I put her on a glucose and salt IV to normalize and regulate her blood pressure, then called her gynecologist. Doctor Burton'll take over from here."

"Emma's all right?"

The corners of his mouth tugged upward. "She didn't want to leave, but didn't want an unexcused absence on her record, either. So, I faxed an excuse letter to her school this morning. She's with her mother, waiting for Burton."

"You do any research?" Miller asked.

"When I wasn't with Kate and Emma, I was on MedLine."

"We still looking for the priest killer, or do you have his body in your morgue?"

"My research convinces me that Granz not only knew he had an inoperable brain tumor, but that time had run out."

"How would he have known?"

"Could've looked up his symptoms on the Internet, or any medical reference."

"What symptoms you talkin' about?"

"Headaches, chewing, staring, spacing out, momentary but total blackouts accompanied by memory loss. Symptoms I observed but didn't do anything about." Nelson sipped his coffee.

"Hell, I noticed those things myself occasionally," Miller admitted. "I figured he was havin' a bad day."

"You're a layman. I'm a doctor, for Chrissake. Kathryn spotted them, too, and asked me what to do."

"What'd you tell her?"

"Someone ought to kick my ass." Nelson snorted. "I should've tried harder—insisted she make him see a doctor, and if she didn't I should've done it myself."

Miller tugged at an earlobe. "Maybe he did, and that's what drove him to set Fields up to take him out."

Nelson nodded. "I thought of that—it's possible."

Escalante frowned. "Why would he go to the trouble of having Chief Fields kill him? Why not eat his pistol like other cops?"

"Life insurance policy exclusionary clauses," Miller explained. "They don't pay on a suicide. He kills himself, Kate, Emma, and the baby don't see a damn nickel."

Escalante looked at Nelson, then at the others. "What about brain surgery to remove the tumor?"

"The cure's worse than the disease," Nelson answered.

"I don't understand."

"The tumor invaded his brain's frontal lobe. That's the center of all higher cognitive functions— appreciation for music and beauty, memory, intelligence, reason, logic—the very things that make us human. Cutting out even a tiny tumor would destroy so much brain function that he'd probably be a vegetable or worse—a slobbering idiot."

"Jesus!" Fields whispered. "No wonder."

"Exactly," Nelson said. "Unthinkable for a man like Granz. He preferred to go out on his terms. How better than to orchestrate a scenario that he could manipulate into a fatal shootout?"

"Fatal for him." Fields' explanation was unnecessary.

"That's right."

"Why me?" Fields' pain was palpable.

Nelson thought. "Most people want someone they know and care about with them when they die—more important, someone who cares about them. He was no different. That's why he chose you. Strange as it seems, it was an expression of affection."

Fields closed his eyes and opened them slowly, then sighed. "Doesn't make me feel any better, but there's a certain weird logic to it."

"That's my point—his brain tumor induced epilepsy, disrupted his brain's electrical impulses, and triggered seizures that screwed up his ability to think and problem-solve."

Nelson interlaced the fingers of his hands behind his head and leaned back in his chair. "I'm absolutely, unalterably convinced Granz went to that church to commit suicide-by-cop."

"I'm not sayin' you're wrong." Miller crossed one leg over the other. "Hell, anything's possible, but someone's gotta play devil's advocate. You've given us a buncha theoretical mumbo jumbo that doesn't add up to squat except a convenient excuse for a friend who's maybe a serial murderer."

Miller held his hands up quickly, palms out. "No offense intended, Doc."

"None taken."

Miller looked at Escalante. "How do you see it?"

"I'm not sure, but—"

She was interrupted by her cell phone's version of Beethoven's Fifth Symphony. She dug it out of her handbag and flipped open the cover.

"Escalante."

She listened for a moment. "I'm in a briefing, George, can't this wait?"

She listened again. "All right, wait a sec."

She covered the mouthpiece with her hand. "My investigative aide's dug up something. Better take it."

"Time for a break anyway." Miller said. "Think I'll hit the john, then grab more coffee, fill the tank up again. Anyone want somethin' from Starbucks?"

"I'll go with you," Fields told him.

"Make it a threesome." Nelson followed Miller and Fields to the door but stopped before they opened it. "Think about it: Why would Granz murder a priest?"

✝ CHAPTER 52

ESCALANTE HADN'T MOVED from her chair when the others returned, and Nelson deposited a sack of pastries in the center of the table with a mushy *thud*.

Miller flipped the plastic lid off a cup and blew the steam away, slurped his fresh coffee, then sat beside Escalante and bit the top off a bran muffin. Fields dropped into a chair beside Nelson's, stripped the safety seal off a pint of Gizdich Farms apple juice, and pointed at the Saint Sebastian High School yearbook on the table in front of Escalante.

"What's that for?" The cover was white with a stylized blue bulldog gripping a football in one front paw and a textbook in the other, elongated ears sticking up through the center of a yellow halo.

"My aide might have just found the answer to Doctor Nelson's question," Escalante told him.

Nelson stopped with a scone halfway to his mouth. "What question?"

"Why Sheriff Granz might murder a priest."

"It was a rhetorical question," Miller said.

"Bullshit." Nelson dropped the scone, looking intense, like he was about to challenge Miller to a duel. "I was serious. Unless you convince me otherwise, I'll keep believing Dave seized an opportunity and committed suicide. Your shooter's still running around loose."

"Be cool, Doc." Miller spoke softly.

"Cool, my ass," Nelson muttered, more to himself than to the others.

Escalante slid the dog-eared yearbook across the table to the doctor. On two pages, Dave Granz' photo was circled in red ink.

Nelson read the caption and scowled in confusion. "Okay, maybe Granz went to Saint Sebastian High School in San Diego, and played linebacker on the freshman football team. So what?"

Miller gulped and spat a mouthful of coffee on his lap. "Shit, I just had these slacks dry-cleaned."

He wiped most of it off and stretched his hand out to Nelson. "Lemme see that."

Fields circled the table and read over Miller's shoulder. "Son of a bitch."

"What's the problem?" Nelson wanted to know.

Fields carried the yearbook back to his side of the table and sagged dejectedly into his chair. "After Davidson's Grand Jury testimony, Miller asked Granz where he went to high school. Granz never said a goddamn word about Saint Sebastian."

"Worse." Miller dabbed at the spilled coffee with a napkin. "He lied—said he graduated from Mira Mesa High School in seventy-three."

"You sure he didn't?"

"Actually, he might have," Escalante interjected. "My aide says his picture didn't appear in any yearbook after this one—nineteen-sixty-nine."

Miller was shaking his head. "Doesn't matter, he never mentioned attending Saint Sebastian at all."

"Maybe he forgot." Nelson's voice rose defensively.

"Fat fuckin' chance. You remember what schools you went to?"

"Of course but—"

"There you go," Miller said with a wry smile.

"I told you epilepsy can erase the memory."

"It's too convenient to remember Mira Mesa but forget Saint Sebastian. When a man doesn't tell the whole truth, he's covering up something."

"Am I the only person here who thinks our friend might be innocent?" Nelson challenged.

Fields, Miller, and Escalante felt a sudden urge to inspect the tabletop. Escalante stirred dust with a fingertip. Fields polished a spot with the tip of his necktie.

Miller broke the silence. "I wanta think Dave's innocent, too, but twenty-plus years as a cop breeds a nasty cynicism that's hard to get past."

"Did Dave say he *didn't* go to Saint Sebastian High School?" Nelson persisted.

As Miller composed his thoughts, he scraped the unidentifiable detritus from hundreds of past meetings into a pile on the table with the edge of a ruler and looked up. "No, but we were investigating a string of ugly murders. An intentional half-truth's bad as a lie, 'specially when it comes from the top cop and sends investigators off in the wrong direction."

Escalante touched Miller on the arm. "Remember what Sheriff Granz said when I mentioned we brought back the yearbooks, and you told him if the shooter was in one of them we'd find him?"

Miller sucked on a tooth and jutted out his lower jaw. "Guess not—jog my memory."

"He asked if we'd looked through them yet and when I said 'no'—"

Miller slapped his forehead. "He offered to do it for us—'to speed things up,' according to him."

"Right."

"He knew his boat had sprung a leak and tried to stick his finger in the hole and stop the flooding."

Nelson's face turned red. "You're implying he was plotting to derail the investigation."

"I'm stating the facts," Escalante responded without emotion. "He asked how long it'd take my aide to go through them. I said three to four days. That was at the Garcia crime scene Friday night."

Miller summed up. "Three days later—Monday night—he turns up at Holy Ascension disguised as a cat burglar and tries to take Fields out."

"Doesn't make sense." Nelson studied the others. "He knew he'd show up in the yearbook. What would he gain by being evasive?"

"Time."

"Not very much."

"You said in his medical condition he didn't need very much."

Nelson shrugged. "So I did."

Fields checked his watch, slid the knot of his tie up tight against his neck, and stood up. "Maybe I can find out why he lied."

"How?" Miller asked.

"By going to San Diego."

"What for?"

"To talk to Granz' parents."

"Maybe someone else ought to interview them," Escalante suggested.

"It's my duty, I shot him."

"You gonna drive down today?" Miller asked.

Fields shook his head. "No way. Southwest commuter flights leave San Jose airport every hour. I plan to be on the next one."

"I'll toss Granz' office while you're gone. We might turn up something that connects him to the killings," Miller said, getting to his feet as well.

"I thought you were his friend," Nelson said without much conviction.

"I'm cop first and friend second. If Granz was sitting here right now he'd be the first to tell you that's the way it is. If he murdered those priests, we've got to know."

Fields walked toward the door. "Let's meet here at five o'clock."

"You got it." Miller looked at Escalante. "We need to get inside their house."

"I'll drive to the hospital while you search his office, ask Kathryn if she'll consent to a search."

"I'm not sure I would," Nelson told her. "Why should she?"

"Because she knows we have a job to do."

Miller snapped his briefcase closed. "And if she doesn't, she knows our next stop'll be in front of a judge with a search warrant."

✚ CHAPTER 53

Door locked behind him, Miller perched self-consciously on the edge of Granz' chair and turned the smiling color portrait of Dave, Kathryn, and Emma facedown before pulling open the desk drawers and rummaging through the contents.

"Holy shit."

From the lower right drawer he pulled out two handfuls of over-the-counter headache remedy and painkiller bottles—aspirin, Advil, Excedrin, Aleve, Tylenol. But he located no prescription meds.

"Looks like a fuckin' pill factory," he grumbled to himself and dumped them all in the waste-basket.

In the center drawer along with pencils, scratch paper, Post-it pads, paper clips, and an assortment of junk he found a certified copy of yesterday's adoption order and a huge, flowery greeting card inscribed in pink, *TO MY DAUGHTER*.

The card was paper-clipped under the flap of a matching envelope. He started to open and read the inside of the card, then reconsidered. Unwilling to invade his friend's most personal privacy, he dropped it into his briefcase to deliver to Kathryn and Emma.

The upper right desk drawer contained a manila envelope whose flap was almost worn out. He lifted the flap and pulled out two bundles of papers, each stapled in the upper left corner.

The first was a printout downloaded from The Brain Tumor Society web site. He flipped through the pages and found several passages highlighted in yellow and underlined in red ink:

... The symptoms are debilitating and the cure rate is very low. Brain tumors cannot be prevented because their causes are still unknown. ...
... A "good" surgical result can still leave the patient with severe physical and mental incapacity ...

The second, Frequently Asked Questions About Epilepsy, was littered with highlighted passages.

Under "Causes and Triggers":

Head Injury & Brain Tumor

On the next page:

In rare cases, seizures can last many hours.

And farther along:

Surgery is used only when medication fails and only in a small percentage of cases where the injured brain tissue causing the seizure is confined to one area of the brain and can be safely removed without damaging personality or functions.

In the same drawer he found a San Jose phone book dog-eared to the neurologists' section in the physicians' listings in the yellow pages with no names marked, a portable, battery-operated voice changer, and a manual LockAid Tool pick gun.

He dropped them in his briefcase, closed the drawer, quickly rifled the remaining drawer, the credenza, and the file cabinets.

Finding nothing more, he sat back down at the desk for a couple of minutes thinking before picking up the desk phone and punching in a four-digit internal number.

"Weapons, records, and evidence, Deputy Rivers."

"This is Miller."

"Hey, Lieutenant, is it true—the Sheriff's dead?"

"Yeah, Rivers, I'm afraid so."

"Jesus! I didn't hear about it till I came to work this morning—thought the guys were yanking my chain. What happened?"

"I'm still investigating."

"Yeah, I understand you can't talk about an investigation that's ongoing. But I was wondering."

"Wondering what?"

"Who's sheriff now?"

"Hadn't really thought about it. I'm Chief of Detectives and Senior Lieutenant. Guess I'm it until the Board of Supes appoints somebody."

"Let me know if I can help."

"Matter of fact you can. How many scoped Remington .308s we got in the department arsenal?"

"Two for each SWAT unit and two spares—ten total, why?"

"Go check the log, see if Sheriff Granz signed any of them out in the past month."

"Why would he do that?"

"Maybe he went to the range."

"I'll check and get back to you."

"Did you hear me! Do it now, I'll hang on."

"Uh—sure, Lieutenant."

Rivers dropped his phone on the counter. Miller rocked the chair back, closed his eyes, and breathed deeply and loudly through his mouth.

Two minutes later, Rivers was back. "Lieutenant?"

"Go."

"If he took one, it ain't logged out."

"Humph! I suppose it wouldn't be, would it?"

"Say again?"

"Never mind."

Miller thought for a moment. "Pull all the .308s, grab a box of M-118 ammo, write my name in the log to check 'em out. I'll be down to sign for 'em."

"You're gonna take all ten of them?"

"You got a hearing problem, Rivers?"

"No, sir."

"Then have the fuckin' rifles ready."

He hung up hard, decided he'd apologize to Deputy Rivers when he checked out the weapons, flipped Granz' Rolodex, found the number he wanted, and dialed an outside line.

"DOJ—Menendez speaking."

"This is Lieutenant Miller at the SO."

"My God, Lieutenant, I can't believe it."

"I'm havin' trouble with that myself."

"How's Chief Fields?"

"He'll be okay."

"Ms. Mackay?"

"In the hospital. Her doctor's watchin' her and the baby close, that's all I know."

"Unbelievable."

"Tell me about it. Reason I called, Menendez, I need a favor."

"Name it."

"If I bring in ten rifles, how long'd it take you to run ballistics comparisons to slugs from the Duvoir and Garcia crime scenes?"

"If I round up a few more criminalists to help, a half hour."

"I'd prefer you do it personally, if you wouldn't mind."

"How soon do you need them?"

"Yesterday."

"Lieutenant!"

"Before five o'clock this afternoon."

"I'll test-fire and put them under a scope while you wait, if you can spare two or three hours."

"That's great."

Menendez pulled back from the twin lens, comparison microscope and digital camera and rubbed her eyes with her fingertips. The scope was bolted to a stainless steel workbench and connected by USB cable to a computer equipped with flat-screen color monitor, keyboard, and printer.

"That's the murder weapon, Lieutenant." She laid her hand on a Remington rifle whose stock sat on the floor with its barrel propped against the workbench, and stepped aside.

"See for yourself," she told him.

Miller leaned over the scope and twisted the focus knobs to compensate for his astigmatism. "Lands, grooves, barrel markings all line up. Which slug's this?"

"Duvoir."

She replaced the slide with a second one that also held two bullets side by side.

He checked them under the scope. "Another match—Garcia crime scene, right?"

"Right." Menendez switched off the microscope's light and pulled out the slide. "No question about it, this weapon fired the bullets that killed Duvoir and Garcia."

Miller sighed. "Considering the results, I don't know if thanks is the right thing to say, but I really appreciate your help, Menendez."

"You're welcome."

"I owe you one."

"Forget it."

"Can you print—"

Miller's cell phone stopped him midsentence. He answered it, listened for several seconds, and said, "Good work—I'll ask her."

Miller covered the mouthpiece. "Am I good for one more real urgent favor?" he asked Menendez.

"Whatever you need."

"Escalante seized a pair of size-ten Nike Airliners."

"Tell her bring them in, I'll compare them to shoe prints from the Benedetti crime scene."

Miller contemplated. "Can you run comparisons on *two* pairs of Nike Airliners rather than one by five o'clock?"

"Sure."

Miller raised the phone to his mouth slowly. "She'll do it on account of my good looks. Meet me at my house before you come to DOJ."

Miller listened. "I'll tell you when I get there."

He glanced at Menendez, flipped the phone's cover shut, and clipped it onto his belt.

"Two pairs?" she asked.

"Just a hunch." He pointed at the coffee stain on his slacks. "Gotta change pants anyway. Where were we?"

"You were asking if I could print something."

"Oh yeah—five sets of ballistics glossies—for me, Fields, Escalante, and Nelson?"

"No problem. I snapped the slides and saved the files on my computer's hard drive."

"And five sets of both pairs of shoe print comparisons?"

"Good thing I don't charge by the page." She loaded a stack of photo-quality printer paper into a HP DeskJet 970cse and punched the Print button on her computer keyboard.

"Who's the fifth set of photos for?" she asked.

"Mackay." Miller cleared his throat. "If she wants to see 'em."

✝ CHAPTER 54

"EITHER OF YOU HEAR from Fields?" Miller asked.

Escalante and Nelson shook their heads.

"Should I buzz his cell phone and reschedule the briefing for tomorrow morning?" Escalante asked.

"It can't wait that long."

"Maybe it should," Nelson observed. "You could use some sleep."

"I'll sleep after we've sorted this mess out. We'll wait for Fields."

After leaving DOJ, Miller met Escalante at home and changed into Sperry Top-Siders with Levi's and a T-shirt that had a silk-screened trombone under the words MUSIC SOOTHES THE SOUL, slipped on his old leather aviator jacket, and drove to the County Building.

He walked to the window, rubbed a peephole through the fog and dirt with the back of his hand, and gazed outside. Rain clouds had choked out the sun and a persistent drizzle had reduced the park to a mud-pocked quagmire. Wind gusts rippled the puddle surfaces before they slammed into the building, rattling the window.

"It looked so pristine under the snow this morning." Anger rose like bile in Miller's throat, lowering his voice to a hoarse growl. "Now the park's ugly and dirty like everything else."

Nelson looked at Escalante, who lifted her shoulders and arched her eyebrows.

Miller banged the window with a fist, turned and sat down. "If I was sheriff, I'd cement the windows over. They're no good anyway, haven't been cleaned in years."

He was wrapped up in thought when the door slammed open and Fields charged in, panting from running up three flights of stairs.

"Sorry, traffic was heavy coming over the hill."

His suit was wrinkled and he'd slid the knot of his tie down and unbuttoned the top shirt button. He dropped into a chair and shifted his gaze around the table.

"How'd it go with Granz' parents?" Nelson asked.

"Not good. I caught his mother at home as she was returning from the hospital."

"Hospital?"

Fields pushed his lower lip over the upper, and composed his thoughts.

"Whoever called them last night screwed up," he said. "Dave's father had a stroke when he heard."

Nelson made a face. "Shit, I called."

Fields grunted in self-rebuke. "Sorry, Doc."

Nelson propped his elbows on the table and lowered his chin into his hands. His breathing was ragged, as if someone had reached into his lungs and was ripping them out in bits and pieces.

"Don't blame yourself," Escalante told him.

"Should've asked the San Diego Coroner to notify them in person, but I thought it'd be easier if someone who knew their son broke the news. Shows how sensitive I can be when I really try."

He dragged in a shaky breath. "How bad a stroke?"

"He didn't make it," Fields answered. "Mrs. Granz was distraught as hell."

"No shit, I wonder why," Miller said. "Her husband and son die the same day."

Fields stared at Nelson before going on. "She gave me these before I left," he finally said. "Told me they might help to explain a few things. They do."

Fields snapped open his briefcase and laid a small packet of old envelopes on the table. They were dusty and yellowed with age and held together with heavy rubber bands that were cracked and brittle.

"What are they?"

"Letters from Granz' parents to John Thompson

and James Benedetti, Saint Sebastian school administrators, and various San Diego Diocese officials, dated late nineteen-sixty-nine and early nineteen-seventy."

He had everyone's attention.

"His mother wrote the first one soon after Dave started high school, asking to meet with Father Thompson about an important matter. The second, a few weeks later—after she didn't hear from Thompson—went to the high school principal."

"What'd the letters say?"

"That Dave said he was being molested by Reverend John Thompson."

Miller wiped his hands on his Levi's as if to scrape off the window grime. "There's motive."

No one answered.

"The others are more of the same," Fields went on. "Back and forth between Granz' parents and the Diocese. Eventually they got a letter from Benedetti—he'd been assigned to investigate, exactly as Bishop Davidson testified."

"Saying what?"

"He claimed he'd interviewed all the boys at length, including Dave, and their stories were the result of vivid imaginations and runaway teenage libido—a total whitewash."

"Did the Granzes follow up?" Escalante asked.

"Yeah, the next letter after Benedetti's snow job went to the Bishop, demanding an investigation or they'd go to the cops."

Fields ran his hand through his thinning hair. "Diocese lawyers wrote them a nasty response, denying culpability and threatening to sue, but also offering *generous reparation*."

"How much?"

"The letter said an amount *to be negotiated*."

"Did the shysters say what the Church wanted in exchange for the payoff?"

"Yeah, it was real specific. It said Dave was a troublemaker and—"

"Sounds about right," Miller interjected with a sad smile.

Fields smiled, too. "The lawyers demanded Dave's permanent transfer to another school plus a statement signed by him *and* his parents recanting the charges. They also demanded that Mr. and Mrs. Granz surrender all written correspondence on the subject."

"Did they take the money?"

"Hell no, the last letter Dave's mom wrote tells them to shove it."

"Did she go to the police?"

"No. To avoid traumatizing their son, her last letter promised not to pursue a complaint if the Church banished Thompson from the teaching and coaching professions forever. She refused money but said she planned to keep the letters, as she put it, *in case they were ever needed again*."

"They agreed?"

"They didn't answer that letter. But as Davidson told the Grand Jury, Thompson was shipped out to Monterey immediately after. He never taught or coached again."

"Gutsy woman," Escalante said. "No telling how many boys she saved."

"For sure. They enrolled Dave at Mira Mesa High School the following fall, to start his sophomore year. She said after that, Dave refused to go to church and as far as she knows, he never did."

"He wasn't lying when he said he graduated from Mira Mesa," Miller observed. "Just left a little bit out."

"Can you blame him under the circumstances?" Escalante asked.

"I can if he murdered Thompson and Benedetti, no matter what the cause."

"So far, we can't prove he murdered anybody."

"If it's got feathers and an orange bill, waddles, quacks, swims, and eats crackers, it's prob'ly a duck."

Miller handed a set of Menendez' ballistics photos to each of them. "DOJ IDed the Duvoir and Garcia murder weapon. A Remington sniper rifle from the Sheriff's Department arsenal."

"Pretty convincing," Escalante said. "But any cop can walk into that arsenal, wave at the deputy on duty, and walk out. I've done it myself."

"You didn't have a motive to murder those priests, neither do other cops."

"You're certain about that?" Escalante challenged.

"Meaning?"

"Granz had no reason to kill Duvoir or Garcia, and the rifle didn't kill Thompson or Benedetti."

"You heard Doc—the psychosis induced by the brain tumor might have generated a hatred for all priests. Not only that, but a .25 automatic killed Thompson, and Granz claims he lost his. Convenient, right?"

"Half the three hundred cops in the Sheriff's Department are Catholic," Nelson speculated. "Newspapers reported that the Boston Archdiocese admitted to eighty-four cases of pedophile priests and paid thirty million bucks to settle the cases. Similar stories came out of Santa Fe, Dallas, New Orleans, Tucson, Los Angeles, St. Louis, Palm Beach, Santa Rosa—every place in the country. Hundreds—thousands—of boys have been molested by priests, and Granz isn't the only cop among them."

"Granz is the only one who disguised himself, sneaked into Holy Ascension, and tried to waste Fields."

"Dave had two overwhelming reasons to commit suicide-by-cop," Nelson surmised, "shame and guilt that all survivors of sexual abuse experience and a terminal medical condition—and he was the *only* one who knew about that setup at the church. He didn't try to kill Fields—he had the chance but didn't do it."

Miller shook his head sadly. "Can't argue with that," he conceded, then told them about the stockpile of pills he'd found when he searched Granz' office. "And that ain't all," he added.

He reached into his briefcase, pulled out the voice changer and pick gun, and laid them on the table in front of him without speaking.

Escalante picked up the voice changer and inspected it. "Why would he have one of these unless he placed those calls himself?"

"Every active and ex-field narc has 'em. When he was Chief of Detectives, he was head of the County Narcotics Investigation team, active in a lot of investigations."

"Okay, I can see the reason for having a voice changer, but why a lock pick—that's how the shooter got into the gym to kill Benedetti."

"I know. They cost thirty bucks on the Internet. Every locksmith has one and for that matter so does every burglary dick I ever knew. We keep 'em in the equipment room—ostensibly to help homeowners who get locked out by mistake, along with SlimJims to pop car doors for folks who lock their keys inside. They might not look good for Granz under the circumstances but they don't mean diddly. What'd Menendez turn up on the shoe comparisons?"

"I'll show you the photographs," Escalante volunteered, bending over to open her briefcase.

"Summarize it, please," Miller suggested.

"After this morning's briefing I drove to the hospital. Kathryn gave me permission to search their house. I seized a set of size-ten Nike Airliners from the Sheriff's closet. On my way to DOJ I stopped by Miller's house and picked up his—they're identical, even the same size. Menendez photographed both pairs, printed transparencies, and overlaid them on the composite prints from the Benedetti crime scene."

"And?"

"Inconclusive."

"That's why I submitted my own shoes," Miller explained. "To prove that this long afterward, with the changes to tread patterns caused by wear, any set of size-ten Airliners might have left the prints at the gym."

Fields' question was direct and blunt. "Are you Catholic?"

Miller stared. "You serious?"

"Damn right."

"Baptist—heathen if you ask my ex-wife. And I've never been sexually molested by a Catholic priest or anyone else. Haven't killed anybody, either."

Nelson removed his bifocals and rubbed the red spots on the bridge of his nose. "Where does this leave your investigation? Half the evidence points to Granz but the other half could point to hundreds of other men, some of them cops."

"If the murders stop, we'll have our answer," Escalante said.

"Not necessarily," Miller told her. "If you were a murderer and someone else went down for your crimes, and if you didn't want to get caught, what would you do?"

"I'd stop killing."

"Exactly."

"So, unless the shooter hits again, or we locate Granz' .25 and match it to the slug that killed Thompson, we can't prove Granz murdered Thompson," Escalante summed up.

"Even if we find his weapon," Miller added, "we won't be able to prove anything because he reported it missing. Filed a police report on Monday after the Thanksgiving weekend."

"How about the throw-down the shooter left by Benedetti's body?" Escalante asked.

Miller looked at her. "What about it?"

"We could go back, look into all the cases Granz handled over the years. If any involved a seized Python, check to be sure it's still in the evidence locker."

"What good would that do?" Nelson demanded.

"We'd know whether or not Granz was the shooter," Escalante answered.

"I know that!" Nelson's face turned red. "You could trace the damn cell phone calls, too. What I meant was—so what if he *was* the shooter and a search of old cases, or a cell-phone-call trace proved it? He's dead, for Chrissake—what good would it do to pin the killings on him except to improve the Sheriff's crime-solving statistics? Can't we leave Kathryn and her daughter Emma the doubt, the dignity of not knowing for certain—leave them with a tiny, loving piece of his memory?"

"I sorta came to the same conclusion." Miller nodded. "Besides, the County changed storage facilities twice in twenty years. There's no indexing system and occasionally we purge evidence from cases after they're disposed—return what we can to the owners, burn the drugs, send guns to Sacramento to melt down. If a Python still exists we'd never find it. Forget it. As for the cell phone calls, I don't give a shit if he placed them or not, wouldn't necessarily prove he killed anyone."

"Thank God for that." Nelson sighed deeply. "Now what, Sheriff?"

"We investigate the names in the yearbooks, see who turns up. If the killings stop, we'll probably never know for sure, and that's fine with me."

Nelson looked at the others. "Is there anything we can do to help Dave's mother?

Fields flicked his tongue over his lips. "I asked her what I could do."

"What'd she say?"

"That I'd done enough."

Miller looked at his friend sadly. "You didn't deserve that."

"I understood. As I was leaving, she said, 'Were you really my son's friend?' I told her I was, and she says, 'There *is* one thing you can do for me.' 'Name it,' I told her. 'Prove my son *isn't* a murderer,' she says."

"What'd you say to that?" Miller asked.

"I promised I would."

"You oughta be more careful what you promise. Nobody can prove he didn't murder those priests—because he prob'ly did."

"I know, but couldn't bring myself to tell her so."

Nelson jutted out his chin. "Even if every shred of evidence that exists points to Dave—even if he actually *did* kill those priests, he didn't know what he was doing or remember that he did it. That means he didn't have the necessary malice afore-thought, so it wouldn't have been murder."

"I feel your pain, Doc." Miller's head wagged skeptically. "But I'm not sure I can buy that."

"The tumor induced epilepsy and seizures that caused blackouts and loss of memory."

"You said the blackouts are momentary."

"I said they're *usually* short-term. But status epilepticus seizures last for hours. They're unusual but not unheard of."

"Not likely though, right?" Miller prodded gently.

"No. But a brain tumor that big could've induced a deep psychosis that caused Dave's rational, justifiable hatred for the priest who molested him, Thompson—and the one who covered it up, Benedetti—to metastasize into an irrational, unjustified hatred for *all* priests."

"Explaining why," Fields filled in, "if he was the shooter, he didn't stop after getting even with the two priests associated with his own molestation."

"Precisely," Nelson confirmed. "Of course, the last three killings could've been copycats as well. But if it was Granz, in his condition killing those priests would've seemed reasonable. Unless someone proves otherwise, and no one can, it adds up to reasonable doubt in my mind that he *knowingly* murdered anyone."

✝ CHAPTER 55

"THANK YOU FOR BRINGING me clean clothes."

Kathryn had dug through the overnight bag while Escalante told her of Mr. Granz' death, then they had both cried as Escalante related to her the ugly story of the sexual abuse her husband had endured as a boy. The catharsis of mutual grief made them feel better for the moment.

Kathryn slipped on clean underwear, tugged her Belly Basics cotton stretch pants over her hips, and buttoned up the matching knit maternity shirt.

"And thanks for driving Emma to school this morning," she added. "She thinks you're the greatest."

"The feeling's mutual."

"How did she seem when you dropped her off?"

"Grieving and worried about you."

"She hadn't left my bedside since Monday night. Getting out of this dreary hospital was the best thing for her." Kathryn managed a small, sad smile. "How can a girl her age be so strong?"

Escalante perched on the edge of the bed. "I'm worried that *you're* strong enough to leave."

"My doctor can't do anything for me in the hospital that she can't in her office."

"I meant strong enough emotionally."

"I can't hide in the hospital."

"I wouldn't call a couple of days in the hospital *hiding*."

Kathryn fingered the bandage on her forehead. "I've got to take control of my life."

"What about the baby's condition?"

Kathryn sat in the chair and slipped on her flat-heeled shoes.

"Doctor Burton says my lowered blood pressure probably diminished the baby's oxygen supply long enough to cause brain damage."

"I'm sorry, Kathryn."

"She also said your quick action and the paramedics' might have saved him. There's no way to be sure until he's born."

"Did she suggest—"

"Yes, but I can't abort Dave's son." Kathryn leaned over the sink, applied her makeup, and studied herself in the mirror. "God, I look terrible."

"Even if I agreed, you have good reason."

"You're always so diplomatic."

Kathryn stuffed the dress, bra, pantyhose, and shoes she wore Monday night to The Shadowbrook into a plastic laundry bag, held it out at arm's length, reconsidered, pulled it back, then held it out again tentatively.

"Seems like I wore these clothes in another lifetime," she said. "The dress has blood on it."

Escalante took the bag. "I'll have them cleaned for you."

"Thanks," Kathryn said. "I'd like to go home now."

✝ CHAPTER 56

ON FRIDAY, JANUARY 17, Kathryn and Emma Mackay flew to San Diego, where Emma met her grandmother for the first time at the funeral of Chester Granz. Mass was celebrated at St. Didacus Parish by the Very Reverend Michael Robinson, an old family friend. Immediately following the ceremony, the three rode a taxi to Lindbergh Field and caught a flight to San Jose.

The next day, James Fields stood on the altar platform inside Holy Ascension Catholic Church and delivered a eulogy to his friend David Granz. Afterward, Mary Enid Granz kissed Fields on the cheek and whispered in his ear. Whatever words she spoke brought tears to his eyes, but he never shared them with anyone.

It was a gorgeous, warm day outside following

the private service, the kind that makes you check the calendar to be sure it's still winter, and the ocean shimmered like a blanket of jewels in the distance.

The sun glinted brightly off the polished-brass trumpet when Sheriff James Jazzbo Miller, in full-dress uniform, played "Taps" on the steps of the church and laid the memory of David Granz to rest.

At eight A.M. Monday, DA Chief Inspector James Fields announced his retirement after thirty-one years' service as a police officer.

That night, Jazzbo Miller fulfilled a commitment to play at the Jazz Club. He opened with a solo instrumental rendition of "When I Fall in Love," which he dedicated to Donna Escalante. They sat together talking quietly over a glass of wine after the combo finished playing and he asked her to marry him.

She said "yes." The next morning she made reservations at Las Hadas Resort in Manzanillo, Colima, Mexico for their honeymoon.

Miller decided that instead of cementing over the Sheriff's conference room windows, he would pay for weekly cleanings out of his own pocket. Later he had the floor carpeted, walls painted pastel blue, replaced the beat-up furniture, and hung No Smoking signs around the room in prominent spots.

Mary Granz put the house where she and her husband had lived for forty years and raised their son up for rent. She moved into Kathryn's condominium, which was being converted to a rental since Kathryn and Emma moved into Dave's house following their marriage. Mrs. Granz said she wanted to be near her grandchildren.

Miller and Escalante's continuing investigation led, through multiple layers of corporations and holding companies, to a retired University of Nevada mathematics professor and his wife, a statistician and computer programmer. They operated Roulette-On-Line from a spare bedroom in their Elko, Nevada, home on a Compaq server fed by three phone lines, running self-written gambling algorithms.

Phone company records disclosed several long-distance calls to the Monterey Diocese at the approximate times Bishop Jeffrey Davidson received telephone death threats. The Bishop declined to press charges.

Under Sheriff Miller's close supervision, his Internal Affairs Officer identified seventeen male Sheriff's deputies who admitted having been molested as boys by Catholic priests, in addition to one female deputy's husband, a CPA. None of the murdered priests was accused of being the violator.

Seized yearbooks yielded four men in Santa Rita and adjacent counties who attended Saint Sebastian High School and played football during Father John Thompson's tenure. Due to the passage of time, most could not account for their precise whereabouts at the exact times that each priest was murdered, but none had criminal records and could not be tied to any crimes. All four were eventually cleared as suspects. None admitted to ever having been sexually molested by a Catholic priest.

No more priests were murdered. Although never officially closed, after months of dead ends the "Holy Homicide Probes"—so dubbed by the media—were placed on the back burner in favor of more urgent investigations.

✝ CHAPTER 57

"Let's take a taxi."

"No way, young lady, if you want to ride the *grande roue* Ferris wheel, we're walking."

"You're riding it with me!"

"The only time I plan to be two hundred feet in the air's on an airplane."

"Chicken."

"You bet I am."

They slept late the morning after they flew into Charles de Gaulle Airport. When the baby woke them, Kathryn ordered a room-service breakfast of coffee, milk, juice, croissants, pains au chocolat, and fresh fruit. It was served on an ornate silver tray with scrolled, arching handles.

Emma sat in a deeply padded high-backed chair, swung around from the table that held the food, holding her baby brother on her lap and swallowing the last of the pains.

"Emma, you ate all the chocolate pastries." Kathryn lay in a robe, back propped against the headboard of the bed with her ankles crossed, sipping coffee from a china cup and watching her children.

"They're my favorites."

"Mine too, thanks a lot!"

"Too late."

The baby kicked furiously at the bottom of his sleeper, broke loose a couple of snaps, then gazed into his sister's eyes and cooed.

"You're a strong little guy," Emma told him, brushing back his hair. "Just like our dad. But sit still so I can feed you breakfast."

She mashed a banana and spooned a taste into his tiny mouth. He gummed it and smacked his lips, swallowed, then bounced up and down, waving his little arms and clenching his fingers, demanding more.

She wiped his chin with a napkin and he laughed. "He sure is a happy baby."

"Happy, hungry, and healthy," Kathryn said, then thought, *Thank you, God.*

She spun the top off a jar of Gerber's cereal that she'd immersed in hot water in the bathroom sink, tested the temperature on her tongue, and handed it to Emma. "Feed him this before he fills up on fruit."

"He likes bananas."

"He sure does, but he's got to eat other food."

"I don't see why you've gotta be too stingy to pay for a taxi," Emma complained, changing mood and direction in the startlingly abrupt manner reserved strictly for teenage girls.

Kathryn smiled to herself, slid off the bed, grabbed a croissant, refilled her coffee, and padded barefoot across the deep paisley carpet to the window.

The maroon-bordered, floral-patterned tapestries were gathered at the middle and tied to the window sash with a thick, maroon felt rope, causing the drapes to hang in an exaggerated K.

The morning light leaked past a thin, streaky cloud cover that portended a cool rather than wet day, and filtered through the gauzy curtains, decorating the floor with delicate patterns drawn of hazy shadows.

Emma spooned cereal into her brother's mouth. He pushed most of it out past his lips.

"Cold out there, huh?" she asked her mother.

"We're walking," Kathryn said.

"It'll prob'ly rain too."

"No taxi."

Kathryn walked over and wiped cereal off her son's face and lifted him into her arms, sending him into a squirming spasm of delight, followed by frantic but futile sucking.

"What if rain gets on Davey's face?"

"Nice try, Em. I arranged with the concierge for an all-day loan of a baby carriage. Go shower while I change your brother's diaper, then we'll take a walk and see the sights."

"Me and Davey'd rather see the sights from the backseat of a taxicab."

"*Davey and I* would rather see the sights from the backseat of a taxicab," Kathryn corrected.

"I'm glad you see it our way," Emma said and grabbed the phone. "I'll call one."

Kathryn laughed and set the phone back in its cradle.

"Cheapskate," Emma accused.

"If we've gotta walk all the way to—" Emma leaned over the table and traced a forefinger across the map, "Tuileries Gardens, be sure you dress Davey nice and warm."

The concierge greeted them in French, then disappeared into a back room and returned pushing an old-fashioned baby carriage with removable rattan basket and red-and-white polka dot fold-up top. It had fat rubber wheels and a shelf underneath onto which Kathryn loaded a diaper bag.

He held the door for them and told Kathryn what she believed equated to "have a nice day."

It was overcast but reasonably comfortable outside and the sweet air smelled of baking bread, fresh-brewed espresso, and distant rain.

Emma checked the baby. He was sleeping with his thumb stuck in his mouth. She fiddled unnecessarily with his blanket, as dictated by her budding maternal instincts, then claimed her usual right to push the buggy.

They strolled down Rue de Rivoli to Rue St. Florentin, then jogged toward the water through the east end of Place de la Concorde.

Beyond the Obélisque and upstream they could see the Seine, swollen and brown with muddy runoff from the past week's storm, roiling angrily around the pilings that supported the Pont Alexandre III bridge.

A maze of concentric circles connected by metal bracing that radiated from the motor-driven hub, La Roue de Paris rose from the concrete pad of Place de la Concorde like a spindly white spider web. A Saturday morning crowd was lined up to buy tickets to ride the self-proclaimed "largest wheel on the continent."

At two hundred feet high, it towered above the landscape, the lone remnant of a decorative Ferris wheel promenade that had bordered the Champs Élysées during Paris' 2000 millennium show.

Kathryn sat on a cast iron and wood bench on the bank of the Seine, humming and rocking the baby, pondering the mysterious cycle of life and death, while Emma bought her tickets. She rode the Ferris wheel three times in a row.

Afterward, they ate sandwiches at a sidewalk café and walked the length of the Champs Élysées, a spectacularly wide, spotlessly clean thoroughfare lined by quaint cafés, ritzy theaters, and upscale shops. It was *the* place Parisians went to see and be seen as much as to shop, eat, and be entertained.

They toured Place Charles de Gaulle and the Arc de Triomphe, built to greet Napoleon's soldiers as they returned home victorious after the Battle of Austerlitz in 1805.

By late afternoon Davey became restless and grumpy, and jet lag sapped their energy, so Kathryn and Emma took turns pushing the buggy back to the hotel. It seemed uphill but wasn't. They ate dinner at the Brasserie.

Over crème brûlée, Kathryn said, "I love you, honey."

"I love you, too."

"Did you have a nice day"?

"Yes but I'm tired. What are we doing tomorrow?"

"Something special. You remember what tomorrow is?"

Emma turned serious. "It's my dad's birthday." She thought for a moment. "And Davey's dad, too."

✝ EPILOGUE

SUNDAY, NOVEMBER 30
PARIS, FRANCE

IT RAINED SUNDAY, so after breakfast Kathryn called a taxicab. They attended mass at Notre-Dame Cathedral. Afterward they lit three candles and said private prayers, then rode in a Mercedes-Benz cab to Rotonde de Ledoux in the Esplanade du Bassin de la Villette and bought tickets aboard a Canauxrama flat-bottom boat.

As the boat entered the center of the channel they moved to the low-lying stern, crossed themselves, and removed the top from a pewter urn.

On November 30, the forty-eighth anniversary of

David Granz' birth, they scattered his ashes and as the Seine sucked them down into its muddy bottom, said goodbye for the last time to their husband and father.

✝ WRITER'S NOTE

THE ASSOCIATED PRESS has reported that at least three hundred civil lawsuits alleging clerical sexual abuse have been filed against Roman Catholic dioceses across the United States. Almost 250 Roman Catholic priests have either resigned or been stripped of their duties in twenty-eight states and the District of Columbia.

On June 14, 2002, the National Conference of Bishops approved a Charter for the Protection of Children and Young People. The following statement of norms was approved on November 10, 2002:

ESSENTIAL NORMS FOR DIOCESAN/EPARCHIAL
POLICIES DEALING WITH ALLEGATIONS
OF SEXUAL ABUSE OF MINORS
BY PRIESTS, DEACONS,
OR OTHER CHURCH PERSONNEL

PREAMBLE

On June 14, 2002, the United States Conference of Catholic Bishops approved a *Charter for the Protection of Children and Young People*. The charter addresses the Church's commitment to deal appropriately and effectively with cases of sexual abuse of minors by priests, deacons, and other church personnel (i.e., employees and volunteers). The bishops of the United States have promised to reach out to those who have been sexually abused as minors by anyone serving the Church in ministry, employment, or a volunteer position, whether the sexual abuse was recent or occurred many years ago. They stated that they would be as open as possible with the people in parishes and communities about instances of sexual abuse of minors, with respect always for the privacy and the reputation of the individuals involved. They have committed themselves to the pastoral and spiritual care and emotional well-being of those who have been sexually abused and of their families.

In addition, the bishops will work with parents, civil authorities, educators, and various organizations in the community to make and maintain the safest environment for minors. In the same way, the bishops have pledged to evaluate the background of seminary applicants as well as all church personnel, who have responsibility for the care and supervision of children and young people.

Therefore, to ensure that each diocese/eparchy in the United States of America will have procedures in place to respond promptly to all allegations of sexual abuse of minors, the United States Conference of Catholic Bishops decrees these norms for diocesan/eparchial policies dealing with allegations of sexual abuse of minors by diocesan and religious priests or deacons.[1] These norms are complementary to the universal law of the Church, which has traditionally considered the sexual abuse of minors a grave delict and punishes the offender with penalties, not excluding dismissal from the clerical state if the case so warrants.

Sexual abuse of a minor includes sexual molestation or sexual exploitation of a minor and other behavior by which an adult uses a minor as an object of sexual gratification. Sexual abuse has been defined by different civil authorities in various ways, and these norms do not adopt any particular definition provided in civil law. Rather, the transgressions in question relate to obligations arising from divine commands regarding human sexual interaction as conveyed to us by the sixth commandment of the Decalogue. Thus, the norm to be considered in assessing an allegation of sexual abuse of a minor is whether conduct or interaction with a minor qualifies as an external, objectively grave violation of the sixth Commandment (Canonical Delicts Involving Sexual Misconduct and Dismissal from the Clerical State, USCC, 1995, p. 6). A canonical offence against the sixth commandment of the Decalogue (c. 1395, §2) need not be a complete act of intercourse. Nor, to be objectively grave, does an act need to involve force, physical contact, or a discernible harmful outcome. Moreover, "imputability [moral responsibility] for a canonical offense is presumed upon external violation . . . unless it is otherwise apparent." (C. 1321, §3).*Cf. Cc* 1322-27.[2]

NORMS

1. Having received the *recognitio* of the Apostolic See on _____, 2002, and having been legitimately promulgated in accordance with the practice of this Episcopal Conference on _____, 2002, the Norms constitute particular law for all the dioceses/eparchies of the United States of America. Two years after *recognitio* has been received, these norms will be evaluated by the plenary assembly of the United States Conference of Catholic Bishops.

2. Each diocese/eparchy will have a written policy on the sexual abuse of minors by priests and deacons, as well as by other church personnel. This policy is to comply fully with, and is to specify in more detail, the steps to be taken in implementing the requirements of canon law, particularly canons 1717–1719. A copy of this policy will be filed with the United States Conference of Catholic Bishops within three months of the effective date of these norms. Copies of any eventual revisions of the written diocesan/eparchial policy are also to be filed with the United States Conference of Catholic Bishops within three months of such modifications.

3. Each diocese/eparchy will designate a competent person to coordinate assistance for the immediate pastoral care of persons who claim to have been sexually abused when they were minors by priests or deacons.

4. To assist diocesan/eparchial bishops, each diocese/eparchy will also have a review board which will function as a confidential consultative body to the

bishop/eparch in discharging his responsibilities. The functions of this board may include

A. Advising the diocesan bishop/eparch in his assessment of allegations of sexual abuse of minors and in his determination of suitability for ministry;

B. reviewing diocesan/eparchial policies for dealing with sexual abuse of minors; and

C. offering advice on all aspects of these cases, whether retrospectively or prospectively.

5. The review board, established by the diocesan/eparchial bishop, will be composed of at least five persons of outstanding integrity and good judgment in full communion with the Church. The majority of the review board members will be lay persons who are not in the employ of the diocese/eparchy; but at least one member should be a priest who is an experienced and respected pastor of the diocese/eparchy in question, and at least one member should have particular expertise in the treatment of the sexual abuse of minors. The members will be appointed for a term of five years, which can be renewed. It is desirable that the Promoter of Justice participate in the meetings of the review board

6. When an allegation of sexual abuse of a minor by a priest or deacon is received, a preliminary investigation in harmony with canon law will be initiated and conducted promptly and objectively (c. 1717). All appropriate steps shall be taken to protect the reputation of the accused during the investigation. The accused will be encouraged to retain the assistance of civil and canonical counsel

and will be promptly notified of the results of the investigation. When there is sufficient evidence that sexual abuse of a minor has occurred, the Congregation of the Doctrine of the Faith shall be notified. The bishop/eparch shall then apply the precautionary measures mentioned in canon 1722—i.e., remove the accused from the sacred ministry or from any ecclesiastical office or function, impose or prohibit residence in a given place or territory, and prohibit public participation in the Most Holy Eucharist pending the outcome of the process.

7. The alleged offender may be requested to seek, and may be urged voluntarily to comply with, an appropriate medical and psychological evaluation at a facility mutually acceptable to the diocese/eparchy and to the accused.

8. When even a single act of sexual abuse by a priest or deacon is admitted or is established after an appropriate process in accord with canon law, the offending priest or deacon will be removed permanently from ecclesiastical ministry, not excluding dismissal from the clerical state, if the case so warrants. (C. 1395, 2).[3]

   A. In every case involving canonical penalties, the processes provided for in canon law must be observed, and the various provisions of canon law must be considered (cf. *Canonical Delicts Involving Sexual Misconduct and Dismissal from the Clerical State*, 1995; Letter from the Congregation for the Doctrine of the Faith, May 18, 2001). Unless the Congregation for the Doctrine of the Faith, having been notified, calls the case to itself because of special circumstances, it will direct the diocesan bishop/eparch to proceed. (Article 13, "Procedural Norms" for *Motu proprio Sacramentorum sanctitatis tutela*, AAS, 93, 2001, p. 787). If the case would otherwise be barred by prescription, because sexual abuse of a minor is a grave offense, the bishop/eparch shall apply to the Congregation for the Doctrine of the Faith for a derogation from the prescription, while indicating appropriate pastoral reasons. For the sake of due process, the accused is to be encouraged to retain the assistance of civil and canonical counsel. When necessary, the diocese/eparchy will supply canonical counsel to a priest. The provisions of canon 1722 shall be implemented during the pendency of the penal process, in accord with Article 15 of this *motu proprio*.

B. If the penalty of dismissal from the clerical state has not been applied (e.g., for reasons of advanced age or infirmity), the offender ought to lead a life of prayer and penance. He will not be permitted to celebrate Mass publicly or to administer the sacraments. He is to be instructed not to wear clerical garb, or to present himself publicly as a priest.

9. At all times, the diocesan bishop/eparch has the executive power of governance, through an administrative act, to remove an offending cleric from office, to remove or restrict his faculties, and to limit his exercise of priestly ministry.[4] Because sexual abuse of a minor is a crime in all jurisdictions in the United States, for the sake of the common good and observing the provisions of canon

law, the diocesan bishop/eparch shall exercise this power of governance to ensure that any priest who has committed even one act of sexual abuse of a minor as described above shall not continue in active ministry.[5]

10. The priest or deacon may at any time request a dispensation from the obligations of the clerical state. In exceptional cases, the bishop/ eparch may request of the Holy Father the dismissal of the priest or deacon from the clerical state *ex officio*, even without the consent of the priest or deacon.

11. The diocese/eparchy will comply with all applicable civil laws with respect to the reporting of allegations of sexual abuse of minors to civil authorities and will cooperate in their investigation. In every instance, the diocese/eparchy will advise and support a person's right to make a report to public authorities.[6]

12. No priest or deacon who has committed an act of sexual abuse of a minor may be transferred for ministerial assignment to another diocese/ eparchy or religious province. Before a priest or deacon can be transferred for residence to another diocese/eparchy or religious province, his bishop/eparch or religious ordinary shall forward in a confidential manner to the local bishop/eparch and religious ordinary (if applicable) of the proposed place of residence any and all information concerning any act of sexual abuse of a minor and any other information indicating that he has been or may be a danger to children or young people. This shall apply even

if the priest or deacon will reside in the local community of an institute of consecrated life or society of apostolic life (or, in the Eastern Churches, as a monk or other religious, in a society of common life according to the manner of religious, in a secular institute, or in another form of consecrated life or society of apostolic life). Every bishop/eparch or religious ordinary who receives a priest or deacon from outside his jurisdiction will obtain the necessary information regarding any past act of sexual abuse of a minor by the priest or deacon in question.

13. Care will always be taken to protect the rights of all parties involved, particularly those of the person claiming to have been sexually abused and the person against whom the charge has been made. When an accusation has proved to be unfounded, every step possible will be taken to restore the good name of the person falsely accused.

FOOTNOTES TO REVISED NORMS

[1] In applying these Norms to religious priests and deacons, the term "religious ordinary" shall be substituted for the term "bishop/eparch" *mutatis mutandis.*

[2] If there is any doubt whether a specific act qualifies as an external, objectively grave violation, the writings of recognized moral theologians should be consulted and the opinions of recognized experts should be appropriately obtained (Canonical Delicts, p. 6). Ultimately, it is the responsibility of the diocesan bishop/eparch, with the advice of a qualified review board, to determine the gravity of the alleged act.

[3] Removal from ministry is required whether or not the

cleric is diagnosed by qualified experts as a pedophile or as suffering from a related sexual disorder which requires professional treatment.

[4] See canons 35–58, 149, 157, 187–189, 192–195, 277§3, 381, 383, 391, 1348, 1740–1747.

[5] The diocesan bishop/eparch may exercise his power of governance to take one or more of the following administrative actions: (cc. 381, 129ff):

    a. He may request that the accused freely resign from any currently held ecclesiastical office (cc. 187–189).

    b. Should the accused decline to resign and should the diocesan bishop/eparch judge the accused to be truly not suitable (c. 157), then he may remove that person from office observing the required canonical procedures (cc. 192–195, 1740–1747).

    c. For a cleric who holds no office in the diocese/eparchy, any previously delegated faculties may be administratively removed (c. 391, §1 and 142, §1), while any de lege faculties may be removed or restricted by the competent authority as provided in law (e.g., c. 764).

    d. The diocesan bishop/eparch may also judge that the circumstances surrounding a particular case constitute the just and reasonable cause for a priest to celebrate the Eucharist with no member of the faithful present (c. 906), and he may strongly urge the priest not to do so and not to administer the sacraments for the good of the Church and for his own good.

    e. Depending on the gravity of the case, the diocesan bishop/eparch may also dispense (cc. 85–88) the cleric from the obligation of wearing clerical attire (c. 284) and may urge that he not do so for the good of the Church and for his own good.

These administrative actions shall be taken in writing and by means of decrees (cc. 47–58) so that the cleric affected is afforded the opportunity of recourse against them in accord with canon law (cc 1734 ff).

[6] The necessary observance of the canonical norms internal to the Church is not intended in any way to hinder the course of any civil action that may be operative. At the same time, the Church reaffirms her right to enact legislation binding on all her members concerning the ecclesiastical dimensions of the delict of sexual abuse of minors.

Visit the
Simon & Schuster Web site:
www.SimonSays.com

and sign up for our
mystery e-mail updates!

◄──────────────►

Keep up on the latest
new releases, author appearances,
news, chats, special offers, and more!
We'll deliver the information
right to your inbox — if it's new,
you'll know about it.

SIMON & SCHUSTER
A VIACOM COMPANY
www.SimonSays.com

POCKET BOOKS   POCKET STAR BOOKS

2350-01